The
Titus
Conspiracy

David Asher

Published by Weyyakin Ranch Publishing, USA.

Library of Congress Cataloging-in-Publication Data
has been applied for.

ISBN: 979-8-9930259-1-9

First Edition, November 2025

Contents

Prologue

Fog meant trouble. Tonight, it smothered the broken streets of Paris, masking the scars of war. The city held its breath. Then— gunfire. Distant. Sharp. A reminder that the fight wasn't over.

Count Otto von Lebenberg adjusted his coat against the damp chill. The courtyard of the Jeu de Paume was silent, except for the clatter of boots as two soldiers loaded the last crates into a waiting Opel Blitz truck. The museum, once a beacon of art and culture, loomed behind them, its grand halls stripped bare, repurposed for something far less noble.

The Jeu de Paume had held some of the finest art in Europe— Impressionists, Renaissance, Dutch Masters—all now amassed and crated under Lebenberg's supervision. The soldiers moved carefully, aware of the historical significance of the orders they followed. The Nazis meticulously marked the crates using a coding system that designated the collection origin and destination. Crates filled with stolen Rembrandts, Monets, and Picassos were destined for storage far from the walls where they once hung.

Under Nazi control, the museum had become a hollow shell of its former self. The ornate walls were stripped bare, replaced with rows of shelves and crates. Priceless masterpieces had been meticulously cataloged under the cold, watchful eyes of German officers. Sculptures were handled like contraband, not art. The names of their previous owners—Jewish, often prominent—were methodically entered into ledgers, their significance reduced to inventory numbers.

Lebenberg had overseen the operation for months, moving treasures as if they were his own. He knew the value of what passed through his hands, not just in Reichsmarks but in legacy. Each piece had a history—a family it belonged to, a story it told. And he knew where most of it was destined: the private vaults of Göring, Hitler's dream of the Führermuseum in Linz, or, for the less fortunate, damp storage depots deep in the Reich. But not this batch, which was headed for a fate more ominous, more strategic.

Lebenberg watched, arms folded, as the men prepared to load the final crate. A sense of quiet calculation flickered in his gaze. The Reich's ambitions extended beyond borders, and this collection—these pieces of beauty—had become part of a different kind of campaign. The war was shifting. So too were his choices.

"*Vorsichtig!*" he said sharply. "Careful." His voice was steady but carried an unmistakable edge. He didn't trust Göring's men. He didn't trust anyone. That was how he had survived this long.

Karl Weber, tall and wiry, took one end of the crate, while Franz Becker, shorter and built like a farmhand, took the other. They worked with the ease of men who had spent years moving burdens heavier than they cared to remember.

Silently, they secured the last crate onto the bed of the truck. Lebenberg approached and ran a gloved hand across the pine wood, staring at the crates as if he could see through them. He turned to the soldiers. "Do you know what's inside these crates?"

"*Nein, Herr*," Weber said.

"Good. And you never will. Now go."

The soldiers climbed into the truck, Weber taking the wheel. Becker shifted uncomfortably on the passenger side, gripping the doorframe, knuckles pale under the strain. His gaze lingered on the side mirror, watching Lebenberg's figure shrink into the distance as they drove away.

The truck rattled along the dark streets of Paris, its tires hissing against wet cobblestones—the only sound that disturbed the night. They drove past rows of elegant, stone buildings with their intricate wrought-iron balconies, designed by Haussmann for Napoleon III. Past shuttered cafés, past the shimmering Seine, and past equestrian statues of French heroes. There were no obstacles to worry about. The city had been largely spared the destruction of war—no bombs, no battles, no craters, no debris.

"You ever wonder what's in them?" Becker asked.

Weber didn't answer at first. His eyes were on the road, scanning for checkpoints. The Allies were closing in, and the city was fracturing. Every street felt like a trap.

"No," Weber said finally.

"Liar," Becker muttered.

Weber glanced at him. "It doesn't matter what's in them. It's not for us to know."

"Doesn't it bother you? Carrying something so important they won't even tell us why?" Becker's voice was a low, raspy whisper. Someone was always listening.

Weber gripped the wheel tighter. "It's above our rank, Franz. Just keep your eyes on the road."

Becker twisted in his seat, glancing over his shoulder toward the crates. From the cramped cab, he could barely make out the rough wood through the small rear window. The boards were hastily nailed together, the marks of someone having pried them off and hammered them back into place. "They're not just paintings," he said, his voice tight.

"No," Weber said again.

"What do you think they are?"

Silent miles stretched on before Weber finally spoke. "If you know what's good for you, you'll do as I say. Eyes on the road."

Back at the Jeu de Paume, Lebenberg paced the gallery—now reduced to nothing more than a storage facility, its halls lined with the spoils of war. He stopped next to an empty space where a painting had hung only hours earlier. The absence felt louder than the art itself.

Lebenberg had always been a man of precision. His life was governed by order, by rules, by the understanding that chaos could only be tamed with discipline. But tonight, standing in the hollowed-out museum, he felt something he hadn't felt in years.

Doubt.

The crates were a risk. He knew that. But risks were all that remained. The Reich was falling apart, and with it, the carefully constructed world he had built. The war was lost. Everyone knew it. The only question was how long it would take for the walls to come down.

He thought of the crates, of what they carried. He didn't know the full story, but he knew enough. Enough to understand their importance. Enough to know that if the Allies got their hands on them, it would be over.

Lebenberg turned away from the empty wall and walked to the far end of the gallery. He stopped in front of a desk, opened the drawer, and pulled out a revolver.

He checked the cylinder. All chambers were loaded.

The Opel Blitz passed the outskirts of the city, the fog thickening as the buildings gave way to open fields. Becker shivered and pulled his coat tighter. The night felt colder out here, the air sharp and heavy.

"Do you think he's coming back?" Becker asked.

"Who?"

"The Count."

Weber shook his head. "He's not coming back."

"How do you know?"

"Because men like him don't come back, Franz. They don't survive when the ship sinks. They just make sure everyone else drowns first."

Becker leaned back against the worn seat, his eyes tracing the rough edges of the metal roof above them. "I hope you're wrong."

They approached the airstrip—little more than a stretch of dirt and gravel, flanked by skeletal trees that swayed in the biting wind. The fog seemed thicker here, swirling in the faint light of a single spotlight mounted on a rusted pole. A Junkers Ju-52 sat at the far end, its fuselage streaked with mud and oil. The engines idled with a low, guttural rumble, the one disturbance on an otherwise quiet night. With its three powerful BMW engines, the plane was a workhorse for the Luftwaffe. Nicknamed "Tante Ju," or "Auntie Junkers," it was rugged and reliable, capable of carrying several thousand pounds of cargo. Where once German paratroopers sat, there would now be crates with unknown contents.

Becker and Weber stepped out of the truck, their boots crunching against the frozen ground. The smell of fuel and damp earth hung heavy in the air. Without a word, they pulled the first crate from the back and shuffled toward the plane. Every step felt heavier than the last, as though the burden of the secrets they were carrying had shifted to their own bodies. They didn't speak, their breaths coming in visible puffs that vanished into the fog. Above them, the stars were hidden, the night sky an unbroken void.

As they reached the plane, a sharp voice cut through the haze. "You're late."

The pilot moved into view, his lean frame backlit by the dim glow of the plane's navigation lights. He wore a patched flight jacket that had seen better days, and his face was gaunt, his eyes restless. A cigarette dangled from his lips, the ember flaring as he took a long drag.

"You think the Americans are waiting for you to show up?" he snapped, tossing the cigarette to the ground and grinding it under his boot. "Get the crates on board. Now."

Weber and Becker exchanged a glance but didn't argue. They hauled the first crate into the cargo bay, the interior of the plane reeking of oil and sweat. The metal floor was slick, the dim lighting casting eerie shadows that danced with each movement. The second crate followed, then the third. Their muscles ached, sweat trickling from their foreheads despite the frigid air.

Becker hesitated as they loaded the final crate. His fingers brushed against the rough wood, lingering as if trying to sense what lay inside. "Where's it going?" he asked, his voice barely audible.

The pilot turned sharply, his eyes narrowing. "You don't need to know that."

The pilot pushed Becker aside and tightened the cargo straps, then moved toward the cockpit. The plane groaned under the strain of the heavy load, its engines sputtering as though in protest. Becker followed Weber, his chest tight with unease as they stepped off the plane and onto the runway.

Becker and Weber stood in silence, watching as the plane disappeared into the fog, its engines fading into the dark. The faint rumble of distant artillery grew louder, a reminder that the world was closing in.

At the Jeu de Paume, Lebenberg sat in a dark corner of the gallery, the revolver resting on his lap. The silence was complete now. The soldiers were gone. The crates were gone. His work was done.

He thought of the plane, of where it might be going. He had his suspicions, but no certainty. That was the nature of war. Certainty was a luxury.

Lebenberg leaned back against the wall, staring at the ceiling. Shadows danced across the pale ceiling, darkness overtaking the last glimmers of light. The museum had once been a place of life, hope, and beauty. Now it was a tomb.

He closed his eyes and picked up the revolver.

CHAPTER 1

Kitzbühel

The snowstorm raged outside the Huberbräu-Stüberl, rattling the windows and muffling the sounds of the lively eatery within. The restaurant stood on a corner of Kitzbühel's old town square, its façade a postcard-perfect reflection of old-world charm. The walls were painted a soft yellow, the wooden shutters a deep forest green. Icicles hung from the sloped roof, glinting like crystals in the flickering glow of the streetlamps. A hand-painted sign above the entrance depicted a pair of crossed beer mugs framed by alpine flowers.

Jack Berman paused under the arched entryway, brushing snow off his jacket. Despite the storm, the warm light spilled from the windows and invited him in, like a refuge from the chaotic world outside. He pulled open the heavy oak door and stepped inside, a rush of warmth hitting him immediately, carrying with it the unmistakable smells of roasting meat, steaming sauerkraut, and spiced Glühwein.

Almost six feet tall, Jack moved like an athlete, light on his feet, with the air of self-assurance of someone who has experienced much in his fifty-seven years. With shortly cropped salt-and-pepper hair that meant business and deep blue eyes on constant alert, he had the lean features and prominent cheekbones of a man who'd spent more time thinking than talking.

Jack surveilled the crowded room, taking it all in as he searched for his friends. The interior was a blend of rustic tradition and mountain-town hospitality. Heavy oak beams crisscrossed the low ceiling, their dark surfaces etched with the marks of time. The walls were lined with dark wood paneling and decorated with sepia-toned photographs of Kitzbühel's past, along with vintage skiing equipment: leather boots, wooden poles, and long, curved skis. An enormous ceramic stove painted with intricate blue-and-white floral designs stood in the corner, radiating heat that could be felt from every corner of the room.

Sturdy, square tables lined the room, covered in red-and-white checkered cloths. Candles flickered in small glass holders, casting a warm, golden light over the patrons. Skiers occupied each table, their faces flushed from a day on the slopes. Some still wore their jackets and hats, snow melting into puddles around their boots. Others had shed their gear in favor of thick sweaters and scarves, leaning back with steins of beer or tumblers of schnapps.

"Jack! Over here!"

Jack turned to the far corner of the room and saw his friend Charlie waving him over. "Took you long enough!" Charlie called out, raising his stein in greeting. The laughter from their group cut through the hum of the room, drawing a few curious glances.

Jack raised a hand in return and made his way toward his friends, some of his closest buddies—he would do anything for them, and they would do anything for him.

Charlie, the self-proclaimed super-shredder, was holding court. Jack had known Charlie the longest; they had trained together at The

Farm for many years. A fellow case officer, Charlie was the best the CIA had at the time. He was Jack's best friend, and Jack trusted his judgment.

Tall and thin, Ryan, Charlie's younger brother, was a history professor with a calm, bookish demeanor that belied his alpine prowess—the days when Jack and Charlie had to ski slowly to let Ryan keep up were long gone.

It was good to see Jason, a finance colleague from his Wall Street days—they had ridden many bulls and bears together. He had known Jason for almost thirty years. Jason was happily married with two grown children. With a strong analytical mind and decisive under pressure, he was a pro at making high-stakes investment decisions. Jason was a very underrated skier.

Mike sat quietly at the far end of the table. He was a lifelong bachelor who worked in fintech and had recently retired. Mike moved to Sun Valley years before him and had raced alpine for Dartmouth College. They tackled Baldy and mountains up and down the Sawtooths together countless times. Mike was, by far, the most accomplished skier on this trip.

This group had a healthy taste for competition—there would be no casual cruising down the mountain.

As he passed the bar at the center of the room, his gaze wandered across the rows of glass steins and bottles of local spirits, arranged with military precision. The bartender, a wiry man with prematurely gray hair, moved efficiently, his hands a blur as he poured drinks and exchanged quick words with the patrons.

Jack slid into the seat nearest the wall, positioning himself so he could see the room. It was a habit he no longer bothered to break. "Snow's coming down hard," he said, brushing melting flakes from his jacket.

Jack and his friends had been planning their Austrian ski trip for months. It had taken some doing. Most of them had wives, families, and other commitments. After recently retiring from a long, rewarding career on Wall Street, Jack was eager to unwind.

He had been a prominent private equity investor at several Wall Street firms, his longest stretch with Kessler & Severin. There he worked with a close group of general partners, building out a niche global investment specialty in identifying undervalued companies in countries most firms couldn't locate on a map. Jack made his mark in private equity, orchestrating complex, international investments and managing extensive portfolios. He had bounced back after a bad bet on a financial services firm in 2008 and expertly maneuvered his funds through the flash crash of 2010 and the global pandemic in 2020.

A discerning investor, Jack had recently retired comfortably, able to travel the world as he pleased.

Before his career on Wall Street, Jack applied his skills in the more secretive chapter of his life—a little-discussed stint with the CIA. His considerable talents didn't go unnoticed at The Agency. After two years spent skiing across the Rockies, Jack began his long CIA career as an intelligence analyst, but was soon promoted to case officer, a position he held for a decade. Working in clandestine human intelligence (HUMINT) collection, his duties included recruiting foreign agents and managing those assets. Over time, Jack became hardened and a little jaded in this uncompromising environment.

Surveillance and countersurveillance, moles, double agents, treachery, disinformation—these were just some of the daily intrigues, all while dealing with the complex internal politics at The Agency. In this world of shades of gray, it was hard to always try to do the right thing. Jack learned that nothing is ever as straightforward as it seems, and never to trust anyone completely.

Occasionally, Jack reflected on the ups and downs, his wins and losses, with The Agency.

Jack smiled, thinking back on his greatest success, a far-ranging CIA operation that put a huge dent in the drug trade in South America and forced the resignation of a slew of high-ranking corrupt officials.

Initially, Operation Snowstorm seemed something more suitable for the DEA. Only later, when the full economic and political repercussions became apparent, was Jack grateful that he had played such a big role in the operation.

In the past few decades, the drug cartels had ruled much of South America, not only selling their product, but laundering their massive profits—corrupting economies, law-enforcement agencies, and politicians.

Jack, almost single-handedly, flushed out the bad actors that ran these cartels, put them out of business, and exposed the wide-ranging corruption. The CIA awarded Jack the Distinguished Intelligence Medal, the details of which the world outside The Agency will never know.

Invariably, his thoughts circled around to just one mission: Operation Silent Ledger.

Operation Silent Ledger started out full of promise—lofty

objectives, intellectual challenges, and enough danger to get some adrenaline flowing. The goal of the covert CIA-led initiative was to dismantle the powerful Russian Mafia-backed money laundering and cyber troll networks.

These were crazy times in Russia. It had been sixteen years since the Berlin Wall came down. Two years after it fell, the Soviet Union disintegrated and the Russian Federation rose from its ashes. In the chaos that followed, the Russian Mafia emerged from the shadows, dominating the wild scramble for wealth and power.

These crime syndicates operated in Russia, Eastern Europe, and beyond. The range of illicit money laundering activities was both expansive and impressive. Billions of rubles, usually converted to Western currencies, passed through real estate acquisitions, fine art sales, and offshore banking.

Jack and his team were embedded with bankers, high-end real estate brokers, and elite art dealers. Jack, posing as a wealthy American investor, traveled extensively, including Moscow, London, and Monaco, usually in style, flying in private jets and sailing on luxurious yachts.

The operations tapped into Jack's extensive financial analysis and investing skills. Using digital surveillance, financial forensics, and recruiting informants, Jack and his team made steady progress infiltrating and disrupting the syndicates' illicit transactions, exposing key players in the money laundering pipeline.

Eventually, the mission went sideways when one of the most powerful syndicates, Solntsevskaya Bratva, suspected a mole in its network and began to brutally eliminate potential informants, including police officers and even a judge who was on its payroll. The carnage led the CIA to publicly disavow all knowledge of the operation, stranding Jack and his team. They were left to fend for themselves without a safety net. Even worse, an internal leak compromised Jack's cover, putting him in extreme danger. Traversing three continents, he finally extricated himself. After that, he could no longer serve The Agency.

Kitzbühel was intended to be a break, an escape with friends, and a chance to clear his head after leaving the financial and intelligence worlds behind. What better way than ripping laps on alpine steeps on a bluebird day? He'd come not just for the skiing but to find inspiration for his next chapter. Jack was fascinated by the town's influence on American ski culture. In the 1930s, Union Pacific Railroad Chairman W. Averell Harriman had hired Austrian nobleman Count Felix Schaffgotsch to find the perfect location for a grand American ski resort. After an extensive search across the Western United States, Schaffgotsch discovered Ketchum, Idaho, which led to the establishment of Sun Valley in 1936.

Now, as Jack sat by the fire, Kitzbühel's old-world charm reminded him why he had chosen to build his retirement home in Sun Valley— a place far from boardrooms and covert ops. A quiet retreat where the mountains did the talking.

And yet even here, with the fire crackling and the fragrance of spiced Glühwein lingering in the air, he couldn't fully relax. Instead of embracing his newfound freedom and shedding the stress of his career, his mind seemed to seek out new distractions—and that long-buried chapter with the CIA was creeping back to the forefront. He still chose seats with the clearest sightlines. He still kept his back to the wall, still catalogued exits. Maybe he wasn't as retired as he liked to believe.

"Heavy snow is perfect skiing weather," Charlie said. "At least for me. You? Maybe not."

Jason rolled his eyes, visualizing Charlie in a face plant with his equipment scattered all around him. "We'll be waiting for your next yard sale, Charlie."

"Impossible and undefeated," he replied, tipping back his beer. "And I plan to stay that way."

Jason laughed and shook his head. "You do realize there's a chance the gondola might not even open tomorrow, right? With this storm?" He gestured toward the frosted window, where snowflakes swirled like tiny white needles.

"Then I'll hike up," Charlie declared, grinning. "Might as well make it legendary."

"Legendary crash and burn," Jason quipped. He took a sip of his beer, the candlelight reflecting in his stein. "Somehow, I think the Streif will survive without you."

Mike, who had been quiet for some time, summed it up nicely: "It will be awesome."

Jack let their banter wash over him, his attention drifting again back to the bar. Vintage photographs lined the wall behind the bar, seemingly chosen as much for their historical weight as their aesthetic appeal. They stood out against the jovial warmth of the room, their black-and-white starkness a reminder of a different time.

One photo in particular caught his eye, and Jack found himself standing before he knew it. His chair scraped against the wooden floor, drawing Charlie's attention. "Where are you going?" he asked.

"I'll be right back," Jack said.

The bartender glanced up as Jack approached the bar. "Need something?" he asked.

"No, thanks," Jack replied, his eyes fixed on the photograph. The black-and-white image of a group of skiers—barely-groomed hair, stiff stances, woolen uniforms—was unmistakably from another era. The rugged men stood shoulder to shoulder on a snowy ridgeline, their skis planted firmly in the ground. They grinned for the camera, their postures brimming with confidence.

But it wasn't their confidence that unsettled him. As his eyes scanned the photo, something tugged at his memory—the crisp ridgeline, the long sturdy wooden skis, the lace-up leather boots, and the broad smiles frozen in time. He knew this photograph. He had seen it before. Back in Sun Valley's lodge, an almost identical photo hung on the wall. Same men, same poses, same unshakable pride. But there, they had stood beneath the Sun Valley rings—symbols of sky, sun, and skiing—resembling the Olympic rings. Here, the rings were gone, replaced with something far darker. His gaze drifted to the background, where a flag hung—a swastika. Jack's stomach churned.

"Something interesting?" the bartender asked, his Austrian accent cutting through Jack's thoughts.

Jack turned to face him. "This picture," he said, pointing. "I've seen one just like it. Same men, same formation. But in Sun Valley—back in America. Without the flag."

The bartender's polite smile faltered. "It's an old photo," he said, his tone clipped. "History."

Jack narrowed his eyes. "Where'd it come from?"

The man shrugged, a gesture that felt too rehearsed. "Local archives, I believe. It's just a photograph, sir."

Jack didn't believe him. He had spent decades learning how to read people, how to spot the tension in a deal, or when someone was lying. The bartender was fidgeting and avoiding eye contact. He was hiding something, and it had nothing to do with old skiing traditions. Jack pulled out his phone and snapped a photo of the image, ignoring the bartender's frown. When he returned to the table, Charlie was grinning at him like he'd just uncovered a secret.

"So, what's the verdict? Fascinated by Alpine history, or just looking for an excuse to talk to the bartender?" Charlie asked.

Jack gave him a look but didn't answer. Instead, he picked up his beer stein and took a long sip, his gaze fixed on the firelight dancing in the hearth. The room seemed louder now, the laughter and clinking glasses a sharp contrast to the weight settling in his chest.

"Jack," Jason said, leaning toward him. "You look upset. What's going on?"

He hesitated. "Just tired," he said finally.

"Right," Jason said, drawing the word out. "You're not convincing anyone."

Charlie raised his glass. "He's brooding, Jason. That's what he does. If we wait long enough, he'll tell us why, and then we'll all feel bad for making fun of him."

Jason chuckled. "Or he won't, and we'll keep teasing him until he does."

Jack forced a smile but didn't reply. His mind was elsewhere, still on the photograph and the uneasy feeling it had stirred. He turned to Charlie's brother Ryan, who had been sitting quietly next to Charlie. Ryan was Charlie's polar opposite, often seeming most content when he blended into the background.

"Ryan, what do you know about this place?" Jack asked as he leaned toward him. "You picked it, right?"

Ryan nodded. "It has quite a bit of history. It's been owned for decades by Josef Steiner, a fixture of Kitzbühel. His family has lived here for generations. His grandfather was once a porter for the aristocratic tourists who came to ski in the early 1900s."

Jack's curiosity intensified. "The early 1900s? So, they were around during the war?"

Charlie cleared his throat "Are you here for skiing or for a history lesson, Jack?" he asked in a loud, booming voice.

"Quiet, Charlie," Jason admonished, then turned back to Ryan. "Go on, Ryan. I love hearing your take on history."

Ryan continued, "It's been said that during the war, Josef's father had worked for a different kind of visitor—men in pressed uniforms who claimed to be preserving European culture even as they stripped it bare. Josef rarely spoke of those years, but he often told stories of his childhood that hinted at the things he had seen and survived."

Jack took it all in. Maybe it was information that he would never use, but it was interesting, nonetheless.

The storm outside was intensifying, its howling wind rattling the windows. Jack glanced toward them and caught a glimpse of his reflection, faint in the frosted glass. He looked older than he had imagined himself to be. The room was filled with all the things he'd been seeking as he stepped into retirement: good food, cold drinks, and warm, lively company. But something felt off, and Jack couldn't quite put his finger on it.

CHAPTER 2

Streif

A swastika instead of Olympic rings. That did not sit well with Jack in the morning—he couldn't shake the photograph he saw above the bar.

It was a bright morning. The storm had cleared, leaving behind a butter-smooth canvas, just waiting for someone to glide through the fresh powder. Jack stepped out into the crisp air, his breath misting in the cold as he made his way to the café where his friends were waiting. The streets of Kitzbühel were quiet, still waking from the storm. Narrow cobblestone lanes twisted through town, lined with brightly colored chalets and small shops displaying handcrafted ornaments, alpine gear, and thick woolen sweaters.

A store owner stepped outside, broom in hand, and tipped his head at Jack in greeting, then started to sweep the new snow off the stoop. Jack pulled his coat tighter around him and glanced over his shoulder. He hadn't slept well; his dreams circled around the photograph he'd seen at the tavern. Why were there two identical photos, one clearly doctored? Did Sun Valley have a hidden connection to the Nazis? He sucked in a breath of cold air and focused his mind on better things: espresso, breakfast, and first tracks.

As he pulled open the café's heavy door, the bell jingled softly to announce his arrival. Inside, the air was filled with the rich aroma of coffee, fresh bread, and the faint sweetness of pastries. His friends were already seated at a wooden table near the corner, their jackets draped over the backs of their chairs.

"Finally!" Charlie called out, grinning as Jack approached. "We were starting to think you bailed."

Jack smirked, sliding into the chair beside him. "Wouldn't miss this for the world."

A waiter appeared, balancing a tray of steaming mugs and plates piled high with food. He was middle-aged, with a neatly trimmed mustache and an easy smile. "*Guten Morgen,*" he greeted, setting down three mugs of coffee and small glasses of freshly squeezed orange juice. "Today, we have fresh Semmel rolls, rye bread, butter, jam, honey, and ham. And of course, eggs however you like."

Charlie, already halfway through a roll, gestured at the waiter. "This, my friend, is the best breakfast in town."

The waiter nodded, his chest puffing slightly with pride. "The best, *ja*. But don't forget the Apfelstrudel. We bake it fresh every morning. Would you like some?"

"Strudel for breakfast?" Charlie asked, raising an eyebrow but smiling.

"In Austria, it's always a good time for Apfelstrudel," the waiter replied with a wink.

"I'll take a slice," Jack said. "And an espresso."

"And for you?" The waiter turned to the others, jotting down their orders with the precision of someone who had worked the same routine for decades.

As the group bantered about the day's plans, Jack let his gaze drift across the small café. Black-and-white photographs lined the walls, and Jack studied each one, his unease from the night before creeping back. But unlike at the tavern, these photos were harmless—skiers in vintage gear posed against the backdrop of the Hahnenkamm, their expressions a mix of pride and exhaustion.

Above the counter, a cuckoo clock ticked softly, announcing it was already 8 a.m. Jack couldn't remember the last time he'd stayed in bed so late—especially on a pow day. Maybe retirement would suit him after all.

He gazed out the window at the town coming to life.

Clusters of skiers filled the streets, bundled in bright jackets and scarves. Some hurried toward the lifts, skis slung over their shoulders. Others milled around or herded their kids like cats and pushed into the rustic restaurants and cafés. A horse-drawn sleigh clattered along the cobblestones, its passengers wrapped in thick blankets. Jack could hear the faint chatter of tourists mingling with the locals, their voices carrying the excitement of a perfect ski day.

When the food arrived, the table fell into a comfortable silence, punctuated only by the sound of knives scraping against plates and appreciative murmurs. The Semmel rolls were warm and crusty, the butter creamy and rich. Jack savored the sweetness of the Apfelstrudel, the flaky pastry giving way to spiced apples and raisins.

"So," Charlie said, leaning back in his chair. "What's the plan, fearless leader?"

Jack glanced out the window at the gondola swaying gently in the breeze, its bright red cars a cheerful contrast to the rugged peaks beyond. "We hit the Streif," he said, his tone calm but resolute. "And I try not to leave you all in the dust," he said, forgetting that Mike was in the group.

Jason laughed, stirring his coffee. "You'd better not. You've been distracted since last night."

Charlie smirked. "Probably planning his victory speech."

Jack shook his head, a faint smile tugging at the corner of his lips. "Something like that."

As they finished breakfast and prepared to head for the slopes, Jack felt a brief sense of calm. The day ahead loomed large, the mountain waiting to test them all. He once again shook off his nerves and let himself enjoy the warmth of the café, the easy laughter of his friends, and the quiet charm of Kitzbühel.

The crisp mountain air whipped around Jack as he approached the Hahnenkammbahn, the main cable car to the top of Hahnenkamm mountain and the Streif. He stepped onto the Hermann Maier (the *Herminator*), the gondola named after the famous winner of the Streif downhill race in 2001—no mean feat—the epic course consists of harrowing turns and massive jumps, with racers reaching speeds over ninety miles per hour. Each gondola commemorated a past winner, including Franz Klammer, one of Jack's downhill racing heroes. Jack gazed at the towering peaks of the Tyrolean Alps. It really was stunning, the snow-covered slopes glistening in the early morning light. As the gondola crept upward, Ryan snapped photos of the view, Jason and Mike discussed the day's route, and Charlie, as usual, boasted about his latest conquests on the slopes. Jack tuned them out, his attention fixed on the majesty of the ridgeline above.

When the gondola docked at the summit station, a rush of frigid air greeted them. Jack stepped out with the others, his boots crunching on the frost-coated wood of the platform. Around him, tourists shuffled and stretched, adjusting their goggles and zipping up jackets. He overheard short parts of conversations—German, English, French, Russian, and even Japanese—echoing in the thin alpine air. Kitzbühel drew a global crowd; many were jetsetters, vacationing at their exclusive destination du jour. The mountain was alive with their energy. It was easy to tell the locals from the tourists. The locals moved confidently, their gear worn but well-maintained. The tourists, on the other hand, carried themselves with excitement and caution, their movements exaggerated as if to compensate for their lack of confidence.

Jack stepped off the platform and onto the snow. He lowered his skis onto the freshly groomed surface, taking his time as he clicked his boots into the bindings. The sound of the bindings locking in place was sharp and satisfying, a sound that always grounded him. No matter what else was on his mind, that sound had a way of pulling him into the present. He adjusted his poles, shifted his weight, and took a deep breath, feeling the tension in his shoulders start to ease.

The group made their way to the trailhead, where they stopped. Ryan asked a young woman to take a group photo and handed her his phone. "Everybody get together!" Ryan said. "The view's incredible. This one is for the history books!"

Indeed, the Streif was a masterpiece of natural design, carved by time and weather into a gauntlet that only the bravest dared to conquer. Jack had studied this course for years, not just as a skier but as someone who understood its significance. The Mausefalle, with its near-vertical drop, loomed just beyond the first descent, and the steep curves of the Steilhang waited like a predator further down the slope. The course demanded respect—and he was ready for it.

As Jack adjusted his goggles, a ski patroller approached, his red jacket and white cross standing out against the snow. He had the rugged, sun-worn face of someone who had spent a lifetime in the mountains.

"Big day for the Streif," the patrolman said, his Austrian accent thick but clear. He looked at Jack's group, sizing them up. "Do you know what you're standing on?"

Jack smiled faintly. "A mountain that eats skiers for breakfast?"

The patrolman chuckled, but his eyes held a seriousness that wasn't lost on Jack. "The last World Cup race here was... brutal. Aleksander Aamodt Kilde took the win. One minute, fifty-three seconds, point two-two. That's the fastest anyone has taken this course in years."

"Fast," Jack said, nodding. "How many didn't make it down?"

The patrolman shook his head. "Four in the hospital. Broken collarbones, concussions, torn ligaments. That's not counting the ones who pulled out before the race even started." He pointed toward the Mausefalle. "You know, that first drop alone? Eighty-five percent gradient. It's not skiing—it's survival."

Jack glanced down the slope, imagining the controlled chaos of the descent. "Kilde must've had nerves of steel."

"Or he just made fewer mistakes," the patrolman said with a

shrug. "That's all it takes. One mistake, and you're in the fence or on a stretcher. Even the best know when to walk away from this one."

Jack looked at the patrolman, his expression neutral. "And those who don't?"

The patrolman gave a wry smile. "They learn the hard way. Or they don't learn at all."

The patrolman tapped his ski pole on the ground and moved on, approaching another group of skiers to offer similar words of caution. Jack turned back to the trailhead, pausing to let the warning of the patrolman sink in. The Streif served as a reminder of how razor-thin the line between victory and disaster could be.

Charlie shot off first, his whoop of excitement trailing behind him as he dove toward the Mausefalle.

Jack waited a moment before pushing off. The rush of cold air hit him like a slap, and for the first time that morning, he felt present. The snow under his skis was perfect, a fresh dusting of powder making every turn effortless. But even as he navigated the twists and drops of the course, something gnawed at him. The photograph from the night before lingered in his mind, an unwanted shadow cast over an otherwise perfect day.

With a knowing smile, and starting last, Mike leaned forward on his ski poles, kicked back with both legs, and dropped into the run, confident that he would be the first one down. He quickly disappeared, leaving behind a puff of crystalline spray.

By late afternoon, Jack had completed several runs, and his legs were burning with fatigue. The mountain's beauty had settled into a quiet rhythm, each descent offering its own release.

One more run—Jack always felt a need to push against his limits. He charged down the mountain, making turns that in his mind could fit on the cover of Ski Magazine. Over his shoulder, he noticed a skier approaching fast, directly toward him. Jack didn't wait to ask questions; he drifted to the more challenging side of the run and picked up the pace. The mystery skier copied Jack's every turn, closing in. Jack couldn't shake him, so he skied into the trees, off-piste. He was a powder hound back in Sun Valley.

Jack slipped between two tree trunks through a gap most skiers would think was too narrow. He cut left, then right, and ducked under a branch, knocking the snow on it to the ground. He continued to make slalom-like turns between the trees. The pursuer could not keep up. When Jack was back on the run, he turned around; there was no one in sight behind him.

As the sun dipped lower and the air turned cooler, Jack paused to detach from his skis, finally ready for a break, still a little shaken by the encounter. His friends were laughing nearby, Charlie recounting another exaggerated tale of his bravery on the Streif. But Jack wasn't listening. His skin prickled with that all-too-familiar feeling of being watched. He spun around, and through a cluster of skiers, his gaze locked onto a lanky man standing near the gondola. The wiry frame and gray hair were unmistakable. Jack's stomach tightened. It was the bartender.

"I need to use the restroom," Jack murmured to Charlie, keeping his voice casual to hide his discomfort. "I'll catch up with you guys at The Lodge." He slung his skis over his shoulder and began walking toward the station. The man saw him coming and turned, disappearing into the crowd. Jack quickened his pace, weaving between skiers and tourists, his heart pounding. The photograph. The conversation. The bartender's tense smile. This wasn't a coincidence.

He caught up with the bartender in a walkway past the base of the lift, near the equipment lockers. "Hey!" Jack called out, his voice firm. The bartender slipped through a side door, and Jack followed him into an empty alleyway. "What's going on?" he called out. "Why are you following me?"

The bartender stopped but didn't turn around. Jack stepped closer, and he spun around suddenly. Jack barely registered the glint of the blade before it came toward him. He jumped back, the knife slicing through the air inches from his chest.

Jack raised a ski pole defiantly. "Who sent you?" Jack demanded, his voice low, edged with anger.

The bartender didn't answer. His eyes were wild, his intentions violent. The bartender lunged again, and Jack used his ski poles instinctively, using one to deflect the strike. The clash of metal echoed sharply against the stone walls of the station.

Adrenaline surged through him, but Jack remained calm—his close-quarters fight training at The Farm serving him well. Jack sidestepped another lunge and swung his pole hard, catching the man's wrist.

The knife clattered to the ground, skidding across the icy surface. But the fight wasn't over. The bartender tackled Jack, driving him back against the brick wall. The impact knocked the air from Jack's lungs, but he kept his footing. He slammed Jack against the wall again.

Bent over and pretending to be hurt, Jack saw an opening. He jammed a thumb into the bartender's solar plexus and followed up with a knee to the groin. With a sharp twist, he broke free, shoving the man off balance. Wearing ski boots, which made movement difficult, both men struggled to stay on their feet.

The bartender slipped, his feet skidding on the ice, and he fell hard. His head struck the corner of a bench with a sickening crack. Then, everything was still. Jack stood frozen, his breath coming in ragged gasps. The bartender lay motionless, blood pooling beneath his head. It was clear he was dead—way too much blood had spilled onto the ground.

Jack's pulse thundered in his ears, and he looked around. He was alone except for a small red blinking light. A security camera guarding the lockers was pointed in his general direction, but Jack couldn't tell if it had recorded the fight.

Jack paused to take stock, checking his ribs and arm. Nothing felt broken despite being knocked down. His injuries were minor, just a split lip and a few bruises, the most painful of which was above his right eye, bleeding slightly. His commitment to fitness—when he wasn't on the slopes, he was in the gym—had paid off.

The bartender's phone lay next to him. Jack snatched it and tucked it away. He grabbed his skis and rushed away without looking back, his heart pounding. He had just killed a man who tried to kill him. Why was he a target? Should he go to the police?

Funny—he'd thought the Streif would be the most dangerous part of this trip. Suddenly, flying down an icy mountain at 80 miles per hour didn't seem so reckless after all.

The streets were beginning to empty as Jack returned to the hotel. The door was unlocked. He slowly pushed it open to reveal a ransacked room. The chest of drawers was pulled apart and his belongings were scattered on the floor. The covers and sheets were removed from the mattress, and it had been prodded and slashed with a knife. The bartender had not been acting alone.

His intuition, which seldom betrayed him, told him that going to the authorities could be a mistake. He needed the advice of someone he could trust.

Marcus Kane, his most trusted friend from the CIA, was just the person.

Jack never again thought he'd be in the kind of trouble that required this call. "Sorry to bother, I need a favor... again."

"The significance of the photograph in the bar is not in your imagination," said Marcus after hearing Jack's story. "Looks like you've stepped into something much bigger than you realize—but there's not enough time to explain now." Aside from being trustworthy, Marcus defined being 'in the know' and had the special skill of being able to see around corners, especially when things got messy.

"You can't go to the police. You won't be treated fairly," Marcus continued. "You need to leave Kitzbühel immediately, before a manhunt is organized and Interpol is notified. I will meet you in Paris tomorrow. Stay at the Hôtel Du Continent—they don't ask questions."

It had been over two decades since he'd served as a case officer in the CIA, yet he effortlessly slipped back into a guarded, analytical mindset. Every second and every movement mattered. He shoved clothes, laptop, and gear into his bag without bothering to fold them, then did a rapid sweep of the room, wiping down the surfaces he'd touched. His phone buzzed with a message from Charlie: *Where are you?* Jack ignored it. The less his friends knew, the safer they would be.

Jack examined the bartender's phone. It wasn't damaged, but there was no way he could unlock it without special equipment—exploring its secrets would have to wait.

Jack turned off his phone to avoid being tracked. He took the back stairs to avoid running into anyone and slipped out through the hotel's rear entrance.

Once outside, he paused, scanning the narrow alley for any sign of movement. The street beyond was dimly lit, the snow glowing faintly under the light of the streetlamps. Jack adjusted the strap of his bag and headed down the alleyway, keeping close to the buildings as he moved. His breath rose in quick plumes as he made his way through the quieter backstreets of Kitzbühel, his boots crunching softly on the snow.

He avoided the main thoroughfares, where tourists and locals were still milling about, many of them returning from the slopes or heading out for dinner. At one intersection, Jack stopped abruptly and stepped into the shadow of a doorway. A police car rolled past, its headlights slicing through the dark. Jack turned slightly, angling his body away from the light. The car didn't slow, and Jack exhaled silently as it disappeared around a corner. He resumed walking, picking up his pace as he heard the hydraulic hiss of the brakes of a train pulling into the station up ahead. Jack struggled to clear his head of the disturbing images of the lifeless bartender as he stepped onto the platform.

The platform was nearly deserted, its flickering overhead lights casting long, jagged shadows across the wet pavement. Behind a grimy glass window sat the station clerk—an older man with wire-rimmed glasses perched low on his nose, a threadbare cap pulled down over thinning gray hair. He thumbed through a battered paperback, barely glancing up as Jack approached.

"Ticket to Paris, please," Jack said, his voice low as he threw a quick glance over his shoulder. The town was getting its second wind as the après-ski crowd spilled into the streets.

The clerk didn't flinch. "Round trip or one-way?" he asked, his delivery flat, eyes still fixed on the page.

Jack hesitated for maybe a little too long. "One-way," he answered, sliding the euros across the counter.

For a moment, all he could hear was the rhythmic ticking of the station clock. The clerk peeled his gaze from the book, his pale eyes flickering to the money before stamping the ticket with a heavy thud. Jack snatched it, his heart racing, and slipped away without another word.

Jack stood in a shadowed corner of the platform until the train arrived, then boarded and settled into a seat near the back. He held his breath until the train pulled away, Kitzbühel fading into the snowy landscape.

What happened in Kitzbühel replayed in fragments, like a spliced film reel. The pursuit. The bartender lunging at him with a knife. The crack of his skull against the bench. Why did the bartender attack him? What about the photograph at the bar, identical to the one in Sun

Valley, aside from the swastika? Was there a connection? Was it a coincidence? Jack had learned long ago that there was no such thing.

Whatever awaited him in Paris, he knew there was no turning back.

CHAPTER 3

Paris

His escape from Kitzbühel had been stressful, but precise and executed quickly, leaving no trace of his presence. Once on the train, it was easy to travel through the Schengen Zone—including Austria, Switzerland, and France—no passport checks at the borders among member countries. Unfortunately, there was no direct train to Paris, so Jack had to change trains in Wörgl and Zurich, but he would still arrive by morning.

In Zurich, Jack boarded a high-speed SNCF train, 1st Class, and slid into a spacious seat for the final leg of his trip. From the back of the car, Jack's eyes scanned every movement in the aisle as the train sliced through the frosted landscape. His bag was wedged between his feet, his coat slung casually on the seat beside him. To anyone watching, he looked like an exhausted traveler. But his mind was anything but calm.

He turned on his VPN, connected his laptop to the Wi-Fi service, and opened an incognito tab to an Austrian news website. So far, there were no reports of a death—but how long would that last?

Jack checked other news sites and social media. He opened the wanted persons page of the Interpol website to check the Red Notices. Nothing—yet.

He had to stay one step ahead of the authorities—by the time Jack finished scouring the internet, he had already devised a plan for getting off the train and to his Parisian hotel undetected.

As the night deepened, the train glided steadily toward Paris. The hours slipped by, and Jack's tension grew. He expected his face to appear on every news channel in France.

When the train slid into Gare de Lyon, the first light of dawn was barely kissing the horizon. The station stood guard over the city, its clock tower piercing the misty sky, keeping silent watch above the Parisian rooftops.

As Jack was about to close his laptop, he glanced at it one more time—a *Breaking News* alert filled the screen:

Unidentified Man Wanted for Murder in Kitzbühel

In a cold sweat, Jack clicked on the link:

There was a photo labeled: "Kitzbühel Killer"

And a story that started with: "A man fitting this description is wanted for questioning."

A grainy image showed him kneeling over the body of the dead bartender. The death was big news in Austria, a country with one of the lowest murder rates in the world.

Jack stepped onto the platform, immediately blending into the flow of early morning travelers—businessmen clutching briefcases, bleary-eyed tourists pulling suitcases, parents shepherding yawning children. Out of the corner of his eye, he noticed a freckled boy stumble as his mother tugged him along, her red scarf fluttering in the crisp breeze. The sight pulled at something deep within him. In an instant, he was a boy again, weaving through Penn Station, his mother's hand wrapped tightly around his wrist. "Even train stations have a soul, Jack," she'd said, steering him past a hot pretzel cart and a sea of rushing strangers. "You just have to know where to look."

If Gare de Lyon had a soul, it was of a quieter sort than Penn Station, though still relentless. Jack moved with purpose, his bag slung low on his shoulder, his coat collar turned up against the cold draft that always seemed to seep into places like this. He glanced at the ornate murals along the upper walls—something his mother would have insisted he pause to admire had she been there. She'd likely know the artist's name, the commission date, and whether it was "authentic deco" or merely a passable imitation. All Jack knew was that the murals lent an air of grandeur to the business of running away.

As he reached the main hall, Jack allowed himself a faint smile. The last time he'd been in Paris, it had been for an entirely different reason, one involving a far-too-public gala and other social commitments. Today, there were no tuxedos, no champagne flutes, and certainly no mingling with Paris' elite. Just the cold, sharp air of the station and the promise of anonymity waiting in the city's labyrinth of streets. Jack adjusted his pace, stepping into the river of commuters with the confidence of someone who'd done this before. He had no plans to linger. After all, as his mother had also liked to say, "Paris is lovely, Jack, but trouble always finds you first."

This time, trouble was already breathing down his neck—he was the target of an emerging international manhunt. As he moved through the station, Jack noted the position of every surveillance camera. He timed his movements past them, taking advantage of the blind spots resulting from their left-to-right oscillations.

Jack moved quickly as he exited the station, keeping his head down as he skirted the line of cabs idling at the curb. Drivers called out, hoping for a fare, but he slipped past without a glance. No credit cards. No paper trail. No questions. He walked instead, his steps purposeful, blending into the streets of Paris as though he'd been born there.

Jack couldn't be sure that he wasn't already being surveilled. He stopped randomly, feigning interest in his phone while studying the reflections in storefront and restaurant windows to see if anyone was following him. Several times, Jack looped back on his route to get behind anyone who might be following him.

Jack circled back to Gare de Lyon and disappeared into the growing throng descending the stairs of the nearby Metro entrance. The train arrived just as he edged his way onto the crowded quai. He took Metro Line 1 to the Concorde station, walked outside, and looked around. At the northwest corner of the Jardin des Tuileries, he immediately recognized the building with tall, arched windows. It was the Jeu de Paume where, during World War II, the Nazis stored thousands of pieces of art confiscated from Jewish families and French museums. He shivered in the morning chill, cleared his head of the troubling vision of looted art, and focused on his destination, just a few minutes away.

The Hôtel Du Continent stood on a quiet street just off the elegant Rue de Rivoli. It was unpretentious, a small boutique hotel that masked its charm behind an unassuming façade. Its five floors were dotted with wrought-iron balconies, each adorned with carefully arranged planters of ivy and begonias, their leaves spilling over the railings.

Inside, the lobby was warm and welcoming. Dark wooden paneling and intricate moldings framed the walls, accented by vintage globes and small brass statues of animals from faraway lands. A faint citrus scent lingered in the air, paired with the muffled ticking of an antique clock mounted behind the concierge's desk.

Jack approached the desk, set his bag down, and reached for his wallet. The concierge, an older man with thinning hair and sharp eyes, looked up, his fingers drumming against a worn leather-bound ledger.

"I need a room," Jack said, his voice low but steady.

The concierge's eyes flicked up, briefly assessing him, then down again. "Passport?"

Jack slid a folded bill across the counter instead. The concierge hesitated, then pocketed it without a word. He reached for a brass key attached to a heavy fob and slid it toward Jack.

"Room 19, monsieur. Second floor. Breakfast is served in the lounge at eight."

Jack appreciated its anonymity—it was where faces blurred together. He silently thanked Marcus for once again being in the know.

Jack took the key, nodding his thanks, and climbed the narrow staircase to Room 19. The room was small but comfortable. The walls were painted a deep green, offset by gold trim and vintage travel posters depicting maps of Africa and Asia. The bed was dressed in crisp white linens, and a small desk stood against the far wall, its surface bare except for a notepad, a pen, a small brass lamp, and a miniature Eiffel Tower.

Jack dropped his bag onto the bed and moved to the window, pulling back the heavy drapes to peer down at the street below. Paris stretched out before him, its streets alive with motion. He could hear the distant sound of laughter from a passing group, the faint hum of a car engine—the rhythm of the city. Jack let the curtain fall back into place and turned around.

No one knew he was in this hotel room, but his training taught him that one can never be too careful. Ideally, he would have a radio frequency (RF) detector to sweep the room for listening devices, but without one, he would have to rely on a physical inspection. Systematically, he scanned the room. Was anything out of place? He examined the objects in the room: the light fixtures, the alarm clock, the smoke detectors, and anything else he could find. He checked the air vents and behind the paintings and mirrors. Nothing—but better safe than sorry.

Jack was not used to being hunted, looking for a hole to crawl into or a tree to climb. He had been the hunter all his life—the one who released the hounds. Game on. He was going operational, not in an official CIA sense, but in every other way. He was no longer a civilian. He would now play by different rules.

His phone buzzed. A message. Short. To the point.

He exhaled slowly, letting the words settle. He had his confirmation.

Taking all the steps to avoid detection, Jack arrived at Les Flâneurs, a small café tucked into the side streets of Montmartre, not far from the

Sacré-Cœur basilica, as the shadows lengthened in the late afternoon. The wooden floorboards creaked underfoot, the air rich with the aroma of roasted coffee and Gauloises cigarettes. Jack hadn't smoked in years, yet the smell stirred a craving—a ghost of old habits. Smoking had once given him a sense of control when life spun out of hand. He could almost taste the tobacco, feel the nicotine threading through his system, steadying his nerves. Some things, at least, had been reliable.

He selected a table near the back, angling his seat to keep both the entrance and the bar in view. A young waiter approached, notepad ready.

"Un café allongé. Extra hot. No sugar."

The order was second nature now—equal parts caffeine and clarity. The waiter scribbled a note and disappeared, returning moments later with the coffee in a simple white cup. Jack nodded his thanks and took a slow sip. The heat steadied him, anchoring him in the present.

Marcus Kane entered minutes later, his sharp eyes sweeping the café, clocking exits, faces, and escape routes before finally settling on Jack. Almost as tall as Jack but heavier, with short dark brown hair and a light tan, he moved with an ease that came from years of slipping in and out of dangerous places unnoticed.

"You always did know how to make headlines," said Marcus, skipping a greeting.

Tacitly agreeing, Jack stood up and extended a hand. Their handshake lingered a second longer than necessary, an unspoken acknowledgment of the years and battles between them. Memories flickered: a rain-slick alley in Istanbul; gunfire tearing through humid air. Marcus yanking Jack out of a wrecked car in Caracas. Jack swallowed hard and forced himself back into the present.

"You look like hell," Marcus said, a faint smirk tugging at his mouth.

Jack started to return the smile, then winced at the pain in his lip. "True, but I sure look better than the other guy."

Marcus grinned as he slid into the seat opposite Jack and signaled for a glass of wine. Jack studied his face, noting the subtle changes in the man he had once seen as invincible. The hair was grayer, the lines around his eyes deeper, but the intensity remained.

"Still finding ways to complicate your life?" Marcus asked.

"Wouldn't want to get rusty."

"What happened to retirement?"

"Turns out being a ski bum wasn't in the cards."

They slipped into the easy cadence of old friends, bound by history. It seemed like a lifetime ago they'd met at The Farm, where Marcus had been an instructor—the kind who commanded attention without raising his voice. His reputation preceded him: a career carved out in the shadows of Cold War Berlin, Tehran, Beirut, and Moscow. Jack had been a raw recruit then, full of potential but rough around the edges. Marcus had a way of testing limits without breaking you, of turning instinct into skill.

Jack never forgot the first lesson Marcus drilled into him: *"Survival is a game of inches. Win enough of them, and you come out alive."*

Years later, their paths crossed again when a mission went sideways in Istanbul. A simple extraction turned into chaos when an asset's cover was blown. It was Marcus who had appeared out of nowhere, pulling Jack out of a firefight in the Grand Bazaar's labyrinth of alleys. "You owe me a drink," Marcus had said as they ducked into the back of a delivery van, his voice as calm as if they were discussing the weather. That debt had been repaid many times over, their relationship forged by a deep trust only shared by men who'd saved each other's lives.

But this was not the time to reminisce—tonight was not a social call.

The waiter returned with Marcus's wine. He took a long sip, watching Jack over the rim of the glass.

"Tell me again, what happened?"

Jack leaned in, voice low. In clipped words, he brought Marcus up to speed on the events in Kitzbühel: the photograph in the bar, the chase on the mountain, the fight with the bartender, the ransacked hotel room, and his face identified as the killer of the bartender.

"I grabbed the bartender's phone. It's definitely encrypted, but hopefully will provide some leads eventually," added Jack.

Marcus listened, his expression unreadable, fingers absently tracing the stem of his glass.

"Like it or not, you're now swimming with the sharks," Marcus said slowly, as if weighing the import of the words. "Have you heard of Eduardo Vilar?"

"Yes, the tech billionaire. He wrote *The Role of Post-Liberal Institutions*. I heard he funds museums, think tanks, and certain political movements and candidates—he's very active in politics—but a little too right-leaning for my taste."

"You'll see his name pop up in places like Davos and the Munich

Security Conference. That's part of his public persona, but there's a lot more. I have a contact in Mossad—'The Office'—who's revealed a much deeper, darker story," said Marcus. "I hope you're not in a hurry."

Marcus continued, talking faster, "Eduardo Vilar. Financier-turned-tech investor, based in Monaco. He's got a reputation—black market dealings, shady connections. Almost impossible to trace his transactions—all blockchain—an encrypted, unalterable digital ledger system. You know as well as anyone, blockchain enables crypto—secure and completely decentralized. But not everyone knows that the transactions can be doxxed with the right tools. Vilar uses shielded transactions—a cryptographic feature of Zcash—to achieve complete financial anonymity. Crypto is despised by law enforcement for its use in this way by criminals worldwide. More recently, rumors have linked Vilar to Nazi-looted art. I have every reason to think this is true."

Jack absorbed the name, turning it over in his mind. His expression remained impassive, but inside, the pieces were shifting.

"Is there a big market in such art?"

"Yes, it's a huge market," said Marcus.

"How big?"

"The total estimated value of these works—if recovered and sold—would likely exceed tens of billions of dollars. One recovered collection alone, the Gurlitt Collection, included over 1,500 pieces and was valued at $200 million, with some estimates as high as $1 billion."

"Wow," said Jack, exhaling forcefully.

"More than 100,000 Nazi-looted artworks are still missing, according to major restitution experts, and I believe Vilar has his dirty fingers in this pie," added Marcus.

"What more do you know about him?" said Jack.

"On the surface, Vilar is a contrarian techno-authoritarian in the mold of several other well-known tech billionaires. His involvement in the stolen art market is the dark underbelly of the beast."

Marcus leaned in, eyes sharp. "You're diving into murky waters, my friend. Nazi-looted art, conspiracy theories—this is the kind of thing that gets people killed. Be careful with Vilar. He may be the deadliest of all—not because he kills with his bare hands, but because he leverages his illicit resources to incite violence and further his ideological agenda."

Jack's jaw tightened. "I didn't come here for a lecture. What more can you tell me?" said Jack, hoping that, even in retirement, Marcus would have the connections to get the information Jack needed.

Marcus paused, then pulled out a beige card and handed it to Jack. "I picked this up for you—I think you'll find it very interesting."

Galerie Moreau, Paris.

The card had striking calligraphy—cursive, black, elegant.

"What's this?" asked Jack.

"Galerie Moreau. An art gallery located in the Marais. It has a reputation for dealing in rare and high-value pieces. Not exactly a storefront for tourists, if you catch my drift."

"My sources indicated this gallery is tied to Vilar," added Marcus. "We have nothing concrete, but if they're involved in moving stolen art, it wouldn't surprise me. Paris is full of places like this—fronts for laundering pieces that shouldn't even exist."

Jack nodded. "Can you dig deeper?"

Marcus drummed his fingers on the table. "I might know someone. Julian Stokes. Financial guy—ex-City of London type. Now lives in Lisbon. Very well connected. He's been poking around these kinds of circles for years—those connections have served him well. Bit of a shady bastard, but useful if you can handle him."

Jack frowned. "Shady how?"

Marcus shrugged. "Let's just say he may not be the most scrupulous character. But if you need someone who can sniff out the financial side of things, he's your guy. Just don't expect him to stick his neck out for free."

Jack filed the name away. He didn't like working with people he couldn't trust—which were most of the people he encountered—but he wasn't in a position to be picky.

Marcus scribbled a few numbers on a napkin, then slid it across the table along with a cheap-looking burner phone. "Call if it gets messy."

Jack smiled, pocketing the phone and napkin. "It's already messy. Keep an eye on that gallery. Let me know if anything interesting comes up."

Marcus raised his glass in a mock toast. "You've got it. But don't wait too long to act, Jack. This kind of game has a way of catching up with you."

Marcus smirked faintly, his fingers tapping lightly on the side of his wine glass. "You sure about this? There's a reason you left all this behind. Why now?"

Jack hesitated, then exhaled. "It's personal. My family..." He stopped, the words thick in his throat. His mother had spent her life tracking down stolen pieces, believing art was more than beauty—it was history, identity, power. She had said that stolen art was about wiping out entire cultures and the histories and identities intertwined with those pieces. Every masterpiece looted and artifact trafficked was a deliberate act of cultural annihilation. Recovering these works was more than restitution; it was a battle against the forces that tried to silence voices and rewrite history for profit and power.

Now, her memory was fading, her time slipping away. He owed her this.

"There's a long history here that started way before Kitzbühel," said Jack. "I have no choice."

"You won't have to deal with Vilar alone. Mossad has been investigating his operation for some time. I'll give Mossad a heads-up about you. They will help you."

"By the way, you're going to need this," continued Marcus, sliding a passport across the table. "The authorities will soon be looking for you by name, followed by an Interpol Red Notice."

Jack nodded appreciatively, drained his coffee, tossed a few euros on the table, and stood. He didn't look back.

"I'll be in touch."

Jack left the café, stepping into the damp chill of the Paris evening. The streets were quiet, the mist curling around the brightening streetlamps like an ethereal shroud. He walked briskly, the faint sound of his footsteps on the cobblestones keeping him company. Jack passed shuttered shopfronts, their displays dim and lifeless, and paused briefly along the side of a square. A lone musician strummed a guitar near the fountain, his notes melancholy but somehow comforting. His thoughts kept returning to Galerie Moreau.

Jack spent the rest of the evening in the hotel room, pacing, too wired to rest. He tried to read, tried to eat, but his mind kept circling back to the gallery—he had to check it out. When night finally came, he made his way there, carefully slipping through the darkened streets. It was tucked into a quiet corner of the city, its elegant façade blending seamlessly with the Parisian streetscape. Jack approached cautiously, lingering in a narrow alley across the street. From there, he could see everything without being seen.

A polished black door bore the name *Galerie Moreau* in understated gold letters. A small brass plaque beneath it displayed the hours, but the gallery had long since closed for the night. Jack noted the security measures: a discreet camera mounted above the door, its lens sweeping lazily across the sidewalk, and the faint shimmer of reinforced glass in the windows. The gallery owner wasn't taking chances, but the measures were subtle enough not to deter its wealthy clientele.

The gallery's large front windows gleamed under the soft glow of streetlamps, revealing glimpses of the curated world within. The displays were immaculate, designed to entice the discerning eye. A striking oil painting dominated the center—a vibrant abstraction of colors and shapes that seemed to shift under the light. To its left, a delicate bronze sculpture stood on a pedestal, its surface catching the light in subtle ripples. Nearby, a glass case held what appeared to be a set of antique jewelry, its ornate gold filigree framing emeralds the size of a thumbnail.

Jack took a long look at the jewelry. It wasn't a typical piece that one displayed for casual browsing. Something told him it was a signal, a marker for those who understood its worth.

As Jack moved into the alley next to the gallery to look around the back, he saw headlights slowing down in the street behind him. He jumped into a narrow space in the shadows between two tall buildings and held his breath as the lights turned toward him.

A roll-up door slid upward as a DHL van backed up to the loading dock behind the gallery. Two men dressed in yellow and red uniforms jumped out. They were met by a man in a dark suit who looked over their paperwork and stepped out of the way.

The men unloaded many large brown cardboard shipping boxes, each too big to handle by one person, and leaned them against the far wall. "*Merde,*" said one of them as his hand slipped and the last box fell to the ground, bending a corner, the sharp crack of splintering wood echoing into the alley.

The man in the dark suit pointed at the box, indicating it should be opened.

The box contained a tan crate, made of rough, unvarnished wood, its faded surface scarred and pitted with age. One corner of the crate was splintered, where it had hit the ground.

Faint faded markings on the side caught Jack's eye: blocky black text in German, a relic of a different time, accompanied by a barely discernible eagle insignia.

His pulse quickened. The crate didn't belong in a Parisian gallery; it belonged in a military archive—or a museum cataloging war crimes.

He scanned the dimly lit space beyond them. More shipping boxes, stacked along the walls, all the same size. Did they all have wooden crates with Nazi markings inside?

Jack took one last glance before disappearing back into the night.

After a restless night, Jack woke to the rustling of the city stirring. The faint clang of a delivery truck echoed in the distance, mingling with the low hum of morning traffic. He dressed quickly, slipping the folded map and notepad into his bag. The beige card was the last thing he picked up, tucking it into his jacket pocket before heading out.

But first, Julian.

Jack stood by the window of his small Parisian hotel room; the closed casement windows hardly muted the sounds of the busy Rue de Rivoli. He held his phone in one hand, the other absently tracing the edge of the beige card from Galerie Moreau. The name Marcus had given him—Julian Stokes—felt like both an opportunity and a liability. He pulled the burner phone and the cocktail napkin from his pocket, carefully entering the number. After a moment's hesitation, he hit dial.

The line rang twice before a clipped, British voice answered. "Stokes here."

Jack kept his voice even. "Marcus Kane said you were worth talking to."

There was a pause, and Jack could hear the faint background noise of a busy café—muffled conversation, the hiss of a milk steamer. When Julian spoke again, he was polite but guarded. "That depends on the conversation."

"I need someone who can follow the money."

Julian hummed, considering. "Tracing money can be delicate work. Expensive, too. What am I looking for?"

Jack glanced at the beige card in his hand. "Galerie Moreau. Paris. Ever heard of it?"

A pause. Then, a quiet chuckle. "I've heard of a lot of things. What's the angle?"

Jack kept it vague. "Word is, they move pieces that don't officially exist. I need to know if they have financial trails worth following."

Julian exhaled thoughtfully. "Smuggling, laundering, or something worse?"

"Maybe all three," Jack said. "I'll send you something encrypted. It's not much, but it's a start."

"I see," Julian said, his tone contemplative. "And you trust Marcus's assessment of me?"

Jack smirked. "I trust him enough to know he wouldn't send me to you unless you could deliver."

"Flattering," Julian said dryly. "Alright. I'll see what I can dig up. Give me a day or two. If anything's moving through the city, I'll find it. In the meantime, you might want to brush up on your French. The Parisians don't take kindly to Americans snooping around their galleries."

"I'll manage," Jack replied. "Let me know when you have something."

"I work in Lisbon, and I don't come cheap," Julian added. "If you want to do some real business, you need to come to Lisbon in two days and bring five thousand euros. You've got my number."

The line went dead, leaving Jack alone with the challenge of what lay ahead. Julian was a risk, but Jack had played riskier hands before. If he could get the money, he was in the game.

Jack got back in touch with Marcus a little sooner than he'd anticipated.

"I talked with Julian. He can get me intel on Vilar for five thousand euros in two days, delivered to Lisbon," said Jack. "Where do I get that kind of money without drawing attention to myself?"

"I've got you covered. Meet me in front of Les Flâneurs in exactly one hour," said Marcus.

No casual observer would have noticed Marcus slipping an envelope to Jack as they passed each other in front of the café an hour later. Executing an undetectable public exchange was a fundamental skill second nature to both men.

Lisbon could be a trap, thought Jack. He needed to clear his head.

In the late afternoon, the streets of Paris were bustling as Jack jogged along the Seine. The sound of his footsteps on the cobblestones echoed faintly, accompanied by the relentless sounds of the city's traffic. The bright sun reflected off the river's rippling surface. Jack kept his pace steady, the cool breeze in his face sharpening his thoughts.

He let his mind wander as he ran, the rhythm of his movements grounding him. The memories came unbidden but familiar. Summers spent on the East Coast, on the wide beaches of Cape Cod, where the days smelled of salt and sunscreen. Winters that revolved around hockey games, his father pacing the sidelines, cheering more out of duty than joy. Jack had idolized him once. Later, he'd come to understand that his father's life on Wall Street left little room for anything else.

His mother had been a different story. She'd spent hours at her desk, immersed in art history books, piecing together the narratives of masterpieces. Jack could still picture her there, surrounded by stacks of notes, her enthusiasm contagious. It was her influence that had opened his eyes to the world of art, though he'd never imagined how deeply that world would one day pull him in.

Jack slowed as he reached a quiet stretch of the river, the faint scent of rain mingling with the cool breeze. His thoughts turned briefly to his wife—never for long, just enough to feel the absence that had reshaped his life. He pushed the thought away, focusing instead on the city around him. Paris always had a way of centering him, even now, when so much was uncertain.

By the time Jack returned to the hotel, his body was tired, but his mind was clearer. He would make a plan. Using the passport Marcus had given him, he was now traveling as Thomas Prescott from New York.

Flying to Lisbon from Charles de Gaulle airport was too risky despite his new passport. At CDG, he would encounter a sophisticated biometric terminal that cross-checked boarding passes against identity documents. There would be little chance of getting past the facial recognition. He couldn't afford that kind of exposure. Trains were his best option. They weren't as fast, but they offered something more important: anonymity—no facial recognition. Cash tickets, regional connections, and a less predictable route would keep him under the radar.

He traced his finger across the map, running through the possibilities. Paris to Madrid was on the way to Lisbon. There was no direct train, but that was OK. He had no intention of taking the obvious route to Lisbon.

His pen moved quickly over the notepad as he sketched out the plan: Paris to Lyon, but indirectly, via Strasbourg and Basel. Lyon to Barcelona through Marseille. From there to Madrid, and finally to Portugal. The route was convoluted by design. He'd make adjustments along the way if necessary.

There would be no advance arrangements for his stay in Lisbon. He was on his own. Fortunately, Lisbon was one of Jack's favorite cities in Europe, and he knew it well. He had a neighborhood in mind where he could find a safe place to stay.

Jack set the pen down and leaned back, exhaling slowly. His mind felt sharper now that the plan was on paper. The beige card from Galerie Moreau sat on the desk beside him, its gold lettering catching the light. Eduardo Vilar. The name lingered in his thoughts, and Jack couldn't shake the sense that Vilar held more than just answers. But for now, planning was enough.

Jack focused his mind on the first leg of his journey: Paris to Lyon. The train station was his next destination, the start of a route that would take him far from here—and closer to the answers waiting in Lisbon.

CHAPTER 4

Lisbon

The Paris morning was damp and gray, the sort of weather that blurred the edges of the city. Jack welcomed it; anonymity was easier in the rain. He moved through Gare de Lyon, once again purchasing his ticket with cash and choosing a seat near the rear of the car, where he could see the entire train without drawing attention.

As the train pulled out of the station, Jack watched the landscape shift from the dense sprawl of the suburbs to the open countryside, his mind elsewhere. His movements felt second nature: he noted the faces around him, tracked glances, and scrutinized behaviors. The Farm had drilled this into him years ago, transforming observation into instinct. A man three rows up checked his phone too often, his eyes darting across the car. A couple argued softly over a schedule, their hands moving with urgency. Jack settled deeper into his seat, outwardly calm but inwardly organizing everything he had observed.

Jack disembarked at Strasbourg's station, letting the crowd carry him toward the exits. Near a café, he spotted a man in a dark coat standing still, his gaze too precise as it swept the platform. Jack shifted course, walking briskly toward the opposite end of the station, where he ducked into a shop and circled back to a quieter ticket counter. Minutes later, he was on the next train, bound for Basel. His circuitous route well underway, Jack took a train from Basel SBB to Lyon.

As the train sped through the Swiss countryside, Jack opened his phone, ensuring location tracking was disabled, and logged into @SnowlineSurveyor, the obscure private Instagram account he used to communicate with a special group from his past while hiding in plain sight. The photo was already queued: a faded alpine lift, its cables sagging slightly under the weight of fresh snow, its caption deliberate: "Old tracks may fade, but they're never truly lost – especially now." The message was layered, a subtle signal to those who understood its meaning. Within hours, replies would appear, coded but clear. Marcus, Sophie, and Elena would know where to find him.

The train sped south from Lyon, cutting through the fertile Rhône Valley past villages with terracotta roofs and vineyards lined up in tight, geometric rows. Several hours later, Jack arrived in Gare de Marseille-Saint Charles. He rushed to catch the next train to Barcelona, departing from a platform five tracks away.

The ride to Barcelona was longer, more than twice as long, but spectacular, hugging the Mediterranean coastline most of the way. Jack couldn't relax enough to appreciate the beauty of the late afternoon sun glimmering off the blue-green waves. As far as he could tell, no one was following him, but he couldn't let down his guard. He arrived at Barcelona's modern Estación de Sants station just after sunset, where he boarded a high-speed AVE train to Madrid. It was almost midnight when the train pulled into Madrid's Puerta de Atocha station. Jack checked into the Only You Hotel Atocha, located directly across from the station.

Early the next morning, he returned to the station and boarded a train to Badajoz, a small city near the Portuguese border—there was no direct train to Lisbon. Jack had not slept well. The events leading him to Portugal swirled in his head throughout the night.

Arriving in Badajoz in the late afternoon, Jack transferred to a regional train that would cross the Portuguese border to Entroncamento, where he would change trains one more time. Three hours later, he jumped on an Intercity train—he was almost there—Lisbon was less than two hours away. An elaborate multi-stop route, daunting for most travelers, barely fazed Jack, who was very comfortable handling complexity.

That evening, Jack arrived at Santa Apolónia station in Lisbon. The city's lights shimmered against the dark surface of the Tagus River, and the humid air clung to his skin. He loosened his scarf but kept his coat buttoned, every instinct on high alert. He had taken every precaution, covered every track, but the specter of the international manhunt still hung over his head.

Alfama was a maze of narrow streets, dark alleys, and steep stairways. This was a double-edged sword for Jack—it was easier to move undetected, but, at the same time, more dangerous if Vilar caught up with him. At a café near the train station, he found a posting, in Portuguese and English, for an apartment for rent. The landlord would be asking no questions if he agreed to pay in cash:

Simple studio. Short-term let. Cash only. No paperwork. Available immediately.

From the window of his rented studio in Alfama, he watched the square below—not for any specific threat, but because the habit had never left him. Observation was muscle memory now, not effort.

Lisbon had always been a city of shadows, its charm concealing a darker history. During World War II, it had been a haven for spies and refugees, a city where neutrality offered safety but no guarantees. Salazar's government had walked a tightrope, selling tungsten to both Axis and Allied powers, enriching itself while playing both sides. It was a delicate game, and Lisbon had become its most significant stage—a city alive with secrets, whispered deals, and coded messages sent under the guise of diplomacy.

For the agents of that era, Lisbon was both a sanctuary and a battlefield. British, German, and American spies operated openly, sharing tables at cafés while trading lies and misinformation. The grand Avenida da Liberdade and the opulent Hotel Aviz became hotbeds of intrigue, where alliances were forged and broken over glasses of port. Refugees filled the city's streets, desperate for passage to the Americas, while couriers slipped through the crowds, carrying messages that could change the course of the war. Ian Fleming had walked these very streets, drawing inspiration for the world's most famous spy, and Jack could almost feel the echoes of those shadowy figures, moving through the city as he did now.

Lisbon's neutrality had preserved it, sparing the city from bombs and bullets, but it had not been untouched. The city carried evidence of its double-dealing, its beauty tempered by a quiet duplicity. Jack leaned against the railing, watching as a tram clattered through the square below. Lisbon was still a city of whispers, its secrets hidden behind shuttered windows and narrow alleys. For centuries, it had been a crossroads where empires converged. And tonight, it felt like he was at a crossroads—a place where his search and the answers he sought converged.

Jack checked his phone. Responses to his old ski lift post had started to trickle in.

Marcus Kane was first: *"No fresh powder in Praça da Figueira, but there's still good shelter near the old lift station. Coffee?"* Jack recognized the cue instantly—the café they'd once used for quiet conversations, tucked into a corner of the square and easy to watch out from all angles.

A close friend followed: *"Whiteouts come and go, but true north stays the same."* Her message was quiet but unmistakable—a reaffirmation of trust, and a readiness to reengage.

Elena Kovaks rounded it out: *"Snowfall always changes, but the mountain keeps its shape."* Her timing was no accident. Elena knew the terrain well—both topographical and political—and her connections to the art world would be crucial.

Jack found the flow of responses reassuring, as he had hoped. Each reply laced with meaning. Each confirming what Jack already suspected: something was happening in Lisbon, and it wasn't just about stolen art.

Now, it was time to meet Julian, who had suggested a private location, such as Jack's flat in Alfama. This didn't sit right with Jack. He knew almost nothing about Julian, and there was no way he would reveal his location.

Julian could be setting him up. Undoubtedly, there was a significant reward for information leading to his arrest. Jack was of two minds. Was he taking too big a risk?

Jack suggested a public setting where Julian could pose no danger. They'd agreed on Miradouro de São Pedro de Alcântara, located in the Bairro Alto neighborhood, a garden with many spots suitable for a discreet conversation. Taking the usual precautions, Jack navigated the winding streets, its ancient alleys offering both concealment and unpredictability. The uneven cobblestones forced a measured pace, but he welcomed it—it gave him time to scan his surroundings. A black sedan idled at the corner, its engine faint but persistent. A man with a newspaper sat at a café across the street, flipping pages too methodically. Jack didn't slow, didn't look twice. He moved like he belonged.

Finally, he reached the upper terrace of the garden, with its spectacular views of Lisbon. On this bright, cool winter day, with clear baby-blue skies, the seven hills of the city were plainly visible. Jack didn't stop to enjoy the panoramic vista; he made sure he wasn't being followed. He continued down a gently sloped gravel path to the lower terrace with its manicured gardens and shaded benches.

A public park could be surprisingly secure. Hiding in plain sight. Looking like tourists would not raise anyone's suspicion, and they were far enough away from other visitors to keep their conversation private.

Jack spotted Julian almost immediately. He matched the description Marcus had given him exactly: slight frame, narrow shoulders, and a patch of thinning blond hair. He wore a tweed jacket and wool pants; his pale complexion and beak-like nose gave him the appearance of a middle-aged English aristocrat. Julian sat on a bench with a coffee, his eyes alert, as if measuring every person who passed by. Even seated, Jack could see that Julian was tall. When he saw Jack, he nodded to a spot next to him.

"Jack Berman, I presume?" Julian said, a hint of a smile tugging at the corner of his mouth.

Jack sat on the bench, glancing out at the skyline of the city below and the São Jorge castle in the distance. Marcus's warning buzzed in his mind, and he weighed his words carefully. "Likewise."

Julian's gaze turned calculating. "Got the money?"

Jack reached into his coat and placed the envelope that Marcus gave him in the space between them. Julian's eyes flicked to it, but he didn't touch it right away. Instead, he took a slow sip of his coffee, then finally handed Jack a thick dark-green folder.

"This should cover everything you need," Julian said, his voice steady. "It's a starting point."

Jack opened the folder, flipping through a stack of photocopies—bank statements, shell company info, and the name Galerie Moreau circled in red ink.

"Five thousand. Count it," Jack said, not looking up.

"I trust you," Julian replied coolly. Then, with a slightly insincere smile, he added, "But let's just say if you need more, you know how to find me."

Jack tucked the folder into his jacket and stood, his movements deliberate. Julian remained on the bench, watching him with quiet amusement. Jack didn't acknowledge Julian, his mind already on the next step. He turned and left the terrace, heading back toward the labyrinth of Alfama's winding streets, relieved that the meeting was over.

Back in his flat, Jack opened the folder and spread out its contents on the kitchen table. Information about Galerie Moreau, but more: A dossier on Eduardo Vilar.

He turned the page.

Eduardo Vilar

Financier. Heir to a Banking Fortune.

Jack massaged his neck, muscles clenched.

Born in Lisbon. 1962. A banker's son. A house in Sintra. A grandfather who looted Europe's art under the Nazi SS insignia.

His eyes skimmed faster.

Eduardo Vilar, heir to the fortune his banker father embezzled from the illicit assets of the Third Reich. While many Nazis fled to South America, Vilar's father and others funneled assets into Lisbon's secretive banking networks, using neutral intermediaries to safeguard their stolen gold, art, and corporate shares.

He was raised on the outskirts of Sintra, a fortress of old money where business was conducted behind closed doors. At the University of Geneva, he studied international finance and art history, and was simultaneously trained in techniques of moving money without a trace. His grooming for operating in the shadows included training on techniques for exploiting Swiss banking laws and how to fabricate provenance for looted works of art.

Financier. Technology venture capitalist. He funds anti-globalist think tanks, far-right politicians, and media conglomerates that push nationalistic rhetoric.

Jack exhaled, sharp and quiet. He glanced up, half-expecting to see someone watching from the balcony.

The dossier's pages smelled faintly earthy. His fingers turned to the next section with curiosity.

The Baur au Lac Hotel. Nazi gold. Lost art. Corporate holdings wrapped in layers of shell companies. Vilar's name never appeared on any official document, but Jack knew that Vilar's empire consisted of a global network of shell companies.

"*Damn!*" Jack said. This isn't a dossier. It's an indictment.

The wood floor creaked under his feet as he shifted his weight in the chair. The words on the page blurred for a second. He blinked and rubbed his eyes.

Then came the American connection. Militia compounds. Media channels.

Jack had so many questions. His fingers tightened onto the sides of the chair.

A long moment passed. His pulse intensified, and he felt momentarily dizzy. He wasn't just chasing a paper trail. He was walking into a war that was still being waged, one that the world believed ended decades ago.

As he flipped to the next page, a heading stopped him cold:

The Institute for Cultural Sovereignty (ICS)

He absorbed the name. Clean. Polished. Unthreatening. An outfit that distributes elegant white papers and hosts wine and cheese symposiums at high-end resorts in the Alps. But he knew better. He was getting the sense that nothing Vilar touched was ever what it seemed.

He read:

A prestigious, well-funded think tank headquartered in Vienna, with satellite offices in Paris, Geneva, and Washington, D.C.

Jack let out a dry laugh. *Of course it is.*

He kept reading—*committed to preserving endangered European identities.*

The phrase was unsettling. Not overtly threatening. Just enough to make certain ears perk up, offering nostalgia as policy.

Ideological laundering machine.

The term sliced right through the page.

Attached was a hand-scribbled note from Julian:

ICS acts as the ideological laundering machine for *Directive 88*:

Cultural exhibitions rewriting history

Virtual museums sanitizing nationalist movements

Academic papers giving political cover to rising extremism

Jack thought, *So ICS is a front. An intellectual smoke screen. But what is Directive 88?*

He scanned faster now, absorbing:

Mainstream politicians were quoting ICS. Governments referenced their research. This wasn't fringe—it was *mainstreamed malice.*

Then came her name:

Dr. Annalise Riedl

Director of Policy and Cultural Strategy

Jack slowed down.

He'd heard of her. Quoted in *Le Monde,* speaking at Davos, always flanked by phrases like *"defender of European legacy"* and *"critic of cultural erosion."* He remembered watching a panel where she dismantled a British MP with frightening efficiency.

Early 40s. Austrian-German. Raised in Salzburg. Sorbonne-trained.

He looked at her photo stapled inside the file—sharp cheekbones, dark eyes, stillness that unnerves seasoned diplomats. She looked like someone who truly believed.

Frames authoritarian drift as a necessary correction.

Jack leaned his head back and stared at the ceiling. He could almost hear her voice—measured, convincing, dangerous in its calm.

She may not even know, he thought. That's the genius of it. She believes she's saving history—not hijacking it.

The title of her paper echoed in his mind. *The End of the Universalist Century.* He thought, *No bullets. No banners. Just white papers and quiet erasure. That's how democracy dies now.*

I've seen enough, thought Jack. He closed the dossier. If there were anything else in there, he would get to it later.

The dossier's weight pressed on him now. This wasn't just about art, or money, or Vilar anymore. The structure Vilar had built was also something else entirely. Jack had seen laundering networks before. This was much more. This was also a scaffolding of influence and power bought with blood money, then cleaned to fund exhibitions, educational grants, and private salons disguised as academic panels. This was about narrative warfare, and they appeared to be winning.

In France, the far-right National Rally has moved from fringe to mainstream; in Germany, the Alternative für Deutschland (AfD) is a central force in German politics, no longer peripheral. Hungary's far-right ruling party had forged a new nationalist alliance inside the European Parliament, while Italy's government, led by a hard-right prime minister, was openly reshaping cultural institutions in its own image. Across the continent, Vilar's worldview and path to influence were no longer on the margins—they were policy.

The influence of *Directive 88* extended beyond the European Union. It promoted unity with authoritarian regimes in China, North Korea, and most notably, Russia, which has a long history of sowing havoc in the political systems of its enemies.

He pushed his chair back, walked to the window, and took in Alfama—its tiled rooftops and winding alleys. A city that had once been neutral during a global firestorm.

Behind him sat the dossier—both an invitation and a warning.

Jack thought, *It's not just the past they're protecting. They're rewriting the future.*

Jack buried himself in the intel Julian had provided until early morning.

As promised, it was more than enough to get started. The problem was knowing where to begin.

That's where Argus came in. Argus wasn't just any off-the-shelf program—it was Jack's custom-built pattern recognition tool, named after the all-seeing giant of Greek mythology. He used it to identify opportunities arising from private equity mispricing across markets. Additionally, over the years, he'd fine-tuned it to spot anomalies in financial transactions, mapping out hidden relationships between entities that weren't supposed to be connected.

Jack took photos of the documents that Argus would be able to analyze and digitized them. He loaded the data on his laptop and launched Argus. As Argus combed through the data, Jack exhaled and rubbed his temple. A progress bar crept forward as the AI-driven tool sifted through transaction histories, searching for patterns. Argus wasn't perfect, but it had one major advantage—it thought like Jack.

A new alert popped up.

MATCH FOUND.

Jack leaned in. The flagged transaction wasn't just large—it was intentional—a wire transfer tied to an art auction in London, six months ago. The money trail started in cryptocurrency wallets, hopped through a shell company in the British Virgin Islands, then landed at the *Geneva Freeport*. He clicked through the details. The auction house had sold three major works: a Basquiat, a Fontana, and a Van Gogh. The buyer? Unnamed. The payment? Routed through an entity he recognized.

It was too clean. The script was familiar: high-value purchases, anonymous bidders, discreet intermediaries. Within weeks, the paintings had vanished into a Geneva Freeport, locked away indefinitely beyond the reach of regulators.

Another alert. Argus flagged a second transaction, and Jack's pulse ticked up. The cryptocurrency wallet funding the purchases had links to a massive embezzlement scandal in Southeast Asia. Billions siphoned. Accounts scattered across Singapore, Switzerland, and offshore trusts. And a name buried in the metadata: Jho Low.

Jack sat back. *That name.*

Low had perfected the art of laundering money through high-profile purchases—real estate, yachts, blue-chip paintings. Vilar wasn't just using the same playbook. He was refining it in his own image.

Jack scrolled through the flagged entries. The more he looked, the clearer it became: Vilar wasn't simply laundering money. He was infiltrating the art world, brazenly manipulating the market itself.

Art was a store of value, a tool for financial concealment in a vault that didn't rust. A painting could cross borders without raising alarms, its value elastic, its provenance murky by design. Vilar and his network understood this better than anyone.

A Van Gogh was liquidity. A Rothko was a dead drop. A forged provenance could add zeros overnight. A discreet auction could launder billions.

Jack looked again at the transaction trail. The art hadn't simply vanished. It had reappeared as leverage—used to secure loans, seed new shell companies, and backdoor investments into media firms and think tanks. Cultural legitimacy masking financial criminality.

Vilar was weaponizing beauty.

Jack returned to the laptop, fingers hovering over the keyboard. The pieces were there. The question was—who else was playing the game?

Jack's attention returned to the dossier. He sifted through the contents for anything he might have missed. As he rifled through, he was pretty sure he had seen everything when a slick, blue and white brochure caught his attention.

What's this?

The Institute for Cultural Sovereignty (ICS) Annual Symposium

Join international thought leaders and global changemakers in stunning Sintra, Portugal, for a transformative gathering focused on preserving cultural identity and a return to time-honored values. At a pivotal point when global forces and ideological extremism threaten the stability of our shared legacy, ICS offers a bold vision for renewal grounded in traditional principles and civilizational excellence.

Jack flipped to the featured speakers. Our distinguished speakers are the architects of the coming new world order.

Polished headshots of the heavy hitters he had just learned about struck formal poses: Eduardo Vilar and Dr. Annalise Riedl.

Venue: Valverde Palácio de Seteais, The Leading Hotels of the World is an elegant 5-star hotel set in the lush hills of Sintra, just outside of the city center. It exudes an atmosphere of elegance and old-world refinement.

By Invitation Only.

A one-day closed-door symposium in two days, tied to Vilar, just thirty kilometers away.

Jack knew he needed to be there. The symposium was a golden opportunity to learn more about Vilar and ICS firsthand. But how would he secure an invitation?

CHAPTER 5

Sintra

Am I getting paranoid—imagining things?

Jack couldn't get the thought out of his head. Several times along the way, on what should have been a twenty-minute walk from Alfama to Lisbon's Rossio train station, he caught a glimpse of a man wearing black jeans and a dark-brown windbreaker.

Just a coincidence?

He wasn't sure. Each time, Jack looped around through side streets and alleys to get behind the man he thought was following him. Each time—nothing.

Arriving at the station in Sintra, he walked twenty minutes through the old town, past colorful shops and cafés, on a garden-lined path and up a hill to Valverde Palácio de Seteais, the luxurious hotel hosting the symposium. In the center of what appeared to have once been an aristocratic estate, two symmetrical wings curved around a central arch adorned with busts, garlands, and bronze medallions. As Jack walked up to the grand entrance, he could see the Moorish Castle and the Pena Palace a short distance away.

Jack had been unable to secure an invitation. Even Marcus, with all his connections, couldn't help. The day before he left for Sintra, Jack created several fake documents at the print shop down the street:

an invitation patterned after one for a symposium he attended years ago, a facsimile of credentials from a conservative think tank, and a transcript touting fabricated academic bona fides.

Inside the foyer of the hotel, the walls and ceiling were adorned with frescoes. Jack imagined that the location was strategically chosen to underscore the symposium's historic theme.

A long white-linen-covered table held a dozen young receptionists, meticulously dressed in matching business outfits. Symposium attendees were lining up to get their passes.

Which receptionist looks the most approachable?

"I'm Dr. Thomas Prescott," said Jack to the third receptionist from the left.

"Please spell your last name," said the receptionist, checking her computer screen. Jack obliged. "One moment."

"I'm sorry, you're not on our guest list," she said curtly.

"There must be a mistake. Would you be so kind as to check again?" said Jack.

Looking again, she said, "There's no mistake. I am sorry, but you will have to leave."

"I'm Dr. Thomas Prescott from the Manhattan Institute for Policy Research in New York," said Jack, raising his voice a little, showing her his makeshift invitation.

"I don't know what this is. Please wait. I need to get my superior."

Jack's mind was racing. *What else can I do?*

"My apologies," said a woman who had been standing a few feet behind Jack.

Jack turned around to face a tall, thin woman with piercing hazelgreen eyes. She had dark hair, pale skin, and high cheekbones, and wore a midnight-blue suit and black stilettos. Her gaze steady, she extended her hand. "I'm Dr. Riedl. And you are?"

Her nametag read: "Dr. Annalise Riedl, Symposium Chair."

Jack flashed back to the dossier: *Early 40s. Austrian-German. Raised in Salzburg. Sorbonne-trained.*

"Dr. Prescott, Thomas Prescott," said Jack, extending his hand in return.

"Pleased to meet you," she said, shaking his hand with an unexpectedly firm grip. She turned to the receptionist. "Please print a nametag for Dr. Thomas Prescott."

"Enjoy the symposium." She bowed slightly, took a step back, turned, and walked away.

What just happened?

Jack wasn't sure; maybe it was his lucky day. He clipped on his nametag and walked down a long hallway to the conference hall. The symposium would start soon, and the hall was filling up fast. Jack sat down on a folding chair in one of the back rows.

Dr. Riedl gave the opening remarks:

"Good morning. My name is Dr. Annalise Riedl, and I would like to welcome you to the annual symposium presented by The Institute for Cultural Sovereignty.

"This year we explore many topics, among them how to preserve our cultural identity and return to time-honored values—a theme that could not be more relevant given the winds of change in Europe and beyond.

"You will hear from many esteemed speakers who are doing their utmost to preserve our culture and push back against the Globalist tide.

"Now, it's my great honor to introduce the founder of the Institute and this great symposium. He is the author of *The Role of Post-Liberal Institutions* and many important papers, including *The Effect of Liberal Democracies on Law and Order*, and *Modern Strategies for Cultural Preservation*, to name just two. Please welcome the distinguished Eduardo Vilar."

After the applause subsided, Vilar presented the keynote speech:

"Look around you. Tell me what you see in the heart of the so-called liberal world. Is it clarity? Is it strength? No. It is a civilization that has forgotten how to speak in the voice of its traditions. Our politics are bankrupt, our institutions paralyzed by contradiction, our borders porous.

"We must regain our historical purpose. Not chaos but disintegration as restoration. A Europe of nations—not market zones or administrative regions, but rooted cultures with time-honored traditions.

"In Hungary, Viktor Orbán's consolidation of a post-liberal state has become a blueprint. Poland, despite recent liberal attempts at reversal, spent years reorienting its judiciary and education under the banner of Catholic-national restoration. In Italy, Meloni's victory represents not just a protest, but a mandate to remember who Italians are, before being Europeans.

"There is a renewal of order in the United States that mirrors the blueprint of post-liberal movements like those in Hungary, Italy, and other countries in Europe. We must support it."

Vilar talked at length, explaining the limitations of populism, how culture and institutions can be used to reshape power, and how art—including World War II-era stolen art—serves as a vehicle for preserving cultural identity:

"You ask why the Nazis stole art. Because they understood that culture is capital. When it reappears under our stewardship, it does not merely correct history—it reorganizes it, placing us in the position of curator, judge, and heir.

"In conclusion, I am not a nationalist. I am an archaeologist of power. I am unearthing the future by restoring the past. Liberal democracy has exhausted its mandate, and societal rebalancing is the proper corrective."

Vilar received an extended standing ovation. Several more speakers gave long, dry speeches.

A panel discussion on "The Importance of Preserving Cultural Identity and a Return to Time-honored Values" followed.

Dr. Riedl introduced the participants. Among them was Vilar, who spoke first:

"We inherit not a world of infinite possibilities, but a civilization that can only support a finite number of traditions. Rule of law, the nuclear family as a foundational unit, moral order—we must not lose our time-honored values. Squander them, and we squander ourselves."

A Russian panelist, speaking in a thick accent with clipped vowels, responded. "We must rebuild, but we cannot rebuild if we refuse to sweep away the rot. And make no mistake, the rot runs deep."

William Harrington, one of the featured speakers, looking very distinguished—his thick head of silver hair gleaming under the lights—agreed. "Yes. Liberalism has become a machine that cannot remember why it was built. It is time to switch it off and start something new."

"The process of preserving cultural identity can involve difficult compromises. Take shared restitution frameworks—while well-intentioned, they aren't always effective," said a scholarly-looking woman sitting at the far end of the table.

"Multiculturalism is not generosity. It is abdication dressed in virtue," quipped another panelist.

"The dilution of time-honored values through multiculturalism has made everything negotiable. Principles once considered immutable, such as national identity, are now subject to interpretation. Reclaiming cultural heritage is how we resist societal disintegration," added Vilar.

The discussion continued for over an hour. Jack wrote down names and made notes to examine later.

An older man, sitting next to Jack, who identified himself as a cultural attaché from Latvia's Ministry of Culture, volunteered an opinion: "We, in Latvia, are still working on the art restitution, but it is a complicated matter."

"A challenging undertaking, for sure. It's difficult to identify original owners of art, and museums are often shortchanged by restitution requirements," said Jack, not wanting to start a debate.

More speakers, breakout sessions, and workshops were scheduled throughout the day.

During another lengthy speech, Jack wandered out to look around the hotel. He noticed a small meeting room to the side of the conference hall. Several folding tables stacked with presentation materials on top and empty cardboard boxes below were lined up against a wall—nothing of interest.

Just as Jack was about to leave the room, he heard two men approaching, two familiar voices, arguing in hushed tones.

"In here," said Vilar, "For some privacy."

There was no time for Jack to do anything but move quickly behind a partially open folding partition in the middle of the room.

"Your numbers are down. We don't have enough sales in the States," said Vilar, raising his voice.

"The FBI and other organizations have been more aggressive in investigating our activities," replied the other man. "Have you heard of the Monuments Men and Women Foundation?"

"No," said Vilar.

"Their people are relentless in the U.S., coming after our art, working to return it to the original owners."

Jack couldn't see Vilar or the other man, whose voice he couldn't quite place. He sounded like one of the participants in the panel discussion that morning.

"That's not my concern. You have a job to do. Go back to your potato farm and find a way," said Vilar.

The conversation grew more heated for several minutes, until Vilar said, "We need to get back to the main hall. The symposium will be ending soon."

Vilar left the room, followed by the other man.

After Jack thought they were gone, he dared to look down the hallway but was too late to catch a glimpse of the man who had been talking with Vilar—someone who, ostensibly, was running Vilar's operation in the U.S.

What Jack didn't know was that the other man was William Harrington from Idaho.

Jack, reflecting on the conversation he had just overheard, was about to reenter the conference hall.

"Mr. Berman, may I have a moment of your time?"

Jack turned to face Dr. Riedl. *She knows my name?* He knew there was no point in insisting he was Dr. Prescott.

"We know who you are, Mr. Berman," said Dr. Riedl. "In fact, we know a great deal about you," she said, as she handed Jack a yellow manila envelope. "Take a look."

Jack opened the envelope to reveal a batch of documents and photographs.

"That's a nice likeness of you in Kitzbühel," she said with a sarcastic smile, adding, "The Austrian police are about to attach a name to this photo, thanks to an anonymous tip they will soon receive."

A chill ran down Jack's spine as he pulled out a handful of photographs.

A picture of him on a street corner near the Galerie Moreau. Several at the Gare de Lyon. Many more around Lisbon—Santa Apolónia station, **Praça do Comércio**, and the streets of Alfama.

"You're sticking your nose where it doesn't belong," she said. "A sure way to get it bloodied."

"You have one day to return to the U.S.," she continued, "Your current identity should get you home. After tomorrow, there will also be an Interpol Red Notice out for your arrest—you will be an international fugitive—making it very challenging for you to travel."

Her eyes narrowed and her smile faded. "And one more thing. If you stay in Europe or even glance again in our direction, you will disappear without a trace. Have a nice flight home."

Jack's mom was right; trouble always finds you first.

CHAPTER 6

Sun Valley

The warning to Jack in Sintra could not have been more explicit—or more grim: stop now or die. The attack by the bartender in Kitzbühel was life-threatening, but the reasons were not well defined. Now, the threats against him were official and clearly spelled out.

These thoughts swirled around in Jack's head, over and over, as he made his way back to Idaho, flying Lufthansa from Lisbon to New York, then Delta Airlines to Salt Lake City, and finally to Hailey. He rented a compact SUV for the twenty-minute drive home.

Stay alert, thought Jack, remembering that the drive had its own set of hazards. Around each turn in the road, a deer could leap in front of a car without warning. And this was Blaine County, where sometimes an overzealous sheriff would be hell-bent to meet his speeding ticket quota for the month.

A few minutes past Friedman Memorial Airport, the shops, restaurants, and cafés in the town of Hailey streaked by in a blur. The drive north took him through serene, wooded areas, past farmhouses, rustic barns, and grazing animals. He drove past the local hospital, while counting his blessings, thinking how often his mad dashes down the mountains could have landed him there. Normally, the serenity transformed the outside world into a personal slice of mountain heaven—not this time—there was too much on his mind. Once in Ketchum, he turned toward Bald Mountain, the final short leg of the drive.

The snow crunched softly under his boots as he stepped out of the SUV, the chilled air sharp against his face. The two-story house he called home, located on the outskirts of Ketchum in the shadow of Bald Mountain, had a welcoming rustic feel. It sat quietly under the faint glow of its porch light, the stillness of the winter night wrapping around it like a blanket. Jack was glad to be home.

On the surface, his return looked ordinary—a man coming back to his quiet mountain retreat after some time away. But beneath the surface, Jack's frustration simmered—his forced exit felt more like exile than a calculated move. There was still the international warrant for his arrest. He was grateful that the US Department of Homeland Security did not automatically act on Interpol Red Notices.

Inside, the familiar stillness of the house greeted him. The fireplace in the corner hadn't been lit since he left for Kitzbühel, and the air carried a faint chill, as if the house itself had grown distant in his absence. He dropped his bag near the door and slumped into the old leather armchair in the living room. The events of the past week replayed in his mind: the threats, the ambush, the sheer precision of Vilar's network. For all his experience, Jack knew he'd underestimated his opponent.

Suddenly, he stopped mid-thought. He noticed some things out of place—furniture had been shifted and books rearranged. Jack pushed himself up from the armchair, looked around, and carefully moved toward his office—all his senses on high alert.

Jack eased the door open, then stopped cold. His desk and filing cabinet drawers were pulled out, and their contents spilled onto the floor. Books brushed off bookshelves. Art and photos torn from the walls. All his family photos slashed to pieces, except one: a black-and-white photo of his grandparents—Holocaust survivors—was intact but pinned to a wall with a rusty Reichsbahn railway spike. The Reichsbahn was Nazi Germany's railway system. The symbolism cut deep as Jack, shaken to his core, was reminded of what his grandparents endured and where he came from.

The message was multi-layered and crystal clear: Abandon any investigation of Vilar's activities and stay silent about what he knows.

Jack reached under the desk. His Glock 19 was still there, held in place by a magnetic holster. He slowly pulled back and released the slide to quietly chamber a round.

Moving slowly, silently, sticking close to the walls, Jack checked the rest of the house—the kitchen, the bedrooms, and the bathrooms. Without turning on the lights, he proceeded down the stairs to the unfinished basement, letting his eyes get accustomed to the near-darkness, and waited until he was satisfied that he was alone.

Jack turned on the lights and walked over to a large cabinet at the far end of the room. He pushed it a couple of feet to the side, revealing that the steel box embedded in the wall was still there.

Jack pulled it free and opened it. Inside were essentials for escape and survival if his predicament became grave enough: Several passports and driver's licenses with different identities; rolls of cash in multiple currencies, including dollars and euros; a SIG Sauer P232, a popular handgun with operatives in his day, and a box of extra ammunition; a wilderness survival kit that included fire starting material, a Swiss army knife, and a map of the region; and a satellite phone. Unfortunately, the phone was obsolete; it would not work with modern satellite networks.

The Canadian passport caught his attention: James Oberling, Pharmaceutical Sales Representative from Vancouver. It was Jack's favorite; he last used it while traveling in Eastern Europe for a CIA assignment. Jack grabbed it, knowing that it might come in handy soon.

As he inventoried the contents, he felt connected to generations of Jews, including his relatives, who had performed a similar ritual. As they were being pursued and persecuted, they had to hide their assets in ingenious ways, such as sewing precious stones into the seams of their clothing.

Returning upstairs, Jack reflected on the ominous message—the spike piercing the photo of his grandparents—left by the intruders.

This message was the final straw. He knew that he could "Never forget." It was time to get to work. *My mind and body are willing. But do I still have it in me?* Regaining his composure, Jack returned to the living room and set the Glock on the coffee table. The intruders had smashed his computer beyond repair, but he still had his laptop, and the data wasn't lost. Years of experience had taught him the value of redundancy. His photos, notes, and contacts had all been backed up to an encrypted cloud server. Jack accessed the backup, breathing a small sigh of relief as the files began to populate. The familiar names and numbers on the screen reminded him that he wasn't entirely in the dark.

Then, a flagged email from Marcus caught his attention. The subject line was innocuous: *Checking In*. But their shared shorthand left little room for misinterpretation. Jack clicked the message. It contained just two lines of text, encoded in a cipher they'd devised years ago. Their cipher was essentially a Caesar cipher, which substituted and shifted the letters in a message. However, it was much stronger because it also added letters from a secret keyword. Decoded, in plaintext, it read:

Gallery linked to Idaho dealer. Quiet but active. Watch for auctions.

Jack stared at the screen in disbelief. An art dealer in his own state was laundering assets for Vilar's operation? The connection between Paris and Idaho seemed absurd at first, but the more he thought about it, the more sense it made. The wealthy circles of Sun Valley, with their seasonal influx of private collectors, provided an ideal cover for moving high-value assets, such as art and antiques. And that explained why the mysterious photograph had appeared in both Kitzbühel and Sun Valley. It must be some sort of message to those on the inside.

The frustration that had been weighing on him now crystallized into determination. Vilar's vast network was not only intricate—it stretched into the places Jack had once thought were safe. And if Sun Valley was part of the puzzle, the fight felt more perilous, and it was on his doorstep.

Jack felt his tension rise as he approached The Pioneer Saloon, affectionately called *The Pio* by locals. From the moment he'd first stepped inside, he'd been drawn to its weathered wooden façade, welcoming atmosphere, good food, and lively company. It was a popular spot where ski bums, ranchers, and tourists all rubbed elbows. Usually, the Pio meant instant tension relief for Jack. Tonight, it was different. Jack wasn't the same man; his home wasn't his refuge anymore.

The antique bar—a polished slab of dark wood lined with well-worn stools, stretching the length of the saloon—was filled with patrons. Overhead, exposed wooden beams bore the scars of time, while mounted antlers and vintage rifles added a distinctly Western feel.

Usually, Jack sat at the bar. Tonight, he headed for the back, sliding into a booth upholstered in cracked red leather. From there, he could take in the room without being in its center.

He watched a group of locals engaged in animated conversation at the bar, their laughter punctuated by the clink of glasses. In the far corner, a couple shared a plate of ribs under a neon sign advertising the saloon's famous prime rib. The faint scent of charred beef and freshly poured whiskey lingered in the air, mixing with the low hum of music from the jukebox.

The Pio wasn't just a watering hole; it was the heartbeat of the town. Ranchers in their work boots mingled with ski instructors in weathered Helly Hansen jackets, while tourists awkwardly sipped cocktails in shiny new gear, trying to fit in. Jack had always appreciated the mix. It made the saloon a perfect place to disappear—where no one stood out, but everyone had a story.

A waitress approached his booth, balancing a tray of empty glasses with one hand. "Haven't seen you in a while, Jack," she said, a faint smile tugging at her lips. "Back for the season?"

Jack offered a forced smile in return. "Hey, Maddie. Yeah, something like that."

She shifted the tray to her hip. "Prime rib?"

Jack nodded. "Wouldn't think of anything else."

"Let's see…" she said, tapping a finger to her forehead. "Medium rare, baked potato, extra horseradish. And a whiskey?"

Jack gave her a full grin. "Impressive."

"I never forget a face—or an order." Maddie smirked, then gave an easy shrug. But before she turned away, her eyes flicked over him— a brief, assessing glance that moved slowly up and down. Had she spotted his injuries? Jack had pulled his woolen hat down low to hide the split over his right eye. There was not much he could do about the healing split lip. The Pio was a place where people noticed things, even if they didn't always ask questions outright. Maddie wouldn't pry, but she'd noticed that something was amiss. That meant others had too.

As she disappeared into the kitchen, Jack leaned back in the booth, surveying the room. The usual low murmur of conversation filled the space, punctuated by the scrape of chairs and the occasional burst of laughter. Then came the tinny hum of the TV mounted above the bar, where a news broadcast had shifted to a blaring political ad.

Bold, sweeping tones of orchestral music filled the room as the camera panned over grainy footage—small-town parades, factory workers, and American flags billowing in slow motion. At the center of it all was the tanned, rugged face of Senator Gerald Cain, a presidential candidate whose rhetoric had been making waves across the country.

Jack's jaw tightened. Cain's voice, deep and authoritative, filled the saloon: *"It's time to take back what's ours. A strong nation, built by its rightful heirs. It's time to replace what no longer works for us."* The visuals cut to images of economic decline—abandoned storefronts, struggling farmers, weeping families—before shifting again. A carefully curated montage followed: clips of immigrants crossing borders, footage of urban protests, a broken window somewhere in Chicago.

Jack exhaled slowly. He'd seen this strategy before. Cain was talking about everyday Americans making ends meet, with white nationalist undertones disguised as patriotism. The ad ended with the senator's slogan emblazoned on the screen: *"Stand for America."*

The rhetoric was populist, but the philosophy echoed what Jack had encountered at the Sintra conference. The focus was on this side of the Atlantic, but one central idea was the same—it was time to replace the failed institutions.

Jack's gaze flicked to the bar, where a few patrons watched the ad with a mix of approval and disinterest. A man in a Carhartt jacket muttered something to his buddy, earning a nod. Another took a slow sip of his beer, eyes unreadable.

The calm, controlled voice of a local newscaster attracted Jack's attention back to the TV.

"Senator Cain is steadily climbing in the polls. Gaining grassroots momentum, he is within striking distance of taking the lead in the presidential election. His campaign has announced that it has surpassed all fundraising expectations."

As Jack studied the poll numbers, a knot of unease twisted in his stomach. The Pio might be a place for laid-back conversation and cold beer, but the simmering undercurrents of allegiance to ideas like Cain's were impossible to ignore. It was the same everywhere these days—divisive politics seeping into the fabric of even the quietest corners. Jack had started untangling Vilar's operation—an empire built on hidden wealth, anonymous transactions, and influence that reached far beyond Lisbon. But money was only one kind of power. Cain represented another.

Jack picked up his whiskey and took a slow sip, thinking about Cain's rise to power.

Before he could dwell on it, the door swung open, letting in a blast of cold air, followed swiftly by a loud booming voice that Jack knew all too well.

"Holy shit—Jack Berman! You're alive!"

Jack looked up just in time to see Charlie barreling toward him, a cocky grin plastered on his face. Before Jack could say a word, Charlie wedged himself into the booth, shoving Jack over a few inches in the process.

"Thought you skied off the Streif or something. What the hell happened?" Without waiting for an answer, Charlie turned toward the entrance, waving wildly at the others. "Over here!" he called, waving them over. "Berman's back from the dead!"

Jack exhaled through his nose, already bracing for the interrogation. He faked a small smile. "Had to take care of some things."

Charlie leaned back, appraising him with exaggerated suspicion. "Yeah? That's why you look like you skied into a tree?"

Before Jack could reply, another, more serious, voice cut in.

"Jack?"

It was Mike. He stood beside the table, hands in his pockets, his eyes scanning him with scrutiny.

Jack sighed, knowing that of the two, he'd be the harder one to brush off.

"Hey, Mike."

"What happened? You just…vanished. We were concerned. We tried calling, but your phone—"

Jack lifted a hand. "It's a long story."

Charlie snorted, clearly itching to pry, but before he could dig in, the rest of their friends trickled over from the entrance and dove into easy chatter, trading stories about the ski season, the latest town gossip, and plans for the weekend. Jack let the conversation wash over him, playing along and laughing at the right moments—but his focus kept drifting.

Not to Mike. Not to Charlie. But to the unfamiliar figure seated at the far end of the group.

"My apologies," said Charlie. "Jack, say hello to Lily. During your vanishing act, we added her to our town."

"Lily is a backcountry guide recently hired by Sun Valley Guides in town," said Mike.

Lily stood up. She was tall and fit, with dark hair and girlish good looks, making it hard to tell if she was in her thirties or forties. Her brown eyes had a warmth that matched her easy smile, though there was a sharpness behind them that suggested she didn't miss much.

"Nice to meet you," said Jack, extending his hand.

"You, too," said Lily, responding with a firm handshake.

"So," Lily said, her manner casual but friendly, "what brings you to Sun Valley? Work or just taking it easy?"

Jack shrugged, giving her a small, polite smile. "A little of both. Sometimes it's good to unplug and reset."

She nodded. "Yeah, I get that. This place has a way of slowing things down."

"Why here, of all the possible places?" said Jack.

"I've heard many good things about Sun Valley," said Lily. "I could ask you the same question."

"I've skied ever since I was in grade school. Since then, I've skied all over North America and Europe, and I've discovered that Sun Valley is the most special place of all," said Jack.

"Wow. I chose the right place," said Lily.

As the conversation flowed around them, Lily chimed in occasionally but mostly listened, her presence more curious than intrusive. Jack found himself studying her out of habit—her confidence, her effortless way of slipping into the group's rhythm. She belonged in the mountains, that much was clear. But as much as she seemed at home there, Jack reminded himself to tread lightly. But there was also something about her that he had seen many times before, a certain demeanor, the way people in the intelligence community carried themselves. One could never be sure, but his gut feelings were almost always spot on; he sensed that there may be a lot going on beneath her polished exterior. Time would tell.

Before they left, Lily slid a napkin across the table toward him, with her number neatly scrawled on it.

"Call me if you ever need a guide." She winked—not flirtatious, but something else.

Jack glanced down at the number, then back at her. She was already standing, zipping up her jacket, her expression unreadable. He liked Lily. There was something familiar about her.

The streets of Sun Valley were eerily quiet as Jack drove home. Snowflakes drifted lazily through the air, and the muffled crunch of his boots broke the stillness. The town's charm, with its glowing streetlamps and snow-covered rooftops, felt almost surreal after the chaos of Lisbon and Sintra. But Jack's instincts were still on edge.

Jack stopped outside Wells Fargo, with its cleared sidewalk and ATM, slid in his bank card, and entered the PIN. He let out a short, involuntary gasp. *What the hell?* His account showed a balance of zero. He understood immediately that this was another attempt to neutralize him.

Thank God he had kept his bank account in Switzerland, set up many moons ago while he was with the CIA—a backup to the backup plans he had in place. In the intervening years, he'd thought about liquidating the account, but never got around to it.

As he turned the corner from the bank, his steps slowed. The alley beside the bank was dark, but he could feel it—that flicker of awareness, the sensing of unseen eyes. Jack kept walking, his gaze watchful, ears tuned to every sound.

A few storefronts ahead, a black SUV idled at the curb. Its engine hummed, exhaust curling into the night air. The windows were tinted and it had temporary license plates.

It didn't belong.

Jack stopped at the crosswalk, pretending to check his watch. The SUV sat motionless. Then, without haste, it pulled away. Not fast. Not slow. Just…deliberate. Jack exhaled through his nose. Not an attack, but a message: *We see you. We know where you are.*

Jack walked to his SUV, brushed off the thin layer of snow from the windows, and started the engine.

His tension didn't ease when he reached his house. If anything, it sharpened. He scanned the quiet street, the rooftops, the windows across the way. Nothing. But as he stepped onto his porch, he noticed it. A small, thin envelope, wedged into the doorframe—no postage, no markings. Just placed there.

Jack pulled it free and unfolded the slip of paper inside.

Two words, written in precise, unhurried script: Last chance.

His jaw tightened. They thought he was done. That the break-in, the threats, the warnings, the emptied bank account—all the show of power were enough to send him running. Jack slid the note into his pocket, unlocked the door, and stepped inside without hesitation.

They were wrong.

There was more work to do. Jack grabbed his laptop. His was razor-sharp. He accessed the cloud server again, reviewing the photos from Lisbon and Marcus's notes. It was tedious work, but he was determined. The partial document labeled Casal Sta Maria (CSM) 83 revealed just enough to raise suspicion. With Argus, he was able to confirm it—the Sun Valley dealer was indeed tied to Vilar's operation. Argus uncovered the telltale signs of illicit transactions in many of the dealer's art purchases and sales, such as missing bank records, too many transactions flowing through freeports, and invoices that didn't match bills of lading.

Outside, snow fell steadily, softening the already quiet town. Jack had spent years honing his instincts, and right now, something felt…off.

A car idled half a block away, headlights off, exhaust curling into the cold night air. A rental.

Jack turned back to his laptop, forcing himself to focus. But then—a knock at the door. Jack's muscles tensed. No one visited at this hour. He slowly reached underneath his desk again. This time, the Glock already had a round chambered. Moving soundlessly, he edged toward the peephole, but kept to the side of the door. A familiar face stared back at him: Julian Stokes.

He flicked the lock and pulled the door open just enough.

Julian, dressed in a dark wool coat, looked completely at ease—except for his eyes. There was an urgency beneath them, something sharp and unreadable.

"What are you doing here?" Jack asked.

Julian smiled, but it didn't reach his eyes. "What, aren't you happy to see me?" He paused, then lowered his voice. "I didn't call because I didn't trust the line. And after what I found, I thought this was worth delivering in person. If you don't agree, you won't have to pay me."

Julian pulled a slim USB drive from his coat and twirled it in his fingers. Jack stepped aside to let him in, quickly locking the door behind him.

"I've done some more digging on that gallery in Paris—Galerie Moreau. It's fascinating, really. On the surface, they're as clean as a whistle. Tax records? Spotless. Transactions? Routine. It's almost too perfect."

"Meaning?" Jack leaned back against the window frame.

"Meaning they're either the most honest art dealers in the world, or they're hiding something clever. Turns out, it's the latter. The gallery is linked to a chain of shell companies. One of them, based in Luxembourg, was recently flagged for being involved in high-value art sales that didn't quite... how should I say it... pass the smell test."

Jack frowned. "What kind of sales?"

"Questionable provenance," Julian said. "Pieces sold through private auctions, conveniently untraceable. If anyone tries to follow the money, they end up running into a maze of offshore accounts."

"Any specifics?" Jack pressed.

"Here's the kicker," Julian continued. "One of these fronts recently sold a painting that matches the description of a piece looted during the war. The sale was routed through Moreau's gallery, though they never technically listed it. It's all very hush-hush."

Jack felt his pulse quicken. "Do we know who bought it?"

"No names yet, but the funds were funneled through opaque accounts in a Geneva bank. And before you ask, I'm working on identifying who is controlling them."

Jack let out a slow breath. "Anything else?"

"Oh, plenty," Julian said, his voice tinged with amusement. "The gallery's director, Luc Moreau, recently took a quiet trip to London. Exclusive, members-only club. No media, no guest records. But I managed to uncover one name on the meeting list—Edward Fischer."

Jack stiffened. "Fischer? I know him. German financier, specializes in 'rare acquisitions.'"

A wave of memories from Operation Silent Ledger washed over him. "Years ago, I suspected Fischer worked with the Russian Mafia, helping launder their dirty money in Europe, but I couldn't make it stick. If he's involved, it's not just art we're dealing with."

"Exactly," Julian replied, his tone sharpening. "Fischer isn't the collector here. He's the one making sure the money stays invisible. Laundering the profits, cleaning up Vilar's mess. Think of him as the fixer."

Jack paced, the tension mounting. "Vilar keeps his hands clean. Fischer handles the dirty work."

"Bingo," Julian confirmed. "Vilar plays the refined statesman—the cultural benefactor, the man of taste. But Fischer's the one pulling the strings for Vilar when it comes to the offshore accounts, the gallery sales, and the *real* transactions."

Jack stopped pacing, his mind racing. "Do you have anything on Fischer's next move?"

Julian hesitated. "Not yet, but there's chatter. An off-the-books auction. High-profile. The kind where buyers don't ask too many questions. I'm working on tracing the invitation list."

Jack's voice dropped, deadly serious. "I need that list. If Fischer finds out we're onto him, we both become liabilities."

Julian's voice stayed calm, but there was steel underneath. "I'm not worried about Fischer, Jack. But you should be. He doesn't make threats. He just *removes* problems. Here, take a look at the USB. You'll find a lot there. I have a plane to catch. I'll be in touch."

Julian turned quickly, got into his car, and left as abruptly as he'd arrived, slipping back into the night.

Jack stood still for a moment, contemplating what he had just learned. The puzzle was finally coming together—but the picture it painted was darker than he'd imagined. Vilar stayed untouchable while Fischer played the enforcer. And if this secret auction was the key, time was running out.

Jack reached into his pocket and pulled out the number he'd gotten earlier.

It's time I learned a little more about Lily, thought Jack.

He dialed.

Lily answered, her voice crisp and professional. "Jack, I wasn't expecting to hear from you so soon."

"I need a guide," Jack said, already making peace with the decision. "There's an old family cabin I like to visit. Off-grid, backcountry. It's not easy to find. I could use some help navigating," knowing it was just an excuse.

Lily paused, clearly intrigued. "What's the catch?"

"No catch," Jack lied. "Just a quick trip. You free tomorrow morning?"

Another pause—just long enough to confirm what Jack already suspected. She'd given him her number for a reason, and it wasn't just for skiing. He hoped his instincts were right about her.

"What time?" she asked.

Jack glanced out at the mountains beyond his window.

"Early." He let the word hang before adding, "There's nothing quite like sunrise over the Galena Lodge."

Jack gathered his backcountry gear, clothing, emergency supplies, and essential avalanche safety equipment: a beacon, shovel, and probe.

Who is she, really?

CHAPTER 7

Galena

The next morning, the first light of sunrise painted the mountains in soft hues of pink and gold, stretching long shadows across the untouched snow. The snow here was pristine, a smooth blanket glittering under the early light. Jack parked at the Galena Lodge parking lot to access the trailhead, the cold biting at his cheeks as he stepped out of the car. His breath hung in the air as he shouldered his pack and adjusted his gear. The silence of the mountains was profound, broken only by the wind rustling the pines.

Despite his low spirits, unable to stop thinking about his ransacked home, Jack was ready to try out the backcountry gear he had spent months researching. The lightweight skis, wide enough to stay on top of the powder and light enough to go for long tours without killing the legs, would be great for today's pow. The bindings perfectly complemented the skis. His boots felt warm and comfortable.

Lily pulled up moments later, just as he pulled out his phone and opened the Gaia GPS app to map out his route. She stepped out of her SUV and unloaded her backcountry setup—a lightweight touring pack, Black Crow skis mounted with Atomic Backland Summit bindings, and adjustable poles, each piece meticulously maintained.

Her layered clothing blended with the rugged landscape. Without a word, she began attaching skins to her skis, designed to grip the snow and allow uphill movement.

Jack walked over and showed her his phone. "Here."

Lily took it, looked at it briefly before flicking him a glance. "Wow. Elevation 10,500. That's quite a trek."

Jack smirked. "That's why I called you."

She studied the plan for a few minutes, seemingly memorizing the whole route. Starting at the base of Galena, the trail was slightly tracked, but as they ascended, it became ungroomed, narrow, and lined with trees. "Alright," she said, adjusting her beanie. "Let's move."

Jack nodded. "Lead the way," he said, fully knowing which way to go.

Most of the route wasn't packed or groomed; Lily broke through the fresh snow with steady, deliberate movements, her skis carving a narrow path as they climbed. Jack followed, his breath rhythmic as he fell into pace behind her. The ascent was steady, the slope increasing as the trees began to thin. The snow was light and powdery, each step sinking slightly before catching on the skins.

As they climbed higher, the landscape opened up, revealing rolling hills blanketed in white and the jagged peaks of the Sawtooths in the distance. The silence was broken by the soft scrape of their skis and the occasional crunch of ice beneath their poles. Jack glanced at Lily now and then, her movements fluid and efficient, her breathing even despite the effort. She didn't say much, and Jack didn't either; the silence suited them both.

After nearly two hours of climbing, they reached a junction where a few other routes converged. A wooden sign marked the way to a nearby hut—one of the backcountry shelters maintained for skiers and hikers. The clearing was windswept and quiet, the type of place where the world felt impossibly large.

"This it?" she asked.

"Yes, a special place, just up ahead," said Jack, leading the way to the shelter.

"It's beautiful up here," said Lily, staring at the glistening ridges and valleys surrounding the rustic, snow-covered structure.

"Yes, I used to bring my family here for years."

"Not anymore?"

"No, I'm divorced, and my son and daughter have both graduated from college and are busy with their lives," said Jack, surprising himself that he was so readily forthcoming.

A lump formed in Jack's throat as he reflected on the toll that working for the CIA took on his marriage—the countless days away from home, the lies and the secrets, all the times he was burned out and emotionally unavailable.

But it wasn't all on me, Jack thought, staring out over the valleys.

"I'm sorry," said Lily.

Jack didn't dwell on the price he paid in service to his country. "It's all good," he said, pulling a couple of sandwiches and two bottles of water from his backpack.

They ate in silence, as if reluctant to disturb the stillness of the quiet majesty around them.

When they finished, Jack nodded toward the trail. "Let's head down."

Skiing down was a completely different experience. Where the climb had been slow and methodical, the descent was pure exhilaration. The untouched powder stretched out before them, a blank canvas inviting them to carve it apart.

Lily pushed off first. Jack watched as she leaned into the slope, her skis slicing through the powder. She moved fast but controlled, her turns crisp, carving a perfect line down the mountain. He found her precision and poise reassuring—he hoped he was right about her—that she was someone who could help him.

Jack followed a few seconds later, letting gravity take him. His skis cut clean, graceful arcs through the snow. His turns sent a spray of powder flying, the weightless feeling reminding him why he'd loved skiing long before it became the central activity of his current life. The snow was perfect—soft yet supportive, each turn a delicate balance between control and freedom. The air rushed past Jack's face, cold and sharp, but he barely noticed. The performance of his new equipment exceeded his expectations. For a time, the weight of the recent events lifted, replaced by the simple joy of the descent. This was why he loved to ski.

They paused halfway down, catching their breath at the crest of a ridge. Below them, the valley stretched wide, the trees dusted with snow and the faint outline of the trailhead just visible in the distance.

Lily pushed up her goggles, her breath curling in the cold air.

"Not bad, huh?" she said.

Jack exhaled, gazing at the valley stretching wide below them. "Best part of the day."

The final stretch was even better, the slope softening slightly as they reached the treeline. Each turn was more satisfying than the last, with a burst of powder spraying off their skis in a fine mist.

Jack unclipped his bindings, ripped off the skins, and shouldered his skis, glancing back at the path they'd carved into the hillside. For a few moments, he allowed himself to enjoy the view—the clean lines, the untouched snow beyond them, the mountains standing silent and vast in the background.

When they reached the parking lot, the sun was dipping low on the horizon, casting long shadows across the snow.

He pulled off his pack and unzipped it. Reaching inside, he pulled out some cash and turned to Lily, holding it out. "Thanks for the help," he said.

She didn't take it. Instead, she just looked at him, her expression unreadable. Her gaze flicked from the money to his face and back again. Finally, she exhaled, waving it off with a flick of her gloved hand.

"Keep it. I had a great time."

Jack watched Lily load her gear into the back of her SUV with the same precision she'd shown on the trail. Each movement was thought out, smooth—precise in a way that didn't quite fit the easygoing, outdoorsy persona she projected.

The descent they'd just finished had been picture-perfect, carving through untouched powder under a brilliant winter sun. But there was something about Lily's skiing—slightly too fluid, slightly too tactical— that made Jack's instincts prickle. She wasn't just good; she was something else entirely.

"Where did you learn to ski like that?" said Jack. "You've had some serious training."

"It's a long story."

"I'd love to hear it," Jack said, testing the waters. "Will you join me for a drink?" He leaned casually against his car.

Lily paused mid-motion, glancing over her shoulder with a faint smirk. "Galena Lodge?" she suggested. "They make the best hot toddy in the valley."

Jack noted the familiarity in her tone. She knew that firsthand.

They walked in silence toward the entrance, low clouds hanging in the sky above them, shifting like they were holding back more snow. Galena Lodge blended effortlessly into the snowy wilderness, its timber frame rising subtly among the dark silhouettes of pines. Fresh snow softened every edge, draping the roof and piling against the base of the building. The air was sharp and clean, laced with the faint scent of woodsmoke drifting from the lodge's stone chimney.

Jack slowed as they reached the entrance, brushing a few lingering flakes of snow from his gloves before pulling the door open for Lily. A wave of warmth and sound spilled out—the low hum of conversation, punctuated by laughter and the occasional clink of a glass. The lodge wasn't flashy, but its presence was steady, its quiet warmth a natural extension of the landscape rather than an intrusion.

Jack and Lily chose a corner table by the window, away from the din of the crowd, where the flickering firelight cast soft shadows over their faces.

Lily didn't glance at the menu. "Two hot toddies," she told the waiter as they sat down, her demeanor casual, like she ordered the same thing every time she came here. Jack made no comment but let his eyes drift around the room. It was familiar territory for her, that much was clear.

"You seem to know the menu," he said once the waiter was out of earshot.

"It's a good spot," Lily replied, leaning back in her chair. "Quiet enough to relax, lively enough to stay anonymous. Perfect after a long day."

Jack studied her, confirming his previous instincts, telling him there was far more to her than she let on. "Anonymous, huh? You strike me as someone who prefers to stand out."

Her lips curved into a faint smile. "And you strike me as someone who asks too many questions."

The drinks arrived, breaking the tension with a brief reprieve. Jack took a sip, savoring the warmth of the whiskey and spices, while Lily seemed content to let the silence stretch. He decided to push.

"You're not just a guide," Jack said finally, his voice low but firm.

"I warned you that it would be a long story," said Lily.

"I want to hear it," said Jack. "Why don't you start from the beginning?"

Lily paused. "From the very beginning?"

"Yes."

Lily took a long look at Jack, then began. "I was born in Haifa, but my parents moved to Tel Aviv while I was still little. No brothers or sisters. My dad worked for the government. He was very secretive—he never told me anything about what he did. Should I go on?"

"How did you learn to ski so well in the desert?" quipped Jack.

"We lived by the sea, but I always dreamed of the mountains. After *tichon*, what you call high school, my dad insisted that I study abroad, so I enrolled at the University of Lausanne in Switzerland, and, at the same time, I went through the IFMGA certification program."

"The International Federation of Mountain Guides Associations?" said Jack. "That's the most prestigious, most intense, mountain guide certification in the world."

She nodded. "Yeah, six years of high-altitude mountaineering, rock climbing, ice climbing, and rescue techniques. Kicked my butt!" she laughed.

"Why are you here?" said Jack, sensing there was a lot more to her story.

"I have another job besides guiding."

The lodge door creaked open, the sound cutting through the low hum of conversation. Jack's gaze flicked toward the entrance, noting the two men who stepped inside. Their heavy boots clumped against the wooden floor, and though their clothes blended well enough with the lodge's casual atmosphere, their movements didn't. They didn't hesitate or pause to take in the room like most newcomers; instead, they moved with intent, scanning the tables with a precision that raised Jack's guard.

Jack leaned forward, keeping his voice low as he addressed Lily. "Don't look up," he said in an even tone. "Two men just walked in. Something's not right." His eyes didn't leave the men as they threaded their way through the room, their strides purposeful, their heads turning just enough to take in each corner. They weren't locals looking for a drink or tired skiers hunting for a snack. Their focus was sharper, deliberate—like hunters closing in on prey.

Lily didn't glance up, but Jack caught the subtle shift in her posture, her muscles coiling like a spring ready to release. "You sure?" she murmured, her tone light enough to be mistaken for casual if not for the quiet sharpness beneath it. Jack gave a barely perceptible nod, his instincts screaming louder with every step the men took toward their table.

Lily didn't turn her head, but her body shifted slightly, tension rippling beneath her calm exterior.

The men made their way through the lodge, their course aimed unmistakably at Jack and Lily's table. Jack tensed, his fingers tightening around his glass, but before he could act, one of the men spoke.

"Evening," the man said, his voice gruff and unemotional. "Mind if we join you?"

Lily smiled faintly, tilting her head. "I'm sorry, do we know you?"

The man's hand dipped toward his jacket, but Lily was faster. In a blur, she grabbed his wrist, twisting it sharply until a compact pistol clattered to the floor. The second man lunged, but Lily met him with a precise strike to the throat, sending him stumbling backward into a nearby chair.

Eyes turned. Movement stirred. The low hum of conversation had snapped into silence. The second man recovered—too fast. He reached for something inside his coat. Jack surged forward, grabbing the back of his jacket and yanking hard. They stumbled into a table, sending plates and glasses crashing to the floor.

Lily drew a small handgun from a concealed holster, her movements fluid and controlled. "Don't." The man hesitated, his hand still halfway to his weapon. Lily fired. Her shot cracked through the air—not at him, but just past his head, shattering a glass display behind the bar. Glass rained down, and both men froze.

Jack picked up the attackers' weapons.

"Time to go," Lily said sharply, grabbing Jack by the arm and pulling him toward the door.

She turned toward the two confused men. "If I see you come out this door, the next bullet won't be for the glass behind you."

They moved fast, slipping through the panicked crowd as the bartender shouted. No one was going to stop them—not after that. Outside, the cold hit like a wall. Lily's SUV was parked near the exit— *not a coincidence,* Jack thought yet again. They reached the car in seconds. Jack yanked open the door and barely had time to slam it shut before Lily threw the car into gear,

The tires spun against packed snow, then caught traction. Jack looked back at the lodge—there was no one coming through the door. The lodge lights faded behind them as Lily cut through the dark, winding roads with smooth precision. Jack exhaled, pulse still hammering. He glanced at Lily from the corner of his eye, her face set in a mask of cold focus. Finally, he broke the silence.

"You want to tell me what just happened back there?"

Jack asked the question instinctively, even though he'd already guessed the most likely answer. This was his third warning. The first had come in Sintra, and the second was the ransacking of his home.

Whatever had happened, the attack at the lodge was the last straw. Jack no longer had a choice; it was an all-out war.

He took a deep breath. He felt his heartbeat slowing as his survival instincts kicked in, supported by his years of training and experience at The Farm.

Lily didn't respond immediately, her hands gripping the wheel tightly. When she did speak, her voice was low and controlled. "You're not the only one looking into things."

Jack raised an eyebrow. "Oh, yeah?"

She exhaled sharply. "You think you're the only one who's noticed Eduardo Vilar?"

The revelation hit Jack like a jolt, but he kept his expression neutral. "Who are you?"

Lily glanced at him briefly before returning her focus to the road. "Someone who knows what they're doing."

"That's not an answer."

"Mossad stationed me here. The Office has been investigating Vilar for some time. His operation spans the U.S., including Idaho."

"Why you?"

"Your friend Marcus Kane provided information to The Office about your involvement. I have known Marcus for a long time. In fact, he suggested this assignment to my superiors."

Jack leaned back, studying her. "How much do you know about Vilar?"

"I know enough to know you're walking into a minefield," Lily said. "And if you don't start being more careful, you won't make it out."

"Look, I can't tell you everything. Not yet. But what I can tell you is this: Vilar's operation isn't just about hiding money. It's about the next level of influence, power, and control. And he's not working alone."

Jack's eyes narrowed. "What do you mean?"

Lily hesitated, as if weighing whether to say more. Finally, she leaned back, her voice softening slightly. "Do you know where cherry tomatoes come from?"

Jack blinked at the sudden shift. "Excuse me?"

Lily smirked. "Humor me."

Jack sighed. "A farm?"

"Israel," she corrected. "Developed them back in the '70s. A hybrid. Resilient, sweet, easy to ship. They became a global commodity almost overnight."

Jack studied her, unsure where this was going. "And?"

"And," Lily continued, "they're a perfect cover. Shipments of tomatoes, produce, anything that seems harmless. You'd be amazed at what you can hide in plain sight."

Jack leaned forward, his voice low. "Like what?"

Lily's eyes met his, her gaze steady. "Let's just say a kibbutz in Sicily."

By the time their conversation ended, the tension between them had shifted, replaced by a cautious understanding. Lily had given him just enough to prove her value, but not enough to reveal her full hand. Jack wasn't sure if he trusted her. Except for Marcus, he could never trust anyone.

Operation Silent Ledger had destroyed his capacity to trust. The directors of this CIA mission, the people he had trusted the most—the people he had trusted with his life—betrayed him. They hung him out to dry. In the end, the wound left on his psyche was permanent, one that refused to heal.

But Jack knew one thing for certain: He couldn't do this alone, and he trusted Marcus's judgment.

"So," he said finally, "what's the next move?"

Lily's lips twitched into a faint smile. "First thing in the morning, we retrieve your car. Then, we take Vilar down and try not to die in the process."

Under the star-filled Idaho sky, their uneasy partnership began.

CHAPTER 8

Ketchum

The drive from Galena to Jack's home took longer than it should have. Several times, whenever there was a car behind them, Jack and Lily pulled over or turned onto side roads to let the car pass. Jack couldn't be too careful—he had to accept that his sanctuary in Sun Valley was no more.

Jack's world was closing in around him. Dr. Riedl had kept her word—the Austrian authorities were tipped off and had put out a warrant for his arrest. He envisioned that his name and picture were being more widely disseminated by the hour. Maybe Interpol had issued a Red Notice. His chest tightened as he imagined law enforcement agencies throughout Europe sifting through a mass of anonymous tips and CCTV footage—all coordinated through Interpol. Soon, they would come looking for him in the U.S.

I'm an international fugitive.

The stark thought haunted him on the short but scenic drive to Ketchum. Pine and aspen lined the road, with an occasional glimpse of the Big Wood River winding below. Clearing his mind, he said, "Let's get some food—I know just the place."

"Lead the way," said Lily. "I'm starved."

Set near the center of town, The Covey was one of Jack's favorite restaurants. Inside, it was bright and welcoming, with a long bar that ran alongside an open kitchen. The walls showcased an assorted collection of children's drawings displayed alongside an original Chagall. The gourmet cuisine featured the inventive and unexpected, a frequently changing offering that depended on the chef's inspiration. A world-class collection of carefully curated wines complemented the menu.

As Jack and Lily walked in, Jesse, the owner, nodded to them from the other side of the restaurant. With a broad, gleaming smile, tanned from skiing and mountaineering, Jesse was a lifelong resident of the valley.

The duo thoroughly enjoyed Jesse's recommendations for trout and bavette wagyu paired with a surprisingly good local wine from Idaho. They finished with house-made date cake and espresso.

"This place almost made me forget why we're here," said Lily, as Jack waved to Jesse on their way out into the crisp evening air.

The car's tires chewed through the icy crust as Jack pulled into the driveway of his home, the headlights sweeping over the modest two-bedroom structure. Nestled near the base of Mt. Baldy and the River Run ski lifts, the place exuded a rugged charm that reflected Jack's personality: functional, unpretentious, and deliberately low-key. The cedar siding and snow-covered roof blended with the surrounding forest, making it seem like part of the landscape.

Like Jack, Ketchum had always been a town of dualities. Born from the boom of silver mining in the late 19th century, it had spent decades as an outpost, populated by dreamers, schemers, and those tough enough to endure a life in the rugged land. But when the silver veins dried up, the town reinvented itself as a haven for artists, adventurers, and seekers of solace. Hemingway had wandered its streets in his final years, leaving behind a legacy of brooding masculinity. Today, Ketchum is a blend of high-end boutiques, rustic saloons, and cozy coffee shops that draws people with wealth and wanderlust. Jack appreciated its balance—a town that looked forward while embracing its past.

Jack cut the engine and grabbed his duffel bag from the back seat. Before he had even shut the door, Lily was already making her way to the porch, pulling her jacket tighter against the wind. She paused at the door, surveying his home with a faint smile.

"Charming," she said, her breath misting in the air. "You could've gone for something bigger."

"Hold on," said Jack, "We have to be careful."

Jack had checked for fresh tire tracks leading up to the home. As he stepped out of the car, he looked for boot prints, broken twigs, tampered locks—signs of snooping or breaking in.

"Wait here," said Jack, and continued surveying the grounds.

Coming around the house and onto the porch, Jack smiled as he slid his key into the lock. "Bigger means more to clean—smaller means more time on the slopes."

It was late in the evening on a moonless night and pitch-black inside. Jack flipped a light switch and looked around—it all looked good.

Jack tossed a log into the fireplace, crouching to add some kindling, and struck a match. Soon, faint popping sounds were replaced by a continuous crackling and a soft warmth. Lily dropped her bag onto the couch and shrugged off her jacket, her eyes scanning the room. The walls were bare save for a few vintage ski posters, an old map of Idaho, and some old-timey skis. A well-worn leather couch sat near the fireplace, its cushions sagging slightly, while the kitchen was tidy but unremarkable, dominated by a sturdy oak dining table.

"It's cozy," Lily said, her voice neutral but edged with approval.

"It's practical," Jack replied, pulling out an RF detector with a built-in spectrum analyzer from his duffel bag. "Does the job, and we have a job, too," handing Lily the bug detector. "Here, scan every inch of this place."

Jack proceeded to look for signs of forced entry or anything missing or out of place.

Lily approached the fire, rubbing her hands together for warmth. Jack slipped out of his coat and hung it over a chair before heading into the kitchen. He heated a pot of coffee and poured two mugs, setting one on the table for her.

He crossed the room to his desk, where he'd stashed the phone he'd retrieved from the bartender in Kitzbühel. He set it on the table with deliberation. "Can you crack this?"

Lily picked it up, turning it over. "Not without help."

Jack frowned. "I was hoping to keep this tight. Fewer people, fewer risks." He reflected on his fugitive status and whether this place could still be a safe haven.

"I get that," Lily said. "But we're running blind here—and based on what just happened at the lodge, we don't have a lot of time."

Jack stared into his coffee, weighing her words. "Who do you have in mind?"

"Alex Lin. He's the best."

Jack looked up from his coffee to meet her gaze. "You know Alex?"

Lily nodded. "Singapore. Cyber-espionage op. He was brought in when things got messy."

Jack sighed, rubbing the back of his neck. "I've worked with him, too. Prague. Corporate gig turned into a money-laundering mess. He's good, but he's... a lot."

Jack knew Alex was very good, but he was also blunt, irreverent, and unpredictable. He was recruited straight out of MIT by a defense contractor. Went on to work with the U.S. Cyber Command. Later, he went freelance—drifting into morally gray territory—a hacker, though more often than not, working for the good guys.

"You mean he's cocky," Lily said.

"That's one way to put it," Jack muttered. "Fine. Call him. But if he screws this up—"

"He won't," Lily said, cutting him off. "I've seen his work.

"Alex did a great job for us in Singapore. He can be trusted. I've been told he now works freelance, living mostly off-grid," said Lily.

She was already dialing. Within minutes, it was set—Alex would arrive the next morning. It still felt like too long, but it was the best they could do.

Jack took a seat by the fire, his fingers tapping absently against the armrest as his eyes darted between the flickering flames and the front door. He'd moved here because it was the only place where he'd ever truly felt safe. But now he felt exposed, like the same men who had attacked them at the lodge could burst through the door at any moment.

Jack thought, *I'm at the center of this.*

"I suspect the reason we were attacked at Galena Lodge was because of me," said Jack. Then he proceeded to tell her about Kitzbühel, Paris, Lisbon, and Sintra.

"When I got back to Sun Valley, I found my home trashed and yet another threat pinned to a wall, this one very personal, aimed at my heritage."

Lily sat in the armchair across from him, hands wrapped around her coffee mug, listening quietly, studying him. "You think they'll come here?"

Jack exhaled through his nose. "I don't know. But apparently someone didn't get the memo that I'm supposed to be in my probationary period."

Lily nodded. "Which means they could be looking for you now. For us."

Lily took a sip of coffee and added. "You always work alone?"

Jack's lips curled into a humorless smile. "Whenever I can."

"Figured," Lily said, leaning back against the chair. "Guys like you always think it's easier that way. Less collateral."

Jack raised an eyebrow. "And you don't?"

Lily paused, then shrugged. "I used to."

Jack watched her carefully. "What changed?"

She met his gaze, deciding how much to give him. "Experience."

Jack huffed. "That's not an answer."

Lily smirked. "You're one to talk." She set her mug down and crossed her legs, stretching them out in front of her. "Things changed after I joined Mossad."

Jack didn't react immediately, but his mind was already clicking through what that meant. "Makes sense—it's a team game."

"Yes, the team holds up the net to catch you if you fall. At least that's the hope," said Lily.

Jack let that one slide. His thoughts turned back to Lily.

"You carry yourself like someone who's been trained to read a room before entering. And you don't flinch when things get messy." He tilted his head slightly. "Field or desk?"

Lily's smile was tight. "Field."

Jack let that settle between them. He knew what it meant for someone like her to make it into fieldwork, especially in an agency like that. Mossad was one of the most feared and effective intelligence services in the world. Small but ruthless, it specialized in surgical precision, covert operations, and deep-cover espionage. Their operatives were known for being relentless, adaptable, and willing to go further than most agencies would dare.

Jack had crossed paths with enough Mossad officers to know you never underestimated their capabilities. If Lily worked in the field for them, she was exactly the type of person he'd want on his side—but it also meant he'd be a fool not to watch his back. People like her didn't just survive in that world; they learned how to win. And if they ever found themselves on opposite sides, he had no doubt she'd do whatever it took to come out ahead.

"Let me guess," he said. "You were top of your class, recruited straight out of university."

Lily smiled. "That obvious?"

Jack smirked. "It's a pattern. The ones who don't have connections? They have to be the best."

Lily's jaw tightened slightly, but she gave a small nod. "After I graduated in Switzerland, I received an advanced degree in International Relations and Middle Eastern Studies from Hebrew University."

Jack let out a low whistle. "Serious credentials."

"My father served," she added, almost as an afterthought. "He was gone a lot."

Jack sensed there was more to that story. "That's why you joined?"

"Mossad, The Office, was very persuasive. They said I had the right skills for the job, especially my survival training."

She paused, then added, "I thought if I was good enough, I'd get answers."

Jack took a sip of coffee. "And did you?"

She exhaled. "Some."

Jack didn't push. He knew the look of someone carrying ghosts they weren't ready to share. Instead, he shifted gears. "And is that where you became an expert in covert tomato farming?"

A flicker of amusement crossed her face. "Now you're catching on. The Office ran winter combat training on Mount Etna. Perfect location—remote, harsh terrain, and completely unremarkable. Just a handful of scientists growing hybrid tomatoes nearby."

Jack shook his head, chuckling. "That's the most creative, low-key cover I've ever heard."

Lily nodded. "The Office thinks outside the box. And you'd be surprised how much funding agriculture projects can get."

Jack leaned back in his chair, watching her. "You're not what I expected."

Lily met his gaze. "Neither are you."

The fire crackled between them, casting flickering shadows against the walls, like dancing phantoms. Neither of them spoke for a while. They had revealed enough for the evening.

Eventually, Jack stretched and stood. "We should get some sleep. Alex will be here in the morning." Jack knew he had to sleep with one eye open.

The next morning, Jack peered out the kitchen window, his senses on high alert. Snow blanketed the house and the surrounding forest, muffling the sounds of the world outside. A fresh set of deer tracks cut through the yard—small imprints that hadn't been there the night before. A reminder that movement never stopped, even when the world seemed still.

Jack brewed a fresh pot of coffee and drummed his fingers on the counter as he waited, racing thoughts whirring in his mind. The phone on the table held answers, but they were locked behind layers of encryption, and time wasn't on their side.

A floorboard creaked behind him. He startled as Lily appeared, bundled in a thick sweater, her hair still damp from the shower.

She gave him a casual smile. "Hope you don't mind, I made myself at home. A hot shower always helps me focus. How'd you sleep?"

"I didn't," he admitted.

The volatility of the situation pressed on him—too many unknowns, too many ways this thing could go wrong. He rubbed his weary eyes, glancing at Lily.

"I made a phone call last night," he said finally. "There's someone else I think we should bring in."

Lily raised an eyebrow. "I thought you didn't like working with teams."

"I don't," Jack admitted, resigned to further intrusions into his sanctuary. "But this isn't something Alex can do alone."

Lily waited.

"His name is Benji," Jack said. "He's—" He searched for the right words. "He's different."

"Different how?"

Jack exhaled. "You'll see. He's the best cryptographer I've ever worked with. Sees patterns no one else can. A few years ago, I watched him crack a Chinese cipher that a forensic team had spent weeks on. He's not field, but his mind works like nothing I've ever seen."

"He's that good?"

"Let's just say he would have given Alan Turing a run for his money. I've yet to see him fail to break a cipher—no matter how long it took. Brilliant linguist. German, Hebrew, French; I forget how many languages he speaks. Worked for the NSA for a while."

Lily tilted her head slightly. "And you trust him?"

Jack hesitated. Trust was a fragile thing. "As much as I trust anyone."

Lily smirked. "High praise."

The coffee machine beeped, and Jack pulled two mugs from the cabinet and filled them. He hesitated for half a second, then handed her the purple ceramic mug that had been his mother's. "You and I both know we have to move on this. If Vilar's network is using embedded encryption, Benji's the one who's going to crack it."

Lily took the coffee, fingers wrapping around the mug. Jack noticed her nails were chewed down to the nub—old habit, maybe— and her index finger was calloused. A trigger finger. Not a fresh mark, but not old enough to be forgotten, either.

She studied him over the rim of her cup. "And he dropped everything to come? Just like that?"

Jack shrugged. "He owes me."

Lily held his gaze for a long moment, then nodded. "Interesting. Maybe you'll tell me the story sometime. I guess we'll see if your guy's as good as you say."

Jack never shared more than was necessary.

By mid-morning, the crunch of tires on snow announced Alex Lin's arrival. Jack watched from the window as Alex stepped out of his SUV, backpack in hand. His wiry frame was bundled in an oversized hoodie, and he scanned Jack's home like someone who didn't miss a thing.

"Nice," Alex said as he entered, his voice light. "Rustic. Cozy. Very off-grid chic. Did you decorate this place yourself, or is there a catalog for retired spies?"

Jack rolled his eyes. "Still a comedian."

Alex grinned, dropping his bag onto the floor. "Keeps things interesting. Nice to see you again, Berman. You too, Lily. Where's the patient?"

Lily held up the phone. "Right here."

Alex's expression shifted, his usual snarkiness replaced with focus. "Good. Let's see what we're dealing with."

The table became a makeshift command center as Alex set up his custom-built laptop, connecting it to the phone with a tangle of cables. His fingers moved rapidly, sending one command after another, lines of code cascading down the screen.

"This encryption is no joke," Alex muttered, half to himself. "Whoever set this up knew what they were doing."

Lily leaned over his shoulder. "Military-grade?"

"Close," Alex replied. "Could be ex-military. Or someone with deep pockets."

Jack leaned against the counter, watching the screen. "How long?"

"Hard to say," Alex said without looking up. "But if there's anything good on this phone, I'll find it."

The room fell into a tense silence as Alex worked, his focus unshakable. Lily occasionally offered suggestions, her technical knowledge keeping pace with Alex's rapid-fire explanations.

The hours passed with little progress. Each of Alex's decryption attempts started out with great promise, then slowly turned into dead ends. Lily was out of suggestions.

A knock at the door broke the quiet. Jack moved to answer it without a word. Benji stepped inside, brushing snow off his sweatshirt, his sharp eyes flicking across the room as he took in the setup. He pushed back his hood, revealing dark, unruly curls. Wire-rimmed glasses perched on his nose.

Alex looked up from the laptop. "You called in backup?"

Jack ignored him. "Benji, this is Lily. And you already know Alex."

Benji gave a small nod in greeting, but he was all business. "I brought some gear."

Jack helped Benji unload two drones, a scanner, tracking devices, a collection of high-powered binoculars and a monocular, and other gadgets from his car. "Do you ever travel without your toys?"

But Benji's attention had already shifted to Alex's screen.

Alex leaned back, folding his arms. "No offense, but I've got this under control."

Benji didn't respond. Instead, he stepped closer, scanning the lines of code flickering across the monitor. The sleeves of his sweatshirt were pushed to his elbows, faint ink stains marking his wrists—a reminder that his skills were as analog as they were digital.

Alex exhaled through his nose, turning his focus back to the laptop. The decryption held steady at 83%, but then stalled. A failed access error flashed across the screen.

Benji finally spoke. "Your algorithm's looping."

Alex's jaw tightened. "I know what I'm doing."

Benji remained unfazed. "Then you know it's not going to hold. The system's designed to detect brute-force attempts. You need a pattern, not raw processing power."

More hours passed. Hope flickered high and low as Alex kept trying. Glancing over at Lily curled up on the couch, sound asleep, Jack finally said, "OK, team, it's getting late. Let's call it a night."

"Are you ready to do it my way?" asked Benji.

Jack watched as Alex hesitated, then sighed and slid his chair back. "Fine. Be my guest."

Benji adjusted his glasses and switched chairs with Alex, ready to take over. He didn't hesitate, didn't second-guess—just adjusted the latest algorithm in real-time, making shifts so subtle that even Alex could barely follow.

Minutes passed, then Alex's laptop let out a soft chime.

Benji leaned back, pushing his glasses up his nose. "We're in."

The phone itself wasn't the goldmine—but it was the key. The decrypted data linked to a secure network, giving them a backdoor into a larger operation. It was the foothold that Benji needed. As he broke into one restricted account after another, the screen filled with encrypted messages, GPS coordinates, and cryptic references.

"Look at these locations," Lily said, wiping the sleep from her eyes, then circling a cluster of points on the map with her finger. "Northern Idaho. One of them is just outside Coeur d'Alene."

Jack frowned, leaning over the table. "What's out there?"

"Nothing good," Benji replied. His speech was clipped, the significance of his knowledge evident. "That area's been a hotspot for militia activity for decades. Far-right extremist groups, survivalist enclaves—a breeding ground for conspiracy theorists and white supremacist cells."

Lily zoomed in on the map, the highlighted locations forming an ominous cluster in remote, forested areas. "It's not just random militia stuff," she said. "These locations look coordinated. Organized."

"They are," Benji confirmed. "A lot of these groups operate under the radar—training camps, propaganda hubs, recruiting centers. Northern Idaho's always been a magnet for this kind of activity. Cheap land, remote terrain, and a network of sympathizers who know how to stay off the grid."

Alex had taken back the laptop and was hammering at the keys with such force that Jack half-wondered if fingertips could bruise.

"The messages are encrypted," Alex said, his voice sharp. "But we're seeing references to large-scale funding—operational budgets, encrypted transfers. And look here—mentions of Harrington Industries."

Jack clenched his jaw. "Harrington? As in William Harrington?"

Jack thought back to how they had crossed paths. "William Harrington was one of the featured speakers at a symposium I attended in Sintra."

"I just Googled him," said Lily, looking at her phone. "It says here that William Harrington is a second-generation industrialist turned crypto-agriculture billionaire. He made a fortune in regenerative agriculture and agri-tech. Harrington developed a proprietary soil analytics platform called TerraFlux, which integrates satellite imaging, AI-driven crop modeling, and blockchain-verifiable carbon credit tracking. He's heavily involved in global sustainability policymaking."

Returning to Alex's laptop, Lily added, "Harrington is big-time— he owns half the agricultural land in northern Idaho. If he's in play, that means we're not just looking at stolen art anymore."

Jack let out a deep sigh. "Harrington Industries. Not only half the agricultural land—through their subsidiary, Harrington Agri Group, they also own half of the water rights in Idaho and key agricultural states. That provides Harrington a lot of leverage."

Jack smirked. "Looking at the big picture, this may be small potatoes, as it were. Harrington Industries supplies vehicles, equipment, and infrastructure to U.S. military bases worldwide. And much more. Harrington's oil and energy holdings are considerable, including several alternative energy initiatives. He has direct ownership stakes in media companies and social media platforms. Need I go on?"

Benji scrolled through another decrypted file. "Harrington isn't just laundering money. He's moving something. Look at this—logistics reports, shipping manifests, coded inventory lists." He glanced up. "Whatever's happening in Coeur d'Alene, it's running through his warehouses."

Jack's mind raced. William Harrington was the perfect puppet. A third-generation industrialist, Harrington had inherited old money and a sprawling agricultural empire. His family's fortune had been built on land, food production, and quiet alliances with people who operated in the shadows. People in Idaho knew the history of the Harrington dynasty.

"Harrington's legacy started with his grandfather, William Harrington Sr.," Jack said. "Rumors have been floating around for years that the old man helped launder Reich assets in the 1940s through Swiss and American banks after the war. Nothing was ever proven, though. Is it possible that now, decades later, the grandson is using those same financial pipelines to move something bigger?"

Lily held Jack's gaze. "So this is the connection. Vilar supplies the stolen art. Harrington hides it behind his agricultural businesses. The money moves through shell companies, then straight into far-right groups, propaganda networks, and political candidates that Vilar can control."

Benji nodded. "It makes sense to hide it under an agricultural front. No one questions farm shipments. It's the perfect cover."

His voice dropped, laced with disgust. "They're funding hate with masterpieces."

Alex frowned, his finger hovering over another message. "But where is the stolen art even coming from? None of this explains how they're getting their hands on it in the first place. Are we talking about gallery heists, private collectors, black-market deals? It's like pieces of the puzzle are missing."

"And then there's Idaho," Lily added. "These white supremacist cells—they're being financed, but how does that connect back to everything else? Are they just the end point, or is there something bigger at play?"

Alex's gaze darkened. "The money flow is deliberate. Auction proceeds hit a shell account, then vanish into encrypted transfers. From there, who knows? A chunk goes toward these groups, but what about the rest?"

"Probably back into the pipeline," Benji guessed. "Recruitment, propaganda, logistics. Whatever it takes to scale up, right?"

"But it's all guesswork," Lily said impatiently. "We're seeing the symptoms, not the source. Until we figure out where the art is coming from and who's pulling the strings, we're chasing shadows."

Benji clicked another log file. "If Harrington's part of this, that means there's physical evidence. He's got to be storing something. The art, the money—maybe even documents linking him to Vilar."

Jack straightened. "Then we're not sitting around. We must act right away—too much is going on. We need to pinpoint Harrington's storage location."

Lily tapped the screen. "There's a Harrington Agri Group agricultural distribution center here." She pointed to a spot on the outskirts of Coeur d'Alene. "It's a farm on paper, but these locations don't match up with its official shipping records. Something's off."

Alex leaned back. "So what's the plan? We walk in and ask for a tour of the potato farm?"

Jack chuckled. "No. I have a more private tour in mind. Uninvited."

CHAPTER 9

Coeur d'Alene

T he sky was still dark as the team set off toward Harrington's agricultural distribution center. Every detail had been perfectly planned—nothing left to chance.

They started in a beat-up suburban that blended with the early morning traffic on the outskirts of town, its license plates swapped out in a desolate parking lot two days prior. At an abandoned gas station on a back road, they switched vehicles, transferring a drone and other gear to a plain, gray pickup. Alex wiped down every surface of the suburban before they left it behind, erasing any trace of them.

By late afternoon, they checked into separate, nondescript motels on the outskirts of Coeur d'Alene, paying in cash. They took the usual precautions to make sure they weren't followed and that the rooms were clear of listening devices.

Jack's room became their base of operations. "Alright, let's do it," Jack said, his tone clipped and professional. "Alex, get the tech ready. Benji, stay on high alert; watch the parking lot. We have one shot at this, and we can't afford to get sloppy."

The group moved quickly; each knew exactly what to do. Alex unpacked his laptop and surveillance equipment, assembling them on the table. Benji walked around the parking lot, making a mental note of the license plates. When he returned, he ensured that the windows and doors were secure and kept watch by the front window. Lily unrolled the map of Harrington's distribution center across the table, her finger tracing the access points they'd identified from satellite images.

"This is where we'll regroup after the recon," she said, tapping the map. "We finalize the approach, hit the warehouse, and get out clean. Any questions?"

Benji shook his head, but Alex glanced up from his laptop. "What about fallback options if things go sideways?"

Lily's expression hardened. "Then we burn everything and disappear. But let's not get to that point."

Jack interrupted. "When we disappear, Alex and Benji, grab a bus to anywhere. Lily and I will take the pickup back to Ketchum."

The group settled into the final stage of preparation. The motel room had become both their refuge and their launch pad for what was to come. After midnight, they gave themselves a few hours to rest, but no one really slept.

As they climbed into the pickup, the sky had deepened into the inky black of pre-dawn, the first hints of light barely touching the horizon. Lily drove, keeping her speed precisely three miles under the limit, her eyes flicking between the rearview mirror and the road ahead.

Every few minutes, Alex adjusted a portable scanner on his lap, monitoring for surveillance signals or trackers. "Clear so far," he muttered, though the tension in his voice said he wasn't convinced it would stay that way.

Their route avoided major highways, weaving through backroads and forgotten trails that cut through dense woods and farmland. At one point, they stopped at a roadside diner for a quick plate swap, replacing the pickup's Idaho plates with a Washington set from a stash in the bed. Benji worked efficiently, tossing the discarded plates into a burn bag they'd dispose of later.

"We're ghosts," he said as he tightened the bolts, though he sounded unconvinced.

Lily and Alex exchanged a glance but said nothing. Ghosts didn't leave trails, but Harrington's network was vast, and none of them could shake the feeling that invisible eyes might already be watching.

Jack could feel them more than anyone. He knew better than to underestimate Vilar, Harrington, and their network, which now included Interpol and law enforcement agencies worldwide.

As they approached Harrington's distribution center, the landscape changed. The thick forests thinned into vast stretches of potato fields unfurling into the horizon. The team fell silent, the air inside the truck growing heavy with unspoken anticipation. To anyone else, this was just farmland—a symbol of honest, hard work. But to them, it was enemy territory, every barn and silo a potential hub for Harrington's sprawling operation.

When they reached the ridge overlooking the center, the first faint blush of dawn crept across the horizon, casting long shadows over the fields below. Lily killed the truck's engine, and the team climbed out, moving quickly. The air was crisp and sharp, carrying the faint, earthy scent of freshly tilled soil.

Jack scanned the property below, already mapping entry points in his mind.

"This is it," Jack murmured, staying low to the ground. He pulled out a pair of high-powered binoculars and raised them to his eyes. "The whole operation is laid out in plain sight."

Harrington's agricultural distribution center sprawled across the valley, a picture of wealth and control. A modernist mansion stood in the center, all steel and glass, gleaming even in the dim light. But Jack wasn't interested in the house. The real focus lay beyond it—the warehouse tucked against the treeline, a fortress disguised as farmland.

Alex joined Lily at the ridge with his own set of binoculars. "Look at the way that storage facility is positioned. Set back away from the main house, with a clear line of sight to the road. Strategic as hell."

Benji dropped to his knees beside them, adjusting the scope of his monocular as he zeroed in on the warehouse. Trucks idled outside the warehouse, cargo bays yawning open as workers loaded and unloaded crates. A forklift beeped faintly, its sound swallowed by the open fields.

"That's a lot of traffic for a potato farm," Benji said, his voice edged with skepticism. "What the hell is he moving?"

Jack noticed the tension in Benji's shoulders—the same unease he felt himself.

"Not potatoes," Lily replied firmly. "This is the heart of his operation. Whatever's in those crates, it's not going to a grocery store."

Jack's gaze locked on the warehouse. "Then that's where we start."

Alex pulled out his laptop and set up the drone controls on a flat rock, his fingers already navigating the touchscreen. "Alright, let's get a closer look."

A soft whir filled the air as the first drone lifted off, disappearing into the pale morning sky. One of a new generation of nearly silent drones, it was almost undetectable. Through his laptop screen, the thermal imaging feed came to life. Bright orange and yellow shapes moved inside the warehouse, clustered around storage racks and machinery.

"Dozens of people in there," Alex muttered, zooming in on a group near the rear of the building. "Look at their uniforms, their coordinated movements. These guys don't look like farmers."

Lily leaned over Alex's shoulder, studying the screen. "Military precision," she said. "This is a supply chain. They're moving something big."

Jack shifted his gaze toward the modernist mansion, noting the sweeping driveway, manicured gardens, and tall walls of windows. "And Harrington sits right there, smack in the middle of it all," he said, his voice filled with disdain.

Lily pulled a small tablet from her pack, flipping through intercepted financial logs. "We're here for proof. Alex, keep the drones on the trucks. I want to know exactly where they're going."

Alex tapped the screen, adjusting the drone's trajectory. The camera zoomed in on a line of boxes stacked inside the warehouse. "Look at that," Alex said. "No markings other than shipping labels. Nothing to indicate what's inside."

Jack flexed his fingers, already calculating. Whatever was in those boxes, Harrington didn't want anyone knowing about it.

"Wait! Zoom in toward the corner. There!" exclaimed Jack.

"What do you see?"

"I see two crates, marked 'ERR R-50' and 'ERR R-51,'" replied Alex.

Jack had seen these markings before on the Nazi stolen art crates.

"It's the same type of wooden crates I saw in Paris, on the loading dock of the Galerie Moreau," said Jack. "They're removed from their shipping boxes."

He wasn't sure about the "ERR," but he knew the rest was code for the owner and inventory number. In this case, "R" for "Rothschild," and they were the 50th and 51st items taken from that collection. This shed light on what might be in the other boxes.

Benji let out a low whistle, shaking his head. "This whole place is a fortress. Every inch of it screams money and power."

"Stolen money," Alex corrected, glancing up from his screen. "And, power abused."

Jack crouched near the edge of the ridge, his fingers brushing against the damp earth. They had enough to confirm suspicion—but not enough to take Harrington down.

"We need to get inside for a closer look—get more information; plant bugs and trackers," Jack said.

After regrouping and restocking, that night, under the cover of darkness, the team crept toward the warehouse. Alex remained at the ridge, his thermal camera mapping every step of the guards' patrols.

Jack motioned to Benji, who crouched near the truck bay and pulled a tracking device from his vest. Lily kept her hand on the Glock at her side, head down, reflexes primed.

They reached the near corner of the warehouse without incident. Jack pressed against the cool metal of a stacked pallet, scanning the area. One guard at the door. Another rounding the corner.

"Surprisingly few guards," said Jack.

"At least those we can see," said Lily.

"Wait here," Jack whispered to Lily and Benji. "I'm taking a closer look."

Moving low to the ground, Jack approached the side of the open door of a loading dock at the far end of the building. With sharp, darting head movements, he peeked into the large receiving area. Two men, with their backs to him, were inserting an antique wooden crate into a padded cardboard box. There was no one else in sight. More wooden crates were stacked along the wall to his left. Next to them, just a couple of yards away, was a small table littered with papers, some stacked, some scattered.

Holding his breath, Jack climbed up onto the dock, grabbed a handful of papers from the table, then quickly retreated, climbing down from the dock. There wasn't anything more he could do.

"Shipping manifests," said Jack, tucking them inside his jacket as he crouched down next to Lily.

It was Benji's turn. Sliding under one of the trucks, he pressed the tracker against the axle and secured it.

As he rolled out from beneath the truck and stood, a flashlight beam cut through the dark. "Hey!" a voice shouted.

"Don't move," Jack whispered to Lily. "There's one guard, and he only saw Benji."

Benji raised his arms high as the guard approached, shining his light on Benji's face.

When the guard was just a few steps away, Jack didn't hesitate. He moved fast, striking before the guard could fully react. His fist slammed into the man's temple with precise force—not enough to kill, but enough to drop him. The guard staggered, eyes rolling back as his knees gave out, and fell to the ground.

Lily spun, activating the thermal camera's strobe function to send a blinding pulse of light into the second guard's eyes as he raised his weapon. The crack of gunfire punctured the air. Benji yelped and hit the ground hard, blood seeping through his sleeve as he crawled behind a stack of crates.

"Fall back!" Lily shouted. She dove behind the crates, grabbed Benji, and hauled him to his feet, wrapping an arm around him. "Cover us!" she yelled to Jack.

Jack took down another guard with a sharp elbow to the throat, then pivoted, firing a controlled burst toward the loading dock. From his safe spot on the ridge, Alex hacked into the warehouse's lighting system, sending the compound into sudden darkness. The confusion gave them the seconds they needed. They ran, vanishing into the night.

Jack cast a final glance over his shoulder. That's when he saw him—Harrington. There was no doubt it was him—silver hair gleaming. He stood along the treeline, silhouetted in the moonlight. He didn't follow, didn't call for his guards to pursue, didn't react. He simply watched them leave, his expression calm and calculating.

It was as if he'd expected them all along.

His mother's words echoed in his ears. Trouble is following him.

"Look behind you," said Jack. Lily and Benji stopped to turn around. They were all well-hidden in the shadows among the trees.

"It's Harrington. He must have watched us run, but he can't see us now," said Lily.

"He's not more than fifty yards away," said Benji, pulling out his SIG Sauer P226, a handgun commonly used by military and intelligence units worldwide. "I can take him out—with a little bit of luck." Benji grimaced, cradling his injured arm against his body.

"Take a shot," said Lily. "His men shot you."

As Benji steadied his weapon at the base of a branch where it joined the trunk of a large tree, Jack thought for a moment, then said sharply, under his breath, "No—it's not right!"

Jack took a deep breath and thought. *We won't be judge, jury, and executioner.*

Benji hesitated, then leaned back, letting the gun tilt upward. "You're right. He must be brought to justice and held accountable the proper way."

When Jack glanced toward Harrington again, he was gone. As Jack headed up the ridge, he knew he had done the right thing, but doubt, nevertheless, crept into his mind.

Have I gotten soft? Would I have let this opportunity slip by in my Agency days?

CHAPTER 10

Rose Lake

The woods were eerily silent as the team fled from Harrington's distribution center. Just as the dense darkness of the forest closed around them, the warehouse's floodlights blazed back to life, cutting through the trees like a spotlight on their retreat. Jack's pulse spiked. They weren't in the clear yet. Adrenaline coursed through his veins, driving his tired legs forward.

Lily led the way, her Glock in hand. Behind her, scanning for any sign of pursuit, Jack stayed close to Benji, whose blood seeped through the bandage pressed against his arm.

"Keep moving," Lily whispered, her voice low but urgent. She turned back to check their formation. "We need more distance." Raising a hand to her earpiece, she pressed the radio button. "Alex, do you copy? We're coming your way. Get ready to head out." Turning toward Benji, she said, "How are you doing?"

Benji's breath came in shallow bursts, his face pale. "I'm fine," he muttered, though his pained voice said otherwise. The makeshift bandage on his arm was soaked through, leaving faint droplets of blood on the underbrush.

The group moved swiftly until they reached Alex and their vehicle. Benji leaned against the side of the pickup truck, catching his breath.

"Next time, remind me to say no," he muttered with a faint sneer. His voice was weak, but the humor was an attempt to lighten the mood.

"What happened?" said Alex. "Benji, are you OK?"

"No time for questions. Everybody get in," Lily replied curtly."

Jack took the wheel and navigated the narrow backroads under Lily's guidance. The pickup rattled over uneven dirt paths, its headlights switched off for the final stretch to avoid detection.

"Where are we going?" asked Jack.

"One of several sites The Office prepared for a situation like this, soon after it started investigating Vilar's operation in Idaho." Lily's voice remained steady as she led him through a labyrinth of winding turns, each one taking them deeper into the woods near Rose Lake— and closer to their destination.

Jack didn't appreciate the mystery—there was enough uncertainty in his life already, but he said nothing.

"Left at the next fork," she said. "Then stay straight until you see the old logging marker. The cabin's beyond that."

Jack's eyes darted to the rearview mirror. "You sure no one's tailing us?"

Lily didn't answer immediately, her gaze fixed on the road ahead. "If they were, we'd know by now."

The house finally came into view, a small, weathered cabin tucked into a clearing surrounded by towering pine trees. Its peeling paint and sagging porch gave it the appearance of abandonment. A rusted water pump sat crookedly beside the cabin, while a stack of firewood leaned precariously against the outer wall.

Alex jumped out and did a perimeter check. "All clear," he

announced. Jack scanned the treeline to confirm. They slipped inside quickly.

Inside, the cabin was stark but functional. A woodstove stood in the corner, its surface streaked with soot. A scarred wooden table was positioned in the center of the main room, surrounded by mismatched chairs. The walls were lined with shelves holding canned goods, medical supplies, and tools. A ladder led to a small loft with two thin mattresses laid side by side.

Benji collapsed into one of the chairs with a groan, his hand clamped over his wound. "Remind me why we couldn't pick a safe house with a *little* more comfort?" he muttered, casting a weary glance around the stark cabin.

Lily ignored him, moving quickly to secure the windows and pull the blackout curtains closed. "It's safe," she said. "That's all that matters."

Jack dug the first aid kit from their gear and knelt beside Benji. He unwound the blood-soaked bandage, grimacing at the jagged graze beneath. "You're lucky," he said. "Another inch, and this would've hit bone."

"Lucky's my middle name," Benji replied, but his voice lacked its usual bite. He looked pale and shaken, his forehead glistening with a sheen of sweat.

Lily exhaled sharply and lifted her shirt just enough to reveal a deep gash along her side.

Jack blinked, masking his surprise—he hadn't realized she was injured. She'd been steady the entire way, never wincing, never slowing down. Without hesitation, she began cleaning her wound, her movements rigid and detached.

"You should let me take care of that," Jack said, glancing at her.

"I've had worse," Lily replied. "We have bigger problems."

Jack didn't push. Instead, he focused on stitching Benji's wound. "It's always the same playbook," he said softly, almost to himself. "Different uniforms, same strategy."

"What do you mean?" Lily asked, glancing up from her wound.

Jack's jaw tightened. "Harrington, Fischer, and Vilar. They're not unique. I've seen this playbook before. Eastern Europe. White supremacists calling themselves defenders of their heritage. All they left behind was ash."

"You fought them?" Lily's voice was softer now.

Jack met her gaze briefly, then looked away. "I tried."

An uncomfortable moment of silence stretched between them. Lily nodded. Her eyes were soft, as if she understood the significance of past battles. "Sometimes trying is the only thing that matters."

Jack exhaled and glanced at Benji, who was still pale, his bandaged arm resting limply at his side. "You're done for now," Jack said, nodding toward the corner of the room. "Get some rest."

Benji groaned but didn't argue. With effort, he pushed himself up and shuffled toward a cot against the wall, lowering himself onto it with a wince.

Jack and Lily joined Alex at the scarred wooden table in the center of the room, cluttered with devices, electronics, and half-empty water bottles. Alex was hunched over his laptop, fingers flying across the keys. His laptop was hooked up to a portable second monitor, giving them a wider view of the data he'd pulled.

In frustration, Lily slammed her fist on the table, the sharp crack cutting through the room. "What a waste," she exclaimed, exhaling sharply. "Our cover's blown, we shed blood, and we didn't even get any proof."

Jack blinked. Lily wasn't one to let emotions slip—at least, not like this. The tension in her shoulders, the edge in her voice, made it clear the mission had pushed her further than she'd let on.

"We have this evidence," said Jack, pulling out the papers from his jacket and showing them to Lily. "These shipping manifests are just a small sample—there were many more. Can you imagine how many shipments of stolen art are flowing through Harrington's distribution center?"

Lily didn't respond.

"Moreover, thanks to the tracker Benji attached to one of their trucks, we'll soon find out where some of these shipments are headed," Jack added.

He gazed at her for a second, debating whether to say anything else, but before he could, Alex spoke.

"There's a lot of proof…" Alex said, barely looking up from his laptop. The glow from the screen cast sharp shadows across his face as he worked. "While you guys were busy making a scene, I got into their system."

Lily's eyes snapped to him. "You hacked in?"

"Had a clean signal from the ridge," Alex said with a smirk. "Figured I'd poke around. Turns out, Harrington's security is good— but not *that* good."

The screens flashed with lines of decrypted code, each one

unraveling another layer of the operation. "Syncing everything now," he said. "Check your phones—I'm pushing the files to the shared drive."

Jack and Lily pulled out their phones as the notification popped up. A moment later, folders loaded onto their screens—dozens of them, packed with images, financial records, and provenance files.

"You wanted proof?" Alex said, tapping a key. "Here's proof."

High-resolution photographs filled his monitor—grainy security cam footage showing silhouettes of workers unloading crates under the cover of night. On their phones, Lily and Jack scrolled through endless images of Harrington's activities, not only in Idaho, but in Europe, South America, and Asia. They saw sprawling warehouses in remote locations, hidden docks along private waterways, and convoys of unmarked trucks moving in precise coordination. The staggering scale of Harrington's operations exceeded their expectations.

The two crates with markings that he and Alex saw in the corner of the warehouse were not the exception; it was clear the crates were filled with stolen Nazi art. Jack skimmed a set of shipping manifests. "This isn't just a smuggling ring," he muttered. "These figures don't add up unless he's moving entire collections." He tapped on an image of a gilded frame leaning against a stack of other artwork. The painting's subject was a serene landscape, its craftsmanship unmistakable. "This piece alone could bankroll months of operations."

They continued opening folders, examining documents, photographs, and videos.

"Lily, did you see this?" asked Jack, tilting his tablet for her to see.

"It's not only stolen art. Look at the markings on these crates—military markings. Harrington is gunrunning."

"It's clear that Harrington has his dirty fingers in yet another pie," said Lily. "This makes him more formidable and dangerous. And, undoubtedly, it's all tied to Vilar."

Alex tapped a folder on his screen, bringing up detailed financial records. "He's moving cash, too—millions of dollars in offshore accounts, most of them flagged for suspicious activity by regulators in Europe. The sheer volume is insane."

"We not only got proof," Lily said. "We got everything." She scrolled rapidly through her files. "It's all here. Provenance records—falsified and sloppy, but enough to convince someone who isn't looking too closely."

Lily clicked through more files, her jaw tightening with each entry. "Vilar has falsified the provenance on all of it. Buyers think they're getting legitimate, rare masterpieces with clean histories. They have no idea they're funding an operation built on the blood and theft of the Holocaust."

Jack's face darkened as he stared at the screen. "So not only is Harrington laundering art, but Vilar's using Nazi-stolen treasures to bait these buyers."

"And tying them to the pieces," Lily added, her voice colder now. "Once they own stolen art, they're vulnerable to blackmail, whether they knew the truth or not. It's a web—and Vilar's at the center of it."

Jack set down the manifest and crossed his arms. "If Harrington's moving entire collections, who's buying this stuff?"

"Not who," Lily said, her tone sharp. "What kind of people. He's not selling to ordinary collectors. He's targeting power players—oligarchs, politicians, corporate elites. Art isn't just money for them. It's leverage."

Jack cocked his head and leaned against the table. "How so?"

"Stolen masterpieces can't be publicly displayed or insured," Lily explained. "The buyers know this, and so does Harrington. Once they own stolen art, they're vulnerable to exposure. Harrington holds that over them."

Jack nodded slowly. "And once he has them tied to stolen art, he owns them."

Alex clicked on a folder labeled *Directive 88*. "This name keeps coming up," he said, pointing to the screen. "Emails, financial logs, internal memos—it's everywhere."

The folder opened to reveal a series of documents in German, many with redacted sections. Maps of Europe and the United States filled the screen, dotted with routes and distribution hubs. Alex enlarged one of the memos, translating it on the fly. "'Expansion Initiative: North American Phase,'" he read aloud. "'Projected targets: political funding channels, media acquisition, and cultural subversion assets.'" He paused, glancing at the others. "This is more than a smuggling operation. It's a takeover."

Lily scanned the text quickly, the light in her eyes dimming with each line. "Check this out—Harrington's laundering stolen art through Vilar's network in Europe, but the profits are being reinvested in political campaigns, extremist propaganda, and media buyouts."

"And weapons," Alex added, clicking on another file. "Look at these shipments. He's using the same trucks to move firearms, encrypted communication systems, even explosives."

Jack exhaled sharply. "Art, money, weapons... this is a full-scale operation. Harrington's a kingpin and a damn general."

As they pieced together the puzzle, the scale of Harrington's operation became disturbingly clear. The stolen art was just the beginning—a means to an end. Each transaction led to another thread: offshore accounts funding white supremacist groups in Idaho, encrypted communications connecting Vilar to Harrington's European counterparts, and financial records tied to Senator Cain's Presidential campaign.

Lily stopped at one file and highlighted a sequence of transactions. "Here's a direct link," she said. "Harrington's funneling money from art sales to Vilar, who's sending it straight into Cain's political action committees. He's bankrolling a fringe candidate with stolen art."

"Why Cain?" Alex asked. "Why not someone more mainstream?"

"Because Cain's of like mind, and he's controllable," Lily said. "Vilar's strategy, the one that has worked across Europe, is to use far-right politicians to cannibalize the center. Germany's conservatives are now working with the far-right AfD. Same thing in France, where the far right is now the largest bloc in parliament. Austria, the Netherlands, and even the U.K. are seeing the same trend. Vilar sees the U.S. as next. He's already using dog whistles and nationalist rhetoric to energize the far right. Harrington doesn't want a known politician. He wants someone who connects with voters' immigration, inflation fears, and can work the system from the inside."

Jack tapped the edge of the table, his eyes narrowing. "If Cain wins, Harrington has a puppet in the most powerful office in the world. The Oval Office. Vilar's concentration of wealth and power will be complete."

Lily pointed to a memo referencing a private event scheduled in four days—a high-stakes auction hosted by Harrington himself.

"Look at this auction at the Galerie Moreau. It will be a gathering of his network. His buyers. His allies. If we can disrupt it... We can take him down," Jack finished, his voice firm. "We must take him down; we must expose the entire operation."

The tension in the room was palpable as they processed the significance of their discovery. Harrington's network was the foundation of a global conspiracy. And with *Directive 88* in motion, and the upcoming high-stakes auction in Paris, the timer was ticking.

CHAPTER 11

Titus Lake

"The world is a dangerous place," quipped the ER doctor, accepting Benji's explanation for his wound. "Be more aware of your surroundings." *Such sound advice*, thought Jack, determined to follow it far more than the doctor could imagine.

The long drive back from Coeur d'Alene to Ketchum was uneventful, except for a near miss with a moose. Initially, there was a lot of excited discussion about the revelations about Harrington, Vilar, Cain, and their global network. But soon the group became quiet as the implications and challenges they would face began to sink in.

The morning light filtered through the frosted bedroom windows of Jack's home, casting a pale glow over the wooden floor. He lay on his bed, staring at the ceiling, knowing sleep wouldn't come. It hadn't all night, though he felt good to be back. Before the Coeur d'Alene operation, Jack worked hard to clean up the mess left by the intruders. But many traces remained—splintered drawers, scratched furniture, cracked picture frames—of how thoroughly someone had ransacked his home.

"You don't look so good," said Alex.

"Good morning to you, too," said Jack.

That morning, Jack dropped Alex and Benji off at Friedman

Memorial Airport in Hailey. Both were leaving for the West Coast.

"I appreciate your work," said Jack. "I may need your help again, soon."

"Understood," said Alex.

"You know how to reach me on short notice," said Benji.

Jack plugged the USB stick Alex had made for him in Rose Lake into his laptop and started looking at the folders again. They contained information he had already seen. Then, he clicked on a folder they had overlooked at the lake.

"Oh, my God," whispered Jack. The folder held documents indicating a hidden lodge near Titus Lake, along with coded references to stolen art.

The lodge's secluded location and its possible ties to Nazi sympathizers in the U.S. made it a compelling lead. More than its isolation, the lake's name carried an eerie resonance: Titus, the Roman general who sacked Jerusalem in 70 CE, was infamous for looting treasures from the Jewish Temple as spoils of war. The historical irony wasn't lost on Jack. If the cache was indeed hidden here, it symbolized a chilling continuum of cultural theft—from ancient Rome to the Nazi regime. Finding the stolen art at Titus Lake would provide not only undeniable proof of the conspiracy's ideological roots but also a powerful counter-narrative to their attempts to rewrite history.

Jack tried to get some sleep again. His body was exhausted, but his mind refused to quiet; a memory would not let him sleep.

His mother's voice, her hands flipping through an old book, the pages brittle with time.

"Art isn't just about beauty. It's about what we value, what we choose to remember."

And what happens when we forget?

Jack exhaled slowly, watching his breath form a cloud in the dim light. He hadn't really thought about faith in years. His Jewish identity had always existed in the background, present but distant, like an old photograph tucked into a drawer. His mother had never pushed it on him, not the way some families did. For her, faith had been a quiet, steady thing, woven into her work, into the way she spoke about the lost and the stolen.

Jack had never fully understood it. Not when he was a kid sitting cross-legged in her study, flipping through art books while she and her closest friend, Dr. Nathan Goldstein, pored over Nazi-looted ledgers. Not until he was a teenager did he begin to grasp the relevance of what had been taken from their ancestors—not just their lives, but their legacies. And not now, as he lay here, preparing to unearth stolen history in a remote stretch of Idaho wilderness.

For his mother, faith had been a source of strength. For his ancestors, it had been something more—something unyielding, something that had made them a target. He couldn't shake the thought: if they had abandoned their faith, had chosen silence instead of defiance, would they have survived?

He wanted to believe in something. Not in God, not in miracles, but in justice. In truth.

And yet, even as he thought it, he knew truth alone wouldn't be enough.

Jack sat up, scrubbing a hand down his face, swung his legs over the side of the bed, and stood.

The past wasn't gone. It had just been hidden. Buried. Waiting.

It was time to go. He picked up his phone and looked up the route to Titus Lake. Then, he dialed Lily's number, knowing there was no way she would miss this for the world.

Jack and Lily said little as they drove the short distance to Titus Lake, less than an hour away. They watched the sun clear the mountain ridges and the sky turn to a bright, wintry blue. The wind howled through the trees, carrying the scent of pine and ice, rattling bare branches like brittle bones.

Jack adjusted the straps on his pack, feeling the weight settle against his shoulders. Beside him, Lily tightened the buckles on her boots, her face set with quiet focus.

Jack gave her a look. The crisp air bit at their cheeks, and for a few seconds, they stood motionless, listening to the quiet creak of the pines swaying in the wind. This was it—the final step before plunging into the unknown. For weeks, their investigation had led them through a labyrinth of connections, shadowy figures, and cryptic documents. But all roads pointed here, to Titus Lake. The stakes couldn't be higher—not just for them, but for the truth they were trying to unearth.

The mission to recover these works wasn't just about justice; it was about reclaiming identity. Jack had absorbed this passion secondhand, listening as Dr. Goldstein described how many of these stolen works had vanished into the shadows after the war. Some were hidden in salt mines, like Altaussee in Austria, or spirited away to private collections. Others were used to fund secret networks of Nazi loyalists who fled to countries like Argentina or even the United States. The idea that such a cache might exist in the remote Idaho wilderness had seemed far-fetched until this recent discovery.

How many untold stories were hidden within the stolen masterpieces? Each painting, each artifact, was a piece of someone's life—a celebration, a memory, a legacy ripped away. His mother's voice had always carried conviction when she spoke about history's silent witnesses, and now those words fueled him. This mission wasn't just an investigation; it was a chance to restore what had been unjustly taken and to stand against the forces that sought to bury the truth.

Jack took a deep breath, the cold air filling his lungs, and looked up at the mountains. "This is it," he said, more to himself than to the others. "This is what we've been waiting for—what we've been working for."

Lily adjusted her hat, pulling it down over her ears. "Looks... inviting," she said, glancing up at the steep trail ahead.

"It'll look a lot less inviting by the time we hit the ridge," said Jack, carefully applying the skins to his skis as Lily did the same. He stepped into his skis, testing the bindings before helping Lily with her gear. "Stay close," he instructed. "The trail's marked, but it's easy to get turned around up here. And watch for signs of avalanche risk." The recent snowfall had been heavy, and with the sun warming the upper slopes during the day, the risk of a slide was real.

"Pay attention to the snowpack," he added, his tone serious. "If we hear any deep, hollow sounds or notice cracks forming in the snow, we need to stop immediately. Stay spread out when crossing steep sections, and call it out if something feels off."

Lily nodded. "Yeah, stay close, don't die."

Lily adjusted her poles and started toward the trailhead, her movements smooth and confident. Jack followed, mimicking her. The trail began as a gentle incline, winding through a dense forest where the trees formed a canopy overhead. The only sounds were the swish of their skis and the occasional call of a bird.

They were alone out here. Or at least, they should have been.

Jack's instincts itched. Something about the quiet felt off.

As they gained elevation, the forest thinned, and the trail grew steeper. The snow was deep and powdery, slowing their progress but muffling their movements. Jack paused occasionally to check Gaia on his phone and survey the terrain, his trained eye scanning for any signs of danger.

"How much farther?" Lily called out, her breath visible in the cold air.

"Not far," Jack replied. "Once we hit the ridge, we'll have a clear view of the lake."

The trail grew more challenging as they approached the ridge, the incline forcing them to dig their skis into the snow for traction. Lily led the way, her pace steady but relentless.

They reached the ridge just before noon. Below, the lake lay frozen and still, its surface glinting like dull glass in the weak sunlight. The landscape was untouched—no signs of recent movement, no tracks in the snow. But Jack knew better than to trust appearances.

"Lodge should be on the far side," Lily said, scanning the treeline.

They descended carefully, the trail winding down toward the lake.

The lodge, if it existed, would be on the far side, hidden among the trees. Jack's mind raced as he considered their next moves. They couldn't afford any missteps.

As Jack adjusted his footing on the icy slope, a thought gnawed at him. How likely was it, he wondered, that Count Felix Schaffgotsch, the Austrian nobleman and Nazi who had once selected Sun Valley for its breathtaking isolation and pristine wilderness, had also covertly discovered this forgotten place? The man had been more than just a ski enthusiast sent to scout America's untapped winter resorts—he had been an agent of ideology, devoted to the Reich's vision. A commitment so absolute that when the war broke out, he didn't remain in the comfort of the Idaho mountains he had so carefully curated. He returned to Europe, donning the uniform of the SS, abandoning luxury for brutality, trading a paradise of untouched snow for the darkness of Nazi service and ultimately paying the ultimate price on the Russian front.

Coincidence felt too thin. There was a pattern, deliberate and precise, layered beneath the snow, echoing through the years. Schaffgotsch's choices weren't random. They were marked by the same obsession with purity, control, and secrecy that had driven the Nazis to loot Europe's art and culture, to hoard beauty while erasing those they had stolen it from. The same quiet precision was here, in the silence of the trees, in the concealed lodge barely visible through the frosted pines.

Jack knew this kind of secrecy didn't just happen. It was built. Cultivated. Passed down through channels of whispered names and numbered accounts. A design of power, not chance—generation after generation guarding the same dark inheritance. And now, as the windswept fresh powder across his tracks, Jack felt that inheritance pressing closer. The same shadow stretching across time, still lingering, still waiting.

The trees seemed to grow closer together as they approached, their branches interlocking to form a cathedral of shadows above the frozen earth. Jack led the way, kicking and gliding through the untouched powder. The wind had picked up, sending icy shards biting against their faces. As the duo moved deeper into the wilderness near Titus Lake, the forest seemed to hold its breath.

Then they saw it.

The lodge was buried in snow, its timbers dark with age, windows frosted over, the heaviness of years pressing against its walls. The wind had blown drifts against one side, nearly swallowing a collapsed outbuilding. The whole place felt abandoned. Forgotten.

As they drew closer, Jack paused, scanning their surroundings, his instincts flaring. He spotted a tree well that would be a perfect hiding place for their equipment. "Let's take our skis off, remove the skins, and set the bindings to ski mode, then hide them over there. On second thought, if we need to escape quickly, we'll need our equipment close by."

"Look at this!" Lily clicked out of her skis and crouched beside him, brushing snow from a faint trail of footprints leading toward the lodge. The prints were fresh. Someone had been here recently.

"Careful," Jack murmured, his breath forming a fleeting cloud in the frozen air. His hand hovered near the weapon holstered beneath his jacket.

They carried their equipment toward the lodge and post-holed, sinking deep into the snow as they went. "Set everything up for a quick exit."

"Expecting company?" Lily whispered.

"Always," Jack replied.

The lodge's door was weathered but sturdy, held fast by rusting iron hinges. Jack tested it gently; it resisted with a groan, then gave way, opening into a cavernous darkness. The staleness of the air hit them immediately—a mix of mildew, decay, and something else, faint but unmistakable: the metallic tang of oil paint and varnish.

Lily swept her flashlight over the space. The room stretched out like a mausoleum. Wooden beams crisscrossed above, their surfaces warped and furred with mold. The walls were lined with crates stacked to the ceiling, their sides stamped with a menacing eagle, the unmistakable emblem of the Third Reich. Everywhere they looked, they saw scattered remnants of a life once lived: a faded rug curled at the edges, a toppled chair, a cracked mirror reflecting their pale beams of light. But the real discovery lay among the crates.

Lily knelt by one, brushing away a layer of dust to reveal the faded swastika. With a crowbar retrieved from a nearby workbench, she pried the lid open, and the beam of her flashlight revealed the contents: a stack of canvas-wrapped frames.

Carefully, Jack pulled one free, his gloved hands steady as he peeled back the fabric. Beneath, the painting's colors glowed even in the dim light—rich umbers, muted greens, and the unmistakable luminosity of Renaissance skin tones. He froze as he recognized the portrait: the piercing gaze of the sitter, his aristocratic features, the folds of his black tunic rendered with almost supernatural precision.

"Raphael," Jack whispered. "Portrait of a Young Man."

"Look at the careful posture, rich textures, and the detail that make for exquisite realism," said Lily.

"Many scholars believe that it's a self-portrait," said Jack. "It was actually housed in one of the oldest Museums in Kraków. It disappeared at the end of the war, and it's rumored that it was transported to Germany to avoid the Allies' invasion."

Now, this masterpiece, thought lost to the chaos of World War II, was resting in the dark heart of this hidden lodge.

Lily stepped closer, her voice hushed. "It's been here all this time," she said, her words tinged with awe. "Hidden in plain sight."

"And here, a Rembrandt that looks to be in near-perfect condition," said Jack.

He pulled the cover off another painting.

"It's a Matisse," said Lily.

"Yes, I know it," said Jack, "It's called Femme Assise. I think it used to belong to Paul Rosenberg, a legendary French art collector and dealer, who had to flee the Nazis during the war."

They found more as they searched—a half-dozen crates filled with priceless works. Each frame told its own story of war and theft, its brushstrokes imbued with a sense of tragedy.

"Jack," Lily's voice was tight. "Look at this."

Jack turned. Lily held an old leather-bound ledger, the edges brittle, the ink faded but legible. Inside were pages filled with codes and names, the handwriting precise and clinical. As Jack took it from her, a yellowed envelope fell out, fluttering to the ground. He knelt to pick it up and realized it was sealed with wax. Breaking it open, he pulled out a single document. Was it a deed of some sort? Then his eyes caught a name scrawled in the margins—a name that sent a shiver racing down his spine.

Before he could share what he'd found with Lily, a noise outside froze them in place. The sound was faint but distinct: the crunch of boots on snow. Lily extinguished the flashlight, plunging the room into shadow. Jack motioned for silence as they pressed themselves against the walls.

Outside, the footsteps drew closer and then stopped. Whoever was out there wasn't moving anymore. They were waiting.

The moment the footsteps stopped, Jack knew they were being hunted. His mind raced through their options, each more dangerous than the last. The stolen art, the ledger, the damning document—they couldn't take it all. They barely had time to save themselves.

Or maybe not.

The first shot came without warning through a window. A sharp crack, shattered glass, and splintering wood just inches from Lily's head.

They dove for cover in opposite directions. Lily rolled next to a stack of chairs propped up against the wall by the open door. Jack slid under the broken window on the other side of the room, his gun drawn.

He stayed low and peeked through the broken glass. "I see a man moving on the other side of the clearing."

Lily checked outside. "Clear on this side. Move now, before he gets closer."

Lily's pre-tour warning echoed in Jack's mind. "Stay close, don't die."

"Let's do it!" Jack exclaimed. He grabbed the ledger and the document, shoving them into his pack before following Lily through the door. Another shot. Too close.

They burst into the open, the cold hitting them like a wall. They clicked into their skis and pushed off. The snow-covered slopes stretched ahead. If they could make it across the ridge, they could lose them in the trees.

Jack skied first, poles stabbing the snow, carving a fast line down toward the valley. Lily was right behind him.

Then—a deep, distant rumble. Faint at first, like something shifting beneath the surface of the world.

Jack's gut twisted. The ground beneath his skis shivered, a subtle, treacherous give, as if the mountain had taken a breath. Then another, deeper. Above them, the trees groaned, brittle branches cracking under an unseen force.

Not a gunshot. Not thunder.

Avalanche!

A sudden *crack* split the air as the snowfield above them fractured. A wall of white broke loose, rolling toward them with terrifying speed.

"Go!" Jack shouted. He knew from his years of skiing that, if caught in the path of an avalanche, wasting even a few seconds could mean the difference between survival and death.

They veered left, cutting through the trees, dodging low branches and half-buried rocks. The ground vibrated beneath them, the avalanche roaring closer, a monstrous tide swallowing everything in its path.

The snow came crashing down just feet behind them, tearing through the trees, breaking trunks like matchsticks. The noise was deafening.

Jack barely saw the ledge before they went over it. For a breathless moment, they were airborne. Then—impact.

Jack hit the slope hard, rolling, his skis tearing loose. Snow exploded around him. He tumbled, arms instinctively shielding his face, the world a blur of white and motion.

Then stillness. Silence. Jack groaned, pushing himself upright. His head throbbed, his gloves sticky with blood from a cut on his temple.

Lily. He turned, searching—then exhaled in relief. She was alive, already moving. "You OK?" she said.

"Yeah," just a little tumble. But, damn, closest I've ever come to a slide," Jack said as he wiped snow from his face, breathing hard. He stepped into his bindings, letting his gloves dangle from his wrists, and adjusted his goggles.

Behind them, the avalanche had slammed into the lodge, knocking down the portico and burying the bodies of whoever had been hunting them.

"We need to keep moving," Lily said.

Jack nodded.

After they skied a safe distance away, Jack said, "Vilar must know about the lodge, and he wouldn't leave a priceless cache of art unprotected, so easy to find and without any attempt to hide its Nazi origins. He may not have expected anyone to find it so soon. I doubt he meant to keep the art here for long."

Lily agreed. "Yeah, maybe this is a temporary storage location for some unknown reason?"

"And what's up with the antique ledger? Who even makes journal entries in paper books anymore?" added Lily.

"It was meant to be dramatic."

The mountain had covered their tracks. For now. But something told Jack that whatever waited ahead was far worse than what they'd left behind.

CHAPTER 12

Stanley

"**D**odging bullets is what we do best," said Jack. "When we aren't outrunning avalanches."

"We used up two of our nine lives today," Lily said with a brave smile. "Good night."

"Good night," said Jack, adding, "How many lives do we have left?"

Lily chuckled but didn't answer.

Jack tossed and turned most of the night. He woke up in a cold sweat—he needed some breathing room to think, to plan. It was imperative to go to a secure location. After the ambush at Titus Lake, Jack knew that Vilar, heir to the fortune his banker father embezzled from the illicit assets of the Third Reich, had eyes and ears everywhere. And, no doubt, Interpol was inching closer. In Sun Valley, he felt vulnerable—like a deer in an open field. Meeting again in Rose Lake was out of the question. Jack had no doubt that it was fully compromised by now, and besides, it was too far away.

Stanley, Idaho, was a place so small and remote it seemed to exist on the threshold of civilization itself. With a population of barely over one hundred, the town clung to the wilderness, dwarfed by the sweeping expanse of the Sawtooth Mountains that loomed in the distance. Winters are long and brutal, isolating the town further, while its sparse grid of streets and wooden storefronts spoke more of survival than prosperity. Once a hub for fur trappers and miners drawn to the area's rugged beauty and hidden resources, Stanley had since settled into a quiet obscurity. Time moved more slowly there, measured more by the changing of the seasons than by calendars and clocks. The streets were quiet—no heavy traffic, just the whistling of the wind blowing through a handful of small buildings.

The cabin sat at the far end of a snow-covered clearing, hidden behind a curtain of towering pines that muffled sound and shielded it from view. It was a modest structure, a simple A-frame with planks worn pale from years of harsh winters. The narrow, unmarked road leading there seemed almost impassable, the truck's tires flattening drifts and skidding on icy patches. Inside, there were wood-paneled walls, a worn leather couch, and a bookshelf lined with survival manuals and novels. A woodstove crackled in the corner, its heat wrestling with the cold seeping through the windows. The cabin felt forgotten by the world, giving them the anonymity they needed.

Jack stepped out of the truck, his boots sinking into the snow. He inhaled deeply, the icy air stinging his lungs. The jagged peaks of the Sawtooth Mountains were shrouded in clouds that glowed faintly in the moonlight. It was beautiful, pristine. And deceptive.

"This is your safe house?" Jack asked, eyeing the rustic cabin. Its slanted roof sagged under the weight of the snow, and smoke curled lazily from a stone chimney. "I wasn't expecting something so... quaint."

Lily smiled as she unlocked the cabin door and glanced over her shoulder at Jack, who was still scanning his surroundings with quiet suspicion, his gaze lingering on the snow-heavy pines and the lack of any visible security features.

"Appearances matter," she said, pushing the door open. A gust of warm air met them, carrying the scent of cedar smoke and something faintly metallic, the smell of old wood and untouched space. "And this place was designed to be invisible."

Jack raised an eyebrow, brushing snow off his shoulder as he stepped inside. "Invisible? You've got a woodstove and a bookshelf full of paperbacks. Feels more like a ski lodge."

Lily shut the door behind them, her expression shifting slightly— still composed, but more serious now. "That's the point. Same as Rose Lake—but much more. The Office had it set up when we realized Vilar's operations extended into Idaho." She unzipped her jacket and hung it on a hook by the door. "At first, we thought it was just another laundering operation—art sales, maybe a few offshore accounts, the usual."

Jack nodded slowly, watching as she moved to the woodstove, adding another log without giving it a second thought, like someone who had lived in the cold before. "So, this is yours? Set up just in case?"

"Exactly." She gestured around the space, her voice calmer now. "Don't judge a book by its cover. This is more than a cabin, more than a safe house; it's a command center. It's secure. More than that, it's… peaceful." She hesitated, her gaze shifting toward the window where the snow was falling more heavily now. "And the backcountry skiing around here? Incredible. Miles of untouched wilderness, no one for miles. If I hadn't been prepping for this, I probably would've used it for touring. But…" Her voice trailed off, her meaning clear.

Jack gave a half-smile. "So, the scenic escape is a bonus?"

She shrugged. "Let's call it professional multitasking."

Jack moved closer to the bookshelf, running his hand over the spines of old spy novels, survival manuals, and foreign language dictionaries. "You really thought of everything."

Lily's expression hardened just a touch. "I had to. The deeper you dig into Vilar's network, the more you realize how connected everything is. If we're going to take him down, we need to control where we work and how we're seen—or not seen."

Jack exhaled, considering their daunting work ahead. "And no one knows about this place?"

"Just The Office and us," she said quietly. "And I'd like to keep it that way."

Jack nodded and relaxed the hold on himself as the warmth from the fireplace began to sink in. The isolation, the careful planning—it wasn't just precaution. It was the way Lily worked. Silent, thorough, untraceable. And now, it was the perfect place to prepare for what came next.

She disappeared into a back room, and moments later, the transformation began. The soft hum of electronics filled the air, and the wooden paneling on one wall slid back to reveal a bank of monitors and servers. Rows of screens blinked to life, displaying maps, live feeds, and encrypted communications. A hidden door opened, revealing a secure satellite uplink and an array of high-tech equipment.

"This is how I stay in touch with The Office without anyone

knowing I'm here," Lily explained, stepping back into the room. "No cell towers, no GPS. I have an off-grid, encrypted satellite system. The footprint is small enough to avoid detection, and security is strong enough to withstand the first 24 hours of brute force attacks. It wouldn't hold against the entire US Cyber Com, but it's as safe as this kind of outpost can be."

"Very impressive. Did you set this up all by yourself?'

"I had a little help."

Jack whistled softly. "And no one knows?"

"No one who shouldn't," she said, her voice matter-of-fact. "Now let's get to work."

The arrival of Benji and Alex added to the buzz of activity. Their flights to Boise landed within minutes of each other, and they continued together to Stanley. Benji immediately commandeered a desk, his laptop open before he even took off his jacket.

"No sling to remind us that you're mortal?" Jack asked playfully, looking at Benji's bandaged arm.

"Bullet bounced off me—I'm an android," replied Benji.

Smiling at Benji's response, Alex carefully scanned the perimeter, nodding his approval at the command center's setup.

"This is a serious setup," Alex said, setting his gear by the door. "You've been preparing for something like this for a while."

Lily nodded. "Preparedness is part of the job."

Benji gingerly handled the keyboard, his arm still tender, as the team gathered around the table. On the main monitor, rows of numbers, names, and coded phrases scrolled past. The ledger they had recovered from the lodge was vast. Benji completely digitized it and was already delving deep into its secrets.

"OK," Benji said, adjusting his glasses. "Here's what we know so far. The ledger lists buyers—some anonymous, but I've cross-referenced a few with known collectors and shell corporations. Two critical nodes stand out: the Sun Valley gallery and a fundraiser in Washington, D.C."

Lily tilted her head. "What kind of fundraiser?"

Benji tapped a few keys, pulling up a file. "High-profile, invitation-only. It's billed as a charity event to support electoral reforms. But in reality, it's a front for laundering money from the art sales into political campaigns."

Jack frowned. "Art sales funding election interference. The Nazis would've approved."

Lily's expression darkened. "We need another set of eyes on this."

"I know someone with a very special set of eyes. Its owner has been in this fight for a long time; she will give us insight and perspective," said Jack as he started typing on Benji's laptop.

He set up an encrypted video call, and moments later, the screen flickered to life, revealing the face of an older woman with sharp eyes framed by silver hair.

"Elena Kovacs," Jack said, gesturing to the group. "Art authenticator, historian, and someone who's been chasing looted art longer than most of us have been alive."

"Elena works closely with Dr. Nathan Goldstein, whom you all know," he continued. "She's based in Geneva, and they've collaborated on many operations for a long time."

"Good evening," Elena said, her gaze sweeping over the group. "It's my pleasure to meet all of you."

"Good evening," replied the team.

Jack stepped forward, holding up a high-resolution photograph of the ledger. "We believe we've found something interesting, something significant," he said. "Does this look familiar?"

Elena studied the image, her eyes narrowing. "More than familiar," she said. "This is an artifact of the Einsatzstab Reichsleiter Rosenberg—the ERR. Operating out of Paris, this Nazi organization cataloged every stolen piece meticulously, sometimes down to the brushstroke."

Mention of the ERR made Jack flash back to his mother and Dr. Goldstein huddled over tattered ledgers and faded photographs—the endless late nights. Each time he reflected on their painstaking efforts to restore what belonged to the Holocaust victims—to those who survived and those who did not—the pain felt more personal.

"What about the Sun Valley gallery?" Lily asked. "Does that ring a bell?"

Elena nodded. "GalerieSV. That gallery has been on my radar for years. They've avoided scrutiny by working exclusively through private sales and laundering through shell corporations. If they're tied to this ledger, they're laundering looted art—and funding something much bigger."

Jack's jaw tightened. "What are the odds they're using this to manipulate elections?"

"High," Elena said grimly. "These networks aren't just about money. They're about control—financial, cultural, and political.

Whoever is running this knows exactly what they're doing."

They ended the call. "Well, that just raised the stakes," said Alex.

Jack leaned back in the creaky wooden chair, the hum of the command center's hidden electronics upstaged by the crackle of the woodstove. He glanced down at his phone, the notification glowing on the screen: Julian Stokes – Update Ready. The message carried equal parts anticipation and apprehension. Julian's intel had been critical so far, but Jack suspected that Julian was not sharing all that he knew. The suspicion lingered in the back of Jack's mind. Pushing those doubts aside, he tapped the encrypted app and set up the video link. If Julian had news, it was time to hear it.

Jack adjusted the video feed. The team gathered around the glowing screen, the tension palpable.

Julian's face appeared, the familiar outline of Lisbon's many hills faintly visible behind him. He looked composed, though traces of fatigue showed around his eyes.

"Good evening," Julian began. "I've managed to untangle a bit more of the web surrounding Vilar and Galerie Moreau."

Jack leaned forward, his hands resting on the table. "We're listening."

Julian adjusted his position, glancing at a stack of notes. "The gallery's finances are heavily insulated, as we suspected. Funds are routed through shell companies, primarily Marigold Holdings. While it's registered in the Caymans, it also operates accounts in Luxembourg."

Jack exchanged a quick glance with Lily, his expression neutral. "Luxembourg and the Caymans. That's not what you said last time."

Julian blinked, his response too slow. "It's both. The funds bounce between the two—typical obfuscation techniques. The Caymans are the endpoint for the transactions, but Luxembourg is part of the layering process. Fischer's handling all of that. He's Vilar's point man for the dirty work."

Lily's reaction was measured but probing. "You mentioned Luxembourg as the hub earlier. Now it sounds like it's just a piece of the puzzle."

"Exactly," Julian said, voice steady. "Vilar stays above it all. The Caymans and Luxembourg structure—that's Fischer's work. Vilar sets the strategy; Fischer moves the money."

Benji tilted his head, studying his laptop. "Makes sense for a layered operation like this. But how'd you pin down Marigold Holdings?"

Julian gave a faint smile. "Let's just say I have contacts who specialize in following this kind of financial footprint. Vilar's too insulated. Fischer's mistakes are easier to track."

Lily leaned back slightly, her gaze narrowing. "And you're confident in those contacts?"

Julian's smile didn't falter. "Absolutely."

Jack shifted the focus. "What about the auction? You said something big was coming up in Paris."

Julian nodded. "Yes, a major auction at the Galerie Moreau—in ten days. It's an off-the-books event, invitation-only. Fischer's running it directly—Vilar's name won't be anywhere near it. There'll be anonymous buyers and some high-profile collectors. If you can intercept it, you'll be right in Fischer's network."

Benji frowned, scrolling through the data on his laptop. "Do you have a guest list?"

"Not yet," Julian admitted. "The invitations are moving through closed channels. Fischer's being careful. I'm working on breaching the distribution system."

"Good," Jack said. "If we can get names, we'll know where to press."

Julian hesitated briefly before continuing. "One more thing—Marigold Holdings authorized a recent transfer linked to an account under the alias 'Victor Adler.' First time the name's appeared, but it's connected to several large transactions."

Jack's eyes narrowed. "Adler? That's new."

"It's a cover," Julian added quickly. "The pattern fits Fischer's usual behavior. Layering it to keep it from pointing back to Vilar. I'm still working on tracing the exact origin of the funds."

It's time Julian and I have a face-to-face, thought Jack.

"Keep at it. I'll need to know as much as possible about the auction," said Jack. "Can you meet me in Paris the day before?"

"I charge extra for in-person consultations," said Julian.

"I'll make it worth your while," said Jack. "Wait for the time and place."

Julian's face softened into a faint smile. "Understood. Stay safe out there."

As the screen went dark, Jack turned to the others, his mind already working through the implications.

"He's thorough, but that shift—making Fischer the point man while Vilar stays clean—feels deliberate," said Lily.

Jack nodded, his voice even. "It's not the change that bothers me. It's the fact that he didn't mention Fischer at all before. Why now?"

Benji shrugged. "Could be he just connected the dots. Or... he wanted us focused on Fischer instead of Vilar."

"Maybe," Lily said, skeptically. "But we should keep both of them in sight."

Jack tapped the table, gaze distant. "For now, we work with what we have. The auction's our best shot at breaking this open. Let's focus there."

The command center felt alive as the group gathered around the table. Maps, blueprints, and satellite images pinned to the walls turned the rustic space into a makeshift war room. The glow of the monitors bathed their faces in cool light. Jack spread out a map of Washington, D.C., marking key locations with a red pen. Beside it, Lily unfurled a detailed floor plan of the fundraiser venue, its rooms and entry points carefully labeled. Benji's laptop displayed real-time financial data tied to the Sun Valley gallery, while Alex meticulously checked their list of surveillance equipment. Nearby, a secondary map of Paris lay pinned to the wall, marked with notes and reconnaissance photos of Galerie Moreau.

"If Elena is right about the gallery in Sun Valley, we need to keep both galleries squarely centered in our sights," said Lily. "Galerie Moreau is the linchpin, but the stream of transactions running through the gallery right in our back yard indicates it's playing an important role in Vilar's plans."

"Yes, but the fundraiser is the key," Jack said, tapping the D.C. map with the pen. "If we can disrupt it, we cut off their primary funding source."

Lily interjected. "But first, we need to know what's really happening at the Galerie Moreau. If Fischer's network relies on the funds from that auction, we can't go into D.C. blind."

Jack nodded, gesturing to the Paris map. "Exactly. We'll head to Paris first. Can you call in any support, Lily? Maybe some friends from Mossad? They could handle external surveillance while we get inside and find the connections between the gallery, Fischer, and the auction."

Benji looked up, curiosity flickering across his face. "A Mossad team?"

Lily's voice was steady, her confidence unwavering. "There is a team I know... Noa, Yaron, and Rafi. I've worked with them before, and they're as good as it gets.

"Noa specializes in surveillance—drones, long-range visuals, and situational monitoring. She's a former Air Force intelligence officer with years of experience in covert observation and remote operations, making her the perfect eye in the sky.

"Yaron is our tech expert, a genius when it comes to network infiltration, data retrieval, and security bypassing. He served in Unit 8200, Israel's elite cyber-intelligence division, where he mastered penetrating secure systems and countering digital threats in high-stakes operations.

"And Rafi? He's our field operative. Trained for close-quarters work, tactical movement, and physical extractions when necessary. He's just back from a tough tour in Gaza, where he led high-risk operations under extreme conditions, making him even sharper under pressure.

"They'll not only cover our weaknesses but give us an edge once we're inside."

Alex folded his arms. "And what happens if we tip our hand at the gallery?"

"That's where coordination comes in," Lily said. "The Mossad team will extract as soon as we're clear. No improvisation, no unnecessary risks. We're there to gather evidence, not start a war."

Jack turned back to the D.C. map. "Once we have the intel from Paris, we move on to the fundraiser. It's a high-security event, but it's also an opportunity. If we can confirm who's handling the funds and where they're going, we can dismantle their network."

Alex leaned forward, his words sharp. "And how do we get into a high-profile fundraiser unnoticed?"

"We will find a way," Jack replied. "Benji and Alex will provide remote support. The Mossad team will recon the perimeter and handle contingency plans."

Lily nodded. "Noa will keep the venue under constant surveillance with drones. Yaron will tap into their internal communications. If something goes wrong, Rafi will extract us."

Benji pulling up a visual on the monitor. "I'm already building fake data trails—buyers, transactions, encrypted communications. The goal is to confuse Fischer's network, make them think they're being attacked from within. If they panic, they'll make mistakes."

"And the gallery?" Alex asked, crossing his arms.

"Still critical," Lily said. "While we're in Paris, we'll plant bugs, cameras, and trackers to monitor activity around the auction. If the gallery is their financial hub, we need to know exactly how the money flows and who's controlling it."

Alex tilted his head. "And if they catch us?"

"They won't," Lily said, her expression unwavering. "Not if we execute this correctly."

Jack's voice was calm but firm. "Everyone memorizes the escape routes. No deviations unless absolutely necessary. If things go hot, we cut our losses and regroup."

Jack thought back to Coeur d'Alene. One cannot be too prepared—even then, under the best of circumstances, things can go wrong.

Jack expected perfect execution and wouldn't tolerate anyone apprehended—especially not him. A long stint in an Austrian prison would take him out of the game and allow Vilar to succeed.

Benji hesitated. "If they figure out we're targeting both locations—"

"They won't," Jack interrupted. "The gallery and fundraiser are connected, but we'll keep our approach compartmentalized."

Alex sighed, leaning back in his chair. "Fine. But I still think we should hit them harder. Take something tangible instead of just monitoring."

Jack met his gaze directly. "We're not looking to score quick wins. This is about dismantling their network piece by piece. If we act too aggressively, they'll shut everything down, and we'll lose our chance to expose them."

Benji broke the tension with a wry grin. "Who needs brute force when you've got me? I'll have their entire system singing before they even realize it's been hacked."

Lily smirked faintly. "Confidence is good, Benji. Overconfidence gets people killed."

"Noted," Benji replied, his grin undeterred.

Jack glanced at the clock. "We don't have time to second-guess. Lily and I leave for Paris next week. Benji, finalize the tech for both locations. Alex, double-check the surveillance equipment. Everyone memorizes the contingency plans before lights out."

The group dispersed, each member retreating into their own tasks. Jack lingered by the maps for some time, his gaze focused on the red circles marking their targets. Lily joined him, her voice low.

"You think this will work?" she asked.

"It has to," Jack replied. "We don't have another choice."

There's one more detail, Jack thought as he retrieved the batch of shipping manifests he had grabbed from Harrington's warehouse. He pulled one out with a faded destination—one almost unreadable. The flight was scheduled in three weeks. *Perfect.* Jack carefully added a new destination, a location in California.

As the first light of dawn crept through the trees, the team stood by the cabin door, their breath visible in the freezing air. The mission ahead loomed large, but for now, they had a plan.

"Ready?" Jack asked.

"Always," Lily replied.

Benji and Alex had other commitments—it was time for them to leave. While on the team, they had pulled their weight and more.

"Good luck," said Benji.

"Stay safe," said Alex.

"Thank you," said Jack, shaking hands with both.

Lily did the same. "I'm very grateful for your help."

With that, they said their goodbyes, and the group split up, the cabin falling silent as the door swung shut behind them.

"Those guys sure pull their weight," said Jack.

Lily nodded. "Let's take another look at what they uncovered."

Benji and Alex were gone, but for Jack and Lily, there was still a lot of work to do.

They sifted through the intel methodically, the cabin eerily quiet without the frenetic energy of Benji and Alex.

In the early afternoon, Jack heard a vehicle approaching the cabin on the snow-covered road.

"Are you expecting someone?" said Jack.

"I thought you might need a friend," said Lily with a smug smile.

Jack opened the door in time to see Marcus step out of his car. "It's good to be back on American soil, snow or not. How was Sintra?" he said.

"They let me into the symposium, but it was a setup—an excuse to warn me to stop, or else," said Jack.

"Over your dead body, I assume," said Marcus.

"That was their idea," said Jack.

"I have some new information about Vilar that you'll find very interesting," said Marcus.

He continued, using his special skill of being able to see around corners, especially when things got messy, "From one of my contacts, I found out Vilar keeps some very important papers in a safe at his estate in Monaco."

"What kind of papers?" said Jack.

"Original documents, dating back to World War II, tied to stolen art. I've been told they include deeds of ownership, shipping manifests, and certificates of provenance."

"Those would be very incriminating," said Lily, adding, "And who knows what else one would find in there."

"We have plans to infiltrate a Galerie Moreau auction happening in ten days," said Jack to Marcus.

"We have a window of opportunity," said Marcus.

"Yes, but it has to be nearly impossible to break into Vilar's estate," said Jack.

After a few minutes, Lily looked up. "It's not impossible. There is a man who can pull off a job like this, but, unfortunately, he won't be easy to find."

"The warrant for your arrest in Europe is serious. Be extra careful when you travel. I think these will help," said Marcus, handing the contents of a small satchel to Jack.

"Here's the new identity I arranged for you: driver's license, passport, bank cards, pictures of your wife and kids, and things to put into your wallet. You're Richard Vandenberg, a retired electronics company executive from Boise and a world-class art collector. You used to work for Silconix Technologies, a shell company I set up precisely for this purpose."

"It doesn't look like me."

"Right. That's the idea. You will use this cleft chin prosthetic kit. Don't forget to apply the makeup to match your skin color. Lighten your hair to match your photos and wear these faux glasses while you're moving around," said Marcus. Then, turning to Lily, "You'll pose as his executive assistant."

"Are you ready to mingle with the rich and famous?" said Lily to Jack.

CHAPTER 13

Monaco

"I'd rather chew glass than jump on a plane to Europe," said Jack. "You'll be OK. Marcus has made special arrangements for us," said Lily. Jack reflected that Marcus has a way of using his special skill of being able to see around corners, especially when things got messy.

In the early morning hours, with the emerging light turning from indigo to orange, Jack, Lily, and Marcus boarded a C-21A at Mountain Home Air Force Base near Boise. They joined a small, uniformed medical group on the military Learjet flying to Istres-Le Tubé Air Base in southern France, about thirty miles outside of Marseille.

"You're a magician, Marcus. I've always been amazed by what you can pull out of your hat," said Jack. "How'd you swing this?"

"Networking," said Marcus. "I know a retired colonel who knows the commander of MHAFB—just friends exchanging favors with friends—I'm going to owe a big one."

"So, who's this mystery man we're meeting in Monaco?" Jack asked Lily.

"For our purposes, his name is Avi. He is the most accomplished jewel thief in Europe who's not in prison. No museum, villa, or vault can keep him out. He does everything, including safe-cracking and high-wire acts. Even though he's getting older, he could make a living performing aerials in a circus," said Lily.

"How do you know him?" said Marcus.

"He's ex-Mossad. I trained with him in Sicily. I was sorry when he left The Office. He was very skilled, a valuable resource. Later, there were stories, which turned out to be true, that he went rogue and was using his considerable talents to take from the rich and to give to himself."

The team settled in for a long trip that required three refueling stops, starting with Dover AFB in Delaware. Twelve hours after leaving Idaho, they arrived at Lajes Field in the Azores, which would include an overnight stay.

The paperwork was pre-arranged, including new passports for all members of the team. The military security personnel gave only cursory glances at their passports at each stop.

At daybreak, Jack stared out the window of the barracks at the lush, green vegetation mixed with rows of purple and white hydrangeas. "Next stop is Camp Mitchell, Naval Station Rota in Spain. Then, on to Istres-Le Tubé Air Base."

"From there, we'll make our way to Monaco, via Marseille, on the train that runs along the Mediterranean coast," said Lily.

"Not exactly," said Marcus.

"What do you mean?"

"I have a friend in Marseille, with a boat, who offered to take us to Monaco," said Marcus. "He's rented a berth in Fontvieille harbor by the Monaco Rock. It will conveniently serve as our base of operations."

"Can we trust this boat captain? How do we know we'll be safe?"

asked Jack, not prepared to place his security in the hands of a stranger.

"I trust the captain with my life," said Marcus. "He's had his share of scrapes with the authorities and knows how to keep a low profile, despite his mode of transportation."

A few hours later, in the waning afternoon, they stopped in Rota to refuel. Then, ending a short last leg, they landed at their destination. A military van dropped them off at the Port de Marseille Fos, Joliette Marina, in Marseille.

"We're to meet him at the marina," said Marcus.

As they walked along the floating dock, a large, bearded man wearing a white yachting cap and a blue polo shirt embroidered with a small logo stepped down from the swim platform of an imposing yacht berthed a few yards in front of them.

"I'm Captain Fontaine. Welcome aboard *La Belle Mer*," said the man. "She's only 26 meters, but she's well-appointed with five guest cabins and doesn't require a crew for short excursions."

"This vessel is also equipped with secure satellite communications," added Marcus.

Jack stepped up onto the smooth teak deck and looked around. Beneath a flybridge overhang, a wraparound sofa with numerous throw-pillows surrounded a low, glass table. To one side, a wet bar gleamed with a large collection of liquor. To the other, there was a buffet table stacked with gold-edged dishes and shiny cutlery. In another lifetime, the luxurious accommodations would have meant he was on a trip of his dreams. Instead of a vacation, he was on a critical mission that could turn ugly, even deadly. Stealth and security, not luxury, were his paramount considerations.

To make the best of it, Jack took a moment to reassure himself of the merits of hiding in plain, although ostentatious, sight. "I guess we won't look out of place in Monaco," he said.

"Yes, we'll look like we belong, in our humble way," replied the captain with a smile.

"Lily, could I have a moment?" said Jack.

"You can talk freely in front of the captain," said Marcus. "He already knows a lot about why we're here."

Less comfortable than before, Jack said, "Alright, we must coordinate on the plan. Lily, do we have the latest intel from Mossad?"

"A member of my team, Noa, working from The Office's headquarters just outside Tel Aviv, has been surveilling Vilar's estate up in the foothills since we left, using a state-of-the-art high-altitude micro-drone equipped with a powerful zoom camera. It's unreal. The drone's camera can identify faces and read license plates. It's too small and flies too high to be visible from the ground," said Lily.

"Noa's logged all the traffic coming and going at the estate. She has a friend staying in the northern end of the principality who launches and retrieves the drone every day," added Lily. "The key to breaking into Vilar's estate is Noa's discovery that Vilar goes to the casino every evening. Monaco fits in with his lifestyle."

"Yes, it does. The Principality of Monaco, a microstate on the French Riviera, is the perfect setting for Vilar to make his home. It boasts the most billionaires per capita in the world, with no taxes on income, wealth, or property—and few questions asked. The principality also features some of the best banking services in Europe, useful for depositing laundered funds. The Casino de Monte-Carlo is the icing on the cake for him," said Marcus.

"That's it, then. We'll access the estate while Vilar is at the casino," said Jack.

"Unfortunately, it's not that simple," said Lily. "Sometimes Vilar is gone three hours or more, sometimes less than fifteen minutes."

Jack thought for a few minutes. "I may have to delay Vilar at the casino to give us the time we need," said Jack. "When does your guy arrive?"

"Avi will join us tomorrow," said Lily.

The captain interrupted. "It's late. We'll get underway and cruise all night to arrive in Monaco early tomorrow," said Captain Fontaine. "Marcus will show you to your cabins. You will find the refrigerators well-stocked. Good night."

Avi arrived in the morning shortly after *La Belle Mer* docked in Fontvieille harbor and introduced himself. A short, slender man with sharp features and thinning hair, cut very short, he exuded confidence and competence.

"You look just as the last time I saw you," said Avi, staring at Lily.

"You look a little thinner," said Lily.

"I try to stay active," said Avi.

"Yes, I bet you do," said Lily.

"Are you still with our former employer?" said Avi.

"Yes, and what have you been doing since you left?" said Lily, knowing full well Avi's activities since leaving The Office.

"I've been trying to make ends meet. I had to get creative since I didn't have the education to be conventionally employed, such as an investment fund manager," said Avi, sounding a little embarrassed.

"You got a raw deal from The Office," said Lily.

"I'm not bitter. I did OK. After a while, I didn't have to work for money—only to test my limits," said Avi.

After Avi was introduced to the captain and the rest of the team, Jack skipped the small talk. "Do you know why you're here, Avi?"

"Yes."

"Has Lily explained the risks?"

"Yes."

"Good. Here's the plan," said Jack. "Vilar leaves his estate for the casino at eight o'clock every evening. You and Marcus will be waiting nearby. I will go to the casino to make sure he's gone for at least thirty minutes. That's the longest time I can reasonably hope to delay him."

"Where is his estate?" said Avi.

"It's in the hills above the center of Monte Carlo. You'll walk to the estate. Should take you about forty-five minutes," said Jack.

"You can get to the center of Monte Carlo by walking through the underground train station. It's the safest way for you to go," continued Jack. "From there, you'll climb a lot of stairs up the hillsides to the estate. The elevators in Monaco all have CCTV systems, but many of the staircases that run alongside them do not."

Jack applied his cleft chin and makeup. Then, putting on his faux glasses, he smiled at Lily. "It's time for Vilar to meet Richard Vandenberg. Would you like to join me?"

"See if any of the dinner jackets in the stateroom closet fit you," said the captain. "The casino has a strict dress code in the evenings."

At seven o'clock, Jack and Lily took a taxi to the Place du Casino. In the circular square, a large, mirrored globe reflected the casino and the rows of neatly parked luxury cars, including Bugattis, Ferraris, and Lamborghinis. On one side of the casino stood the Café de Paris, on the other, the Belle Époque-style Hôtel de Paris Monte-Carlo.

Jack took a deep breath to steady his nerves as a line of valets helped elegantly dressed women out of their cars, and impeccably uniformed doormen with white gloves ushered them through the heavy wood and glass doors.

"Wait for me here," said Jack, as he checked his earpiece, turned, and walked up the steps into the casino.

As the taxi sped away from the harbor, Marcus and Avi walked twenty minutes through the historic Condamine district to the nearest train station entrance, Fontvieille / Le Rocher.

From there, it took five more minutes through the station to reach the Monte-Carlo exit, a short distance from the casino. They walked past the casino square and on to streets filled with luxury apartments and stores.

On the hillsides, the lengthy stairs did not disappoint. Avi and Marcus would sleep well that night.

They stopped a block from the estate, out of view.

Vilar's estate was high in the hills of the most exclusive part of Monaco, in the district of Monte Carlo, the name often synonymous with the principality itself. It was a classic Mediterranean villa, with white stucco walls and a terracotta tile roof. A tall limestone wall covered with green vines and multi-colored bougainvillea surrounded the spacious grounds.

Soon, they saw a white Rolls-Royce Spectre exit the estate. "It's confirmed," said Marcus, listening to Noa in his earpiece. "That was Vilar leaving."

"Where are the guards?" said Avi.

"Noa has an infrared camera mounted on her drone. She says most of the guards are in the kitchen, probably having dinner. The rest are patrolling the outside walls. The east wall is monitored by only one guard, walking back and forth. You may be able to get in behind him," said Marcus.

"OK, Avi, it's all yours, now," said Marcus, "Watch out for the security cameras. I'll be on lookout and warn you if necessary."

"Wish me luck," said Avi, as he turned, crouched, and crept toward the east wall. Marcus watched as Avi, nimble as a cat, scrambled over the wall, just yards behind a guard walking away from him.

Inside the grounds, Avi sneaked toward a corner of the house to a security camera blind spot. He quickly climbed up a drainpipe onto the tile roof, above all the cameras. Then he disappeared.

"I'm in." Marcus heard Avi whisper in his earpiece. "Had to unlock a skylight."

Marcus's hands were cold and sweaty, as if it were he who was inside Vilar's estate.

After what seemed like a very long time, Avi said, "There's so much magnificent art everywhere. I'm in front of a large Picasso—a painting of bathers by the sea."

Avi moved from room to room, keeping close to the walls, jumping past doorways. He looked for a safe in all the places that his years of experience had found them to be—behind mirrors or paintings, inside closets or bookcases, under floorboards or rugs.

"Did you find the safe?" asked Marcus, attempting to keep Avi focused.

"Not yet. I've looked everywhere—the office, the living room, the basement—only a few more places it could be."

Minutes later, "I found it! Behind a Renoir in the bedroom. It's a German-made Döttling, one of the best in the world. Can't wait to challenge it."

Jack took in the opulent, baroque interior of the main gaming room. Every part of it exuded elegance—wood-paneled walls adorned with frescoes and murals, a luxurious, multi-colored carpet, and brilliant crystal chandeliers hanging from the ceiling. Well-dressed guests crowded the roulette and blackjack tables.

Out of the corner of his eye, Jack could see a tall, silver-haired man enter the casino. Elegantly dressed in a dark tuxedo, Eduardo Vilar, heir to the fortune his banker father embezzled from the illicit assets of the Third Reich, stopped briefly to glance at the room. For a moment, the chatter subsided as guests paused to look in his direction.

He turned toward the private baccarat and chemin de fer salons. A floor manager quickly approached him, and Jack could hear the manager announce the bad news: "I'm very sorry, sir. This evening, we do not have any chemin de fer players."

"*C'est la vie*," said Vilar, with an impatient sigh, and turned to leave.

Jack moved quickly to cut off Vilar. "Good evening, Mr. Vilar. I must tell you how immensely I enjoyed your superb presentation at the Sintra symposium."

"I'm pleased to hear that. And you are?" said Vilar.

"Richard Vandenberg," said Jack, without presenting his hand. "It's my pleasure to make your acquaintance, sir."

"The annual symposium in Sintra is one of my great successes," said Vilar, launching into a monologue, expounding on topics from promoting post-liberal ideology to preserving European cultural purity—until he caught himself. "My apologies, Mr. Vandenberg. I often get carried away."

"No need to apologize—I find it fascinating," said Jack, cringing, then adding, "You said you own an art gallery. I must admit that I'm a discerning art connoisseur. I'm particularly interested in unique pieces that aren't offered to the average collector."

Vilar thought for a moment, then said, "You must attend my auction of fine art at the Galerie Moreau in Marais this weekend, Mr. Vandenberg. You'll find my eclectic collection well-suited to your refined taste. I will place you on the guest list."

Vilar thought again, pulled out the familiar beige card, and scribbled his initials. "Take a tour of the gallery before you go to the auction," he said, handing Jack the card and walking away before Jack could say another word.

Not quite thirty minutes had passed.

"Vilar's leaving the casino," Noa announced in Jack's earpiece as Jack watched Vilar step through the casino doors into the square.

"Vilar's on his way back. He left the casino early," said Marcus to Avi. "Get out of there. We'll come back another day."

"Just need a couple more minutes," said Avi.

"Go, now," said Marcus. "Vilar's car is approaching the gate."

Minutes later, Avi ran toward Marcus, shouting, "Let's get out of here. They saw me!"

Marcus and Avi sprinted away from the estate, checking behind them every few steps to see if anyone was in pursuit. Eventually, they stopped to catch their breath.

"Just as I opened the safe, I had to run for my life," said Avi. "I saw what looked like leather-bound binders in the back of the safe. They were too far back, behind too much jewelry—I could not reach them in time—I could only grab a souvenir," he added, showing Marcus a small brooch, studded with pearls and diamonds.

"Let's move," said Marcus.

They retraced their steps down three long flights of stairs, again avoiding the elevator. At the bottom, they slowed down to look up behind them. They could see someone at the top of the stairs, too far away to pose a threat, much less catch up with them.

Suddenly, Avi stiffened, coughed, followed by a sharp sound from the direction of the estate. A flow of blood appeared at the corner of his mouth as a bullet hit dead center in his back.

No way, from that distance, thought Marcus.

He grabbed Avi and started to move, but Avi stopped him, slumping to the ground. "It's too late. There's nothing anyone can do for me. Leave me here. I never betrayed my country. Tell Lily I never betrayed Zvi's country. Take this. Go."

A whistling sound close to his head was Marcus's cue to leave—he took the brooch from Avi's hand, turned, and moved quickly toward the Pont Sainte-Dévote entrance of the underground train station near the casino.

Noa talked into Marcus's earpiece. "Vilar's men are approaching Avi, but you're all clear. Keep going through the train station directly to Fontvieille harbor."

Avi's words haunted him as Marcus proceeded through the station to the last entrance, near Fontvieille, side-stepping the security cameras as much as possible. *Who's Zvi?* Back above ground, it was a short walk to the harbor and *La Belle Mer.*

By the time he returned, Jack and Lily were already back from the casino. On the yacht, the mood was somber among the team.

"We lost Avi, but he tried his best. He's a true hero," said Marcus. He held up the brooch. "We have this piece he took from Vilar's safe. It's fitting this was Avi's last act."

Marcus turned to Lily. "Avi's final words were peculiar. He said to tell you he never betrayed Zvi's country."

"Avi was forced out of The Office on suspicion of being a double agent—but the evidence was not conclusive. I never thought the charges were true."

"Who's Zvi?"

"Zvi Zamir. He's my father," said Lily, her eyes welling up.

"*The* Zvi Zamir, the former director of Mossad, is your father?" said Jack, seeing tears from Lily for the first time. "During my training at the CIA, we studied his Wrath of God operation to extract retribution for the horrific Munich Olympic Massacre. He orchestrated the hunting down and elimination of the Black September terrorists and others responsible for killing in cold blood eleven members of the Israeli team that participated in the 1972

Munich Olympics."

"My dad told me stories about that horrible September day when the Israeli team was taken hostage, and how he watched helplessly as the German authorities' incompetent rescue attempt resulted in the deaths of the hostages. He vowed the killers would get what they deserved. My life's work with The Office is in honor of my dad," said Lily.

"Your dad would be very proud of you."

Lily softened but pivoted quickly. "Let me see the brooch," she said. I recognize it. It's from an Austrian Rothschild collection, at one time thought to belong to Alexandra Feodorovna, the last tsarina of Russia."

"How do you know?" said Jack.

"I consult with an operations unit at Mossad that specializes in recovering stolen jewels and valuables not classified as art. I'm holding one of the prominent items in our catalog."

Jack let out a long breath. "The stakes have risen again. Vilar's operations are more extensive than I imagined, now including trafficking in stolen jewels and other valuables, with possible dealings in Russia."

"Yet another reason we must bring him down. What's our next move?" said Lily.

"Marais. We head into the eye of the storm," said Jack, pulling out the beige Galerie Moreau card.

CHAPTER 14

Marais

Jack's world streaked by at 300 kilometers per hour through Provence. Earlier that afternoon, he took a regional train from Monaco to Nice. There, he boarded a TGV First Class train to Paris. His Mr. Vandenberg identity was holding up, for now. He settled into his seat, leaned his head against the headrest, and closed his eyes. Not a catnap but a reset. Years earlier, he had mastered the art of quickly shifting gears by slowing his breath, clearing his thoughts, and recharging. It was a survival strategy.

Scenes from the morning played in his mind. Jack said goodbye to Lily and Marcus on the yacht, knowing he and Lily would reconvene soon in Paris. They thanked Captain Fontaine and said *Kaddish* for Avi.

"I wish there were a way to clear his name," said Lily.

Lily and Marcus returned to Marseille with Captain Fontaine. From there, she took a flight to Paris. As far as she knew, she was on no one's radar. Marcus did not reveal his plans.

Arriving in Gare de Lyon in Paris, Jack by now could recite the drill in his sleep—synch up with surveillance camera blind spots, check behind in window reflections, loop back through stores and walkways, and squeeze into crowds—the same drill he performed inside and outside many other train stations.

Half a block outside the station, Lily pulled up beside him in a small black Peugeot sedan, suitable for squeezing through the narrow streets of typical Paris neighborhoods. It had lightly tinted windows and local license plates.

The black sedan eased to a stop on a quiet, tree-lined street in the Marais, its engine settling into silence with a low mechanical sigh. Jack stepped out first, the winter air sharp against his face as he scanned the quiet surroundings. The street was nearly deserted, the cafés long shuttered, their terraces empty, save for a few frosted chairs stacked in the corner. The lingering scent of baking bread, faint but unmistakable, curled through the cold air. The delicious aroma reminded Jack he hadn't consumed anything except for black coffee in 24 hours. Eating would have to wait.

To the casual observer, the Marais seemed serene, even picturesque in its stillness. But Jack knew better. This was a neighborhood shaped by both beauty and betrayal, its cobbled streets whispering stories few cared to remember. Once the heart of Jewish life in Paris, these narrow corridors had borne witness to unimaginable loss. Families torn from their homes. Doors smashed open. Lives cataloged, as ruthlessly as the stolen art that once hung behind those same walls.

And now, under the cover of darkness, a team of Jewish operatives returned—not as victims, but as seekers of justice. The irony wasn't lost on Jack. Here, where history had once conspired against them, they were here to uncover the signs of that very history. To expose the remnants of stolen culture, to trace the shadowed threads of art that had been plundered and hidden by the very men who once sought to erase those they belonged to.

The street's silence felt less like peace and more like a hush before revelation. The Marais wore its history lightly now, its labyrinth of narrow streets ideal for both concealment and observation—just as they had been decades earlier, when collaborators watched windows for signs of resistance. Tonight, however, it was a different kind of watchfulness that filled the air. Jack could feel it in the way the Mossad team moved—silent, precise, unyielding. Not merely reclaiming artifacts, but confronting the ghosts of unfinished history.

Jack adjusted his scarf and nodded toward the others. They moved as one, their steps echoing lightly off ancient stone. Justice had a long memory. And tonight, it walked these streets once more.

Lily emerged next, her gaze sweeping the rooftops, cataloging exits, blind spots, and the slow drift of a pedestrian who had passed their vehicle twice. Her scarf shielded her face from the cold but did little to hide her focus. Her movements were calm, but Jack could see her scanning too, noting the same details he did—the alleyways, the distant hum of street noise, the rhythm of the city. They approached the safe house, a nondescript door tucked between a quaint bookshop and a café, its humble façade masking the high-tech operation within. The safe house entrance, tucked discreetly between a bookshop and a shuttered café, bore no distinguishing marks—no doorbell, no number. Only the subtle glint of a reinforced lock hinted at what lay beyond. As Lily knocked, the door opened almost instantly, the Mossad team expecting them.

This was not an ordinary Mossad safe house. A few years after World War II ended, the newly formed State of Israel—proclaimed in

1948—immediately had to defend itself against its enemies. It needed an organization to identify and counter threats from abroad. Israel's intelligence agency, Mossad, created the following year, hit the ground running, establishing safe houses in the Middle East, Europe, and beyond to support its clandestine operations. The location in Paris was one of the first and most sophisticated.

The art on the walls was deliberately generic, the furniture worn but functional. It wasn't a home. It was a command post, perfectly suited for the work ahead.

Inside, they were greeted by Noa, Yaron, and Rafi.

Lily's team appeared to be twenty-somethings. Yaron, six feet tall, balding with thick-rimmed glasses, had all the hallmarks of a hacker. He wore loose-fitting clothes. Rafi, stockier and more muscular than Yaron, had a dark complexion. His eyes shone like tiny flames. And finally, Noa, who played a critical support role in Monaco. Looking the youngest, she was a petite woman with piercing brown eyes and black curly hair. Her style was Mediterranean boho-chic.

Each member of the Mossad team exuded competence; their introductions were brief but professional.

Except for Rafi, his eyes fixed on Jack. "Lily, have you lost your mind? This man is hotter than the gunmen who shot up the Bataclan theatre."

Lily frowned. "I take full responsibility for this man. Despite the risks, he's key to our operation."

"Interpol and police agencies throughout Europe are looking for him," said Rafi, not convinced.

"We have ways to make him nearly invisible," said Lily, ending the discussion.

"Glad you made it," Noa said, guiding them into the secure flat. She gestured to a wall of monitors displaying live feeds of Galerie Moreau. "We've been watching the gallery for 48 hours. There's a pattern, and it's tight, but not impenetrable."

Yaron, already seated at his workstation, glanced up from his laptop. "The network security's good, but not unbreakable. I'll need internal access to finish the job."

Rafi, seemingly placated, leaned casually against the wall. "And if it gets messy," he said, smirking, "that's where I come in."

Jack took in the setup: reinforced windows, signal jammers, encrypted communication lines—it made the cabin in Stanley seem bare-bones. Everything was carefully designed for the delicate operation ahead. Lily stepped closer to Noa as she brought up a dossier on one of the monitors.

"Luc Moreau," Noa said, gesturing to the screen. A crisp photo of a middle-aged man with a sharp suit and a sharper gaze appeared. "Gallery director. Took over a decade ago after his father's sudden death. No criminal record, but he's been flagged by Interpol for suspected involvement in black-market art sales."

"Let me guess," Jack said, crossing his arms. "Nothing stuck."

"Correct," Noa replied. "He uses top-tier lawyers to deflect investigations. Socially, he's well-connected—politicians, financiers, and recently, an associate of Edward Fischer."

German financier, specializes in 'rare acquisitions,' thought Jack.

"So, he's a gatekeeper," Lily said, her voice thoughtful. "If we pressure him, he might lead us straight to Fischer."

Noa nodded. "But we need to play it carefully. He doesn't crack easily."

"She's in position," proclaimed Noa, referring to the drone above the building housing the gallery. "We can see anyone approaching the gallery from three blocks away on all sides."

The soft whir of the drone's rotors was barely audible against the Parisian night sky. Noa crouched low on the rooftop across from Galerie Moreau, her gloved hands steady on the controls as the compact device hovered near the upper windows. From the drone's camera, the gallery's grand façade filled her screen—a masterpiece of modest wealth with tall arched windows and delicate wrought-iron balconies. It was a fortress disguised as elegance.

In the safe house, Yaron and Rafi watched the feed from her drone on a split-screen display alongside heat signatures from inside the building. The soft crackle of encrypted comms filled the air.

"Two security guards in the main gallery," Noa whispered, adjusting the drone's angle to capture the interior through a high window. "Cameras on the upper floor and the lobby. Movement is minimal. Moreau's personal office light just went off."

"Confirmed," Yaron replied. "I'm cross-referencing building schematics now… Looks like he uses biometric locks on the private storage areas in the basement."

Lily, standing behind Yaron with her arms crossed, frowned. "Biometrics and rotating guard shifts for an art gallery? This place is over-protected for what they're showing publicly."

Jack nodded, watching as the drone feed zoomed in on the loading dock at the back of the building. "Because what's behind those locks matters more than what's on display."

Yaron shifted the screen to display a digital catalog they had intercepted from the gallery's internal database. Each image was pristine, high-resolution, and curated for its wealthy collectors.

Impressionist masterpieces dominated the list—Monet's soft blues and lavenders, Renoir's tender portraits, Cézanne's faceted landscapes. Then came the darker, more brooding Post-Impressionist works—Van Gogh's swirling turbulence, a haunting Munch sketch titled *Summer Night at the Beach*, and several pieces attributed to artists with questionable provenance.

Lily leaned in closer as Yaron clicked open the provenance records for a Degas pastel of a ballet rehearsal.

"The gallery lists this as 'rediscovered' after the war," Yaron noted. "No prior documentation, just a vague reference to a Swiss banker in 1945."

Jack's expression stiffened. "That's right after the fall of Paris. Looted pieces from the Einsatzstab Reichsleiter Rosenberg catalog."

Lily traced the entries on the screen with a gloved finger. "This one—Renoir's *La Liseuse*—was last documented in the Louvre before the occupation. Then it turns up in Buenos Aires. No coincidence."

Noa chimed in through comms from the roof. "We're not just talking about stolen art. This is generational theft—cultural erasure. The fact that these pieces have resurfaced here means Moreau's not just complicit. He's a central player in laundering them."

Jack nodded grimly. "The paintings themselves are the cover. The real value here is the network they're cleaning."

"We'll get a privileged tour of the gallery tomorrow," said Jack.

"Indeed," said Lily, "A glimpse at what very few people get to see."

"Including a closer look at their security system," said Jack, checking his watch. "It's time to meet with Julian."

The location, Café La Promenade in the 11th Arrondissement, within walking distance of the safe house, came highly recommended—Marcus had suggested it.

Jack discreetly positioned himself a block away and pretended to type into his cellphone. He had arrived twenty minutes early so that he could check the surroundings, and he would join Julian only after making sure no one had followed them.

Julian entered the café a few minutes before the predetermined time. Jack waited. He looked up and down the street, checking the traffic, cars, and pedestrians, trusting his training and instincts to detect any surveillance. Convinced that it was clear, Jack walked into the café and sat down at the table Julian had chosen by a window.

Jack kept the niceties to a minimum. "Thank you for coming to Paris. What do you have for me?"

"It's nice to see you, too," said Julian, sarcastically. "I was able to get more intel about the day-to-day operations of the gallery."

"Is it incriminating?" said Jack.

"It could be," said Julian, showing Jack a mishmash of notes. "I was able to uncover these transactions, both buying and selling, routed through these shell companies—occurring almost daily."

"Let me take a look," said Jack, noticing that he knew about some of them already.

"And here," said Julian, pointing to a handwritten log, "More Marigold Holdings transactions tied to the Luxembourg accounts I told you about."

Jack paused and thought, *Now, it's my turn.*

"There's something I want you to help me with," said Jack, opening a portfolio folder and pulling out the altered Harrington shipping manifest.

"What is this?" said Julian.

"It's a shipping manifest from Harrington's warehouse in Coeur d'Alene," said Jack. "It's clearly for an upcoming shipment of stolen art."

"Yes, I can see that," said Julian.

"Look at the destination," said Jack. "What do you see?"

Julian stared at the manifest for a long minute. "The destination seems odd. Not a place I would expect Fischer to receive shipments."

"That's what I needed to hear," said Jack. "The destination is near one of Harrington's agri-businesses in California."

"Does that mean...?" said Julian.

"Yes, I think Harrington is diverting some of the art that passes through his Idaho warehouse to himself," said Jack. "Thank you for the confirmation."

"If Fischer only knew...?" said Julian.

"There's no need to help Fischer," said Jack. "I assume you'll keep this conversation just between us."

"Yes, of course," said Julian, hesitantly.

Julian would not have survived for very long in the information-trafficking business had he not been extremely observant. He had noted the date and time of the flight on the manifest, not just the suspicious destination.

He had a decision to make—one of three choices: He could honor his promise to Jack and say nothing to anyone. He could alert Fischer, which would earn him a lot of goodwill. Better than that, he could offer Fischer this information for a hefty fee. Lastly, he could tell Harrington that Jack was on to him, but that didn't seem like a good option.

Concluding, *I'm a professional—I buy and sell information.* Julian pulled out his cellphone to make a call.

The next afternoon, Jack and Lily arrived at Galerie Moreau, their roles as wealthy American collectors impeccably rehearsed. Jack wore an elegant charcoal suit, subtle but clearly expensive. Lily chose a soft-gray cashmere wrap over a minimalist black dress. Their cover was complete with a fabricated backstory—a recently inherited art collection and a desire to expand discreetly.

The gallery's entrance was pure European elegance, with tall arched doors opening into a grand space of white marble floors and ambient lighting designed to cast subtle halos on the artwork.

Luc Moreau awaited them near the center of the gallery, his lean figure framed against a large Monet of water lilies. His dark, close-cropped hair was graying at the temples, and his smile was somewhat formal, warm but impersonal—the smile of a man who closed deals in silence.

Jack presented the card that Vilar had given him in Monaco.

"*Bienvenue*, Monsieur Vandenberg. I've been expecting you," Moreau said smoothly, extending his hand. "I trust your journey was pleasant?"

"Very," Jack replied, returning the handshake with the perfect balance of assertiveness and restraint. "Please meet my assistant, Vivian Sterling."

Luc kissed Vivian on both cheeks. "Pleasure to make your acquaintance, Madame Sterling."

"We've heard remarkable things about your collection, Mr. Moreau," said Jack.

Luc gestured toward the gallery. "You are most kind. Please, allow me to show you our finest pieces."

The first thing Jack noticed was the discreet placement of security cameras in each room, deliberately hidden to avoid making visitors uncomfortable. He memorized the location of each one and turned away from them as much as he could.

"We pride ourselves on offering the finest," Luc said, his voice smooth as he gestured toward a bold Monet of water lilies. "Each piece has been carefully vetted for both its authenticity and artistic significance."

The next thirty minutes unfolded with the polished rhythm of a carefully curated presentation. Moreau spoke at length about the exquisite condition of a Kandinsky, the pristine lineage of a Josef Albers, and the artistic significance of a rare Lyonel Feininger—each description underscoring the gallery's emphasis on postwar abstract and Bauhaus movements.

Jack noted the meticulous documentation displayed beside most works—clearly legitimate, with detailed histories tracing back to estate sales, artist foundations, and postwar exhibitions. Yet, when Lily paused before a Monet landscape, the atmosphere shifted slightly.

Lily's gaze drifted across the carefully curated collection, lingering on a Cézanne still life of fruit, its rich ochre and crimson hues glowing under the gallery's carefully positioned lighting. She approached the painting, tilting her head as though admiring the brushwork. "This is remarkable," she said, her tone light but probing. "The individual brush strokes create a nearly tangible volume as if elevating the still life to a portrait. You know what Picasso said of Cézanne, of course? He is the father of us all. Oh, please share, what about the provenance?"

Luc's smile brightened, his posture subtly more relaxed. "Ah, yes. That one comes from a distinguished private collection in Vienna. The family safeguarded it for generations—an extraordinary story of preservation."

Jack, standing a few steps behind, spoke without shifting his gaze from the piece. "Safeguarded? Through the war?"

There it was—the slightest hesitation. A flicker, a heartbeat too long before Luc responded. "Indeed. Remarkably, it was never confiscated."

The phrasing was polished but vague, too careful in its wording. Lily caught the brief shift, noting how Luc's smile recovered almost instantly, flowing back into his rehearsed charm.

"You must have quite the network to source works like this," she offered, letting the compliment linger.

Luc inclined his head gracefully. "Years of dedication and trust, madame. But as you can imagine, the rarest treasures never make it to public view."

But then there was the Van Gogh.

It hung slightly apart from the others, a haunting piece with streaks of blue and gold swirling like a storm trapped on canvas. The gallery's plaque described it as *"Rediscovered in Zurich, 1951."* No gallery or estate attribution. No chain of ownership.

Lily stopped, studying it for longer than she had the others. "This one... It's breathtaking," she said, voice soft but edged with curiosity. "I noticed the provenance states it was 'rediscovered.' What does that mean, exactly?"

Luc's polished exterior held, but just barely. The smile remained, though a shade tighter than before. "The art world is full of surprises, madame. Pieces long thought lost sometimes find their way back. This one resurfaced postwar, through an estate sale managed by a Swiss collector."

Jack stepped closer, examining the brushwork. Genuine. Powerful. But the timeline didn't sit right. Zurich, 1951—convenient. Postwar enough to obscure the gaps, distant enough to evade deeper scrutiny.

"Which collector, exactly?" Jack pressed, voice calm but deliberate.

There was the briefest pause. A fraction too long. "Unfortunately, certain wartime records were lost during the occupation," Luc replied smoothly. "However, our experts have verified its authenticity with the utmost care."

The answer was polished, almost reflexive, yet just opaque enough to raise doubts.

Jack met Lily's gaze across the room. No words were exchanged, but the conclusion was clear—the Van Gogh was the outlier here. The gallery had taken great care to emphasize the legitimacy of every other piece. But this? The language was different, the history too vague. And Zurich, 1951—a known hub for trafficked art after the war.

They didn't need to press further. Luc Moreau was skilled enough to deflect without outright lying. The gallery was legitimate, but the Van Gogh wasn't.

And he knew it.

While Lily continued asking polite questions, Jack scanned the gallery's security setup. The guards, dressed in plain suits, were positioned near the entrance and by a discreetly marked staff-only door. Cameras were angled for broad coverage, though Jack noted a minor blind spot near the rear staircase. Likely unintentional.

Jack noticed hidden speakers lining the baseboards. Silent alarms, perhaps, wired for remote activation.

On the way out, Jack slowed his pace near the restricted door marked Private Collection Access.

He noted the biometric scanner and reinforced steel door, far more secure than anything protecting the main floor pieces. This wasn't just extra protection for rare art. It was a vault.

Before he could linger, a guard shifted position slightly, shooting Jack a glance with quiet authority. Jack offered a casual smile, then returned to Luc and Lily, filing the detail away for later...

Back at the safe house, Noa played the drone footage while Yaron scrolled through intercepted gallery communications.

"Look at this," Yaron said, pulling up a flagged email. "A secure message from Moreau to an unregistered server. Reference to a 'private Paris event—VIP clientele only.' Looks like they're moving forward with the auction."

Lily leaned over the monitor. "And the artwork we saw?"

"Several were tied to the same offshore account," Yaron confirmed. "Marigold Holdings. The same shell company Fischer used in Vienna."

Jack exhaled slowly. "It's not just stolen art. Moreau's gallery is a clearinghouse. Fischer's laundering art and using the sales to fund his network."

The evidence was clear, but it wasn't enough yet. Jack knew they needed something more direct to expose Vilar and prevent the election of his puppet, Cain, to the Oval Office. Something inside that basement vault.

He turned back to the gallery's layout on the monitor. "We're going back in. Next time, we're not leaving without answers."

"Every piece with questionable provenance is a puzzle piece in a larger network," Jack said.

"Rumor has it that Fischer possesses Gustav Klimt's *Bildnis Fräulein Lieser* and that he's found a buyer," said Lily.

"I've heard of it—supposedly worth tens of millions of euros," added Yaron. "All traces of the painting disappeared during World War II; historians long feared that it was lost forever."

"Moreau's cleaning these works for Fischer's buyers, and in return, they're funding something much bigger."

"Bigger like what?" Rafi asked.

"Control," Lily replied. "Cultural, financial, and political. These pieces are leverage."

"The Klimt is key," said Jack. "If we can confirm Fischer has the Klimt, that will put the first nail in his coffin."

As they prepared for the next step, Jack knew they were inching closer to the heart of the conspiracy. But with each layer they uncovered, the risks grew exponentially.

Rafi reiterated his concerns. "The risk of Jack being identified is too great. If not at the gallery, then by the police in Paris."

Lily responded quickly. "We need Jack. He knows what to look for more than anyone here. If we get into trouble, that's where you come in to extract us, and Yaron has been working on some special precautions."

"But can't Jack just brief us on what to look for and remain in the background?"

"Trust me on this, Rafi. It's worth the risk."

"Easy for you to say. You're not risking decades of prison time," said Rafi.

"Jack?" said Lily.

Jack crossed his arms over his chest. "Don't worry about me. I'm the least of our concerns."

"My mission, Jack's mission, our mission, is to take down Vilar," said Lily.

CHAPTER 15

Rue de Seine

The operation began the next night. Rafi staged a power surge in a nearby building, causing a brief blackout at Galerie Moreau. As the lights flickered, the guards scrambled to restore order. Jack and Lily, posing as clients who'd lingered after hours, used the distraction to slip into the restricted storage area.

The basement was dimly lit, rows of crates and locked cases filling the space. Jack's flashlight swept over the crates, stopping on one with faded German markings.

"Here," he whispered, prying it open carefully.

Inside was a painting, its vibrant colors preserved beneath layers of protective wrapping. Beside it lay ledgers, their pages filled with detailed entries in German.

Lily flipped through one ledger, her expression grim. "These match the ERR's cataloging system. This is Nazi-looted art."

Jack nodded, his jaw tightening. "This confirms Moreau's involvement."

Upstairs, Yaron worked swiftly from the van, hacking into the gallery's network using a device Jack had planted earlier.

Yaron said over the comms, "They're selling art and funneling money through shell companies tied to Fischer. And there's chatter about an upcoming event—a private auction."

Jack and Lily continued their search, uncovering more ledgers and an encrypted tablet. At the bottom of a crate, Jack found a small envelope embossed with gold lettering. Inside was a coded invitation detailing a secret auction set to take place in Paris in three days.

The team regrouped at the safe house, their discoveries laid out before them. The implications were staggering: a conspiracy involving Nazi-looted art, financial manipulation, and high-level political players.

Jack stared at the invitation. "If we can disrupt this auction, we can expose the whole network."

Lily nodded. "But we have to move fast. This changes everything."

More than that, thought Jack. Disrupting the network would also expose the conspiracy to set up Jack for a murder that was self-defense, clearing his good name.

Outside, the city pulsed with its usual rhythm, oblivious to the storm brewing within. Inside the safe house, the team prepared for the next step, knowing the stakes had never been higher.

Jack and Lily navigated the labyrinthine streets of Paris's 6th arrondissement separately, each taking meticulous care to avoid detection. Their destination was La Palette, a historic café and brasserie located at 43 Rue de Seine, renowned for its artistic heritage and vibrant ambience.

Jack arrived first, slipping into the intimate bar room adorned with ceramics from the 1930s and numerous paintings—a testament to the café's rich history as a gathering place for artists and students from the nearby École des Beaux-Arts.

He chose a secluded corner table, the dim lighting casting soft shadows, providing the discretion they required. Moments later, Lily entered, her eyes scanning the room before settling on Jack. She approached with a subtle nod, and they exchanged brief pleasantries as she took her seat.

Immaculately dressed, they were convincing as art connoisseurs, with budgets robust enough to pick up a valuable painting or two at an art auction. In addition to their sophisticated attire, they wore discreet earpieces.

A waiter approached, and they ordered modestly—two espressos, in keeping with the café's tradition of light fare available throughout the day.

As the waiter departed, Jack leaned in, his voice barely above a whisper. "Everything set on your end?"

Lily nodded, her expression composed. "Yes. The gallery's security has a blind spot at the rear entrance. We'll have approximately ten minutes to make our move once inside."

Jack glanced toward the window, taking in the charming terrace outside. Picturesque, with old, weathered, wooden tables and chairs arranged randomly on an uneven stone floor, filled with people talking and drinking coffee.

"La Palette has seen its share of clandestine meetings," he mused, recalling the café's history as a favored haunt of artists and intellectuals.

Lily allowed a brief smile. "Let's hope it continues to keep its secrets."

Their espressos arrived, and they sipped in silence, each mentally rehearsing the steps to come. The clinking of cups and murmur of patrons provided a comforting backdrop, a momentary calm before the impending storm.

Finishing their drinks, they settled the bill and left a tip.

They rose and headed for the front door. Suddenly, Jack froze. "Don't look, but the two policemen in their car across the street may be surveilling us."

"Just pretend to chat for a minute. If they make a move, we'll make ours, and eventually meet back at the safe house," said Lily.

After a few minutes, the police moved on. With a final, understanding glance, they exited the café, crossing Rue de Seine toward Galerie Moreau. The evening air was crisp, the city's lights casting shadows on the cobblestone streets.

As they approached the gallery, Jack's voice was steady. "Remember, we stick to the plan. In and out, no unnecessary risks."

Lily's eyes met his. "Understood. Let's make this count."

The plan was simple in theory. Observe. Gather intel. And most importantly, find Gustav Klimt's *Bildnis Fräulein Lieser*. Was it sold?

Together, they disappeared into the dark, their partnership a blend of precision and unspoken trust, ready to face the challenges that awaited within the gallery's walls.

Jack stepped through the grand entrance of Galerie Moreau. The dim lighting of the auction room cast long, dramatic silhouettes across the marble floor. The now-familiar gilded frames and sculptures stood like silent witnesses to the wealth and power gathered in the Marais that evening. Velvet ropes sectioned off rare pieces on display, while waiters in crisp black and white uniforms offered champagne to the elegantly dressed crowd.

Lily followed closely, her gray cashmere wrap draped over her shoulders, her dark hair styled in a simple but sophisticated twist. The subtle elegance of her attire blended perfectly with the other guests, though her sharp gaze swept the room with clinical precision. Each corner, each face, was carefully cataloged for later review.

Noa and Yaron watched through a live feed from the safe house, multiple camera angles giving them a bird's-eye view of the event. Yaron adjusted his headset, his eyes narrowing as he sifted through the gallery's digital architecture. "Hold position. I'm expanding the net," he murmured, typing in several instructions. A fresh window of cascading code filled the screen.

"I have a bad feeling about this," said Rafi. "It's tough to fool modern face recognition systems, even with the best countermeasures. We shouldn't have let Jack go back to the gallery."

"Jack's disguise has been effective so far," said Yaron. "For added security, I'm adjusting the neural network weights of the gallery's facial recognition system to make Jack's face virtually undetectable. In effect, I'm creating a blind spot in the system that will propagate to the security cameras—Jack will be able to move around like a ghost."

Yaron had been with Unit 8200 for six years. The Holocaust deeply scarred his family's history; his grandparents had survived the camps, their lives forever altered by the horrors they witnessed. After the war, they emigrated to Israel, determined to rebuild and protect their heritage. This legacy fueled Yaron's sense of duty, driving him to become a specialist in cyber operations, mastering the art of digital infiltration. He knew how to burrow into complex systems without a trace, leaving behind no signatures but complete control. The virus he'd deployed wasn't just for observation—it could alter access permissions, manipulate logs, and even trigger controlled shutdowns if necessary.

"Jack, Lily, you're both clear," Noa's voice came through their discreet earpieces. "Security patrols are tight, but standard. Stick to the plan."

Simple enough, thought Jack. *Most importantly: find the Klimt.*

Jack and Lily plucked flutes of champagne from a tray offered by a waiter and mingled, nodding politely to other guests while the auctioneer on the podium presented a surrealist piece, bidding escalating in clipped European accents. Jack noted the intense focus among the elite bidders, a silent battle of wealth and influence being waged through subtle nods and flicks of the wrist.

Lily whispered, "I see Fischer. Far right, by the Monets."

Jack turned slightly, scanning the crowd. Edward Fischer's presence confirmed their suspicions. His involvement wasn't subtle— he was orchestrating the whole conspiracy on behalf of Vilar.

"Keep your eye on him," Jack muttered. "I'll take a look inside."

Meanwhile, Yaron worked his way deeper into the gallery's digital infrastructure. With Unit 8200 tools at his disposal, he had deployed a sophisticated multi-layered infiltration program. He launched a virus designed not only to mirror all keystrokes but to create a backdoor for full remote access at their discretion. Every keystroke, every transaction was being recorded and relayed back to their secure network.

"Rootkit is working," he announced. "Keylogger active. We'll see every keystroke from here on out."

"Nice work," Noa replied. "Rafi, be ready. We may need a distraction if this goes south."

In the gallery, Lily gestured toward the restricted area guarded by a single security officer. "The Klimt won't be on public display. It has to be back there."

Jack nodded and set down his flute of champagne. He needed both hands. "Stay close to Fischer. I'll make my move."

He confidently approached the security guard. "Bonsoir, I'm quite interested in a private showing. I was told some of the most important works were in the secured collection?"

The guard's expression remained impassive. "I'm afraid that area is not open to guests, sir."

Jack's smile remained unyielding. "I'm sure the gallery wouldn't mind for a collector with a... significant interest." He discreetly offered a folded bill, crisp euros, enough to loosen even the tightest lips.

The guard hesitated, then nodded once, unlocking the door with a keycard. Jack slipped inside.

The secured collection was colder, the lighting more subdued. Crates lined the walls, some still sealed. But what drew his attention was a single painting under a protective glass case—Gustav Klimt's *Bildnis Fräulein Lieser*. The portrait depicted a young woman draped in a delicate, shimmering gown with floral patterns blooming across the fabric, Klimt's signature golden hues accentuating the ethereal beauty of the figure. Her gaze was soft yet haunting, framed by delicate brushstrokes that blurred the line between realism and symbolism. The layers of gold leaf caught the dim light, reflecting a subdued brilliance, while the background melted into a haze of intricate patterns that seemed to pulsate with hidden meaning.

Jack took a slow, steady breath. The piece was breathtaking, but its presence here—under Fischer's control—was a travesty. He captured high-resolution images with his watch's hidden camera for later verification.

Jack's earpiece crackled. "Jack, I'm seeing an active financial transfer starting now," Yaron warned. "They're moving funds from tonight's bids straight into a Luxembourg account."

Suddenly, a shadow moved. Fischer had followed him inside.

Fischer's voice echoed softly through the dimly lit gallery, a smooth yet unmistakably menacing tone. "What are you doing here, Mr. Vandenberg?" He took a measured step forward, hands clasped behind his back, the subtle click of his polished shoes breaking the silence. "This area is off-limits to our guests."

Jack's mother's words rang in his ears: "Trouble always finds you first."

Fischer's gaze shifted to the *Bildnis Fräulein Lieser*, its golden hues catching the low light. "Remarkable, isn't it? A masterpiece, lost for nearly a century, shrouded in mystery, and now..."

Jack held his ground, eyes locked on Fischer while keeping his body between the painting and the man who had so brazenly claimed it. His voice was calm, controlled, but tinged with contempt. "My apologies. I heard this masterpiece was in your possession. I could not resist taking a peek—it's magnificent! What do you want for it?"

Fischer tilted his head, the corner of his mouth curling into a thin smile. "Profit is a byproduct of our work, Mr. Vandenberg. What we do here transcends wealth. These works, these pieces of history, they represent far more than paint on canvas. They are power. Symbols of legacy, influence... control. People will pay for that. Kings, tycoons, politicians. I'm simply providing a service—facilitating the preservation of power in capable hands. I'm sorry to say this painting is not for sale."

Jack's fists clenched at his sides. His pulse quickened, but his expression remained impassive. "Capable hands?" said Jack, thinking: *You mean the same hands that looted homes, erased families, and destroyed entire cultures? This painting—this piece of a family's soul—was stolen.*

"Did it once belong to the Lieser family?" asked Jack, knowing that it did, to a family wiped out during the Holocaust. And someday, Fischer would be selling it as if the blood on it had dried.

Fischer's smile faded, replaced by something more sinister. Dead eyes and a snarling mouth to match. He took a step closer, the space between them shrinking. "History is written by those who survive, Mr. Vandenberg. Those who control it dictate how it is remembered. The Liesers... they are gone. But the power this art holds? That remains. And I assure you, it's far better kept with those who can appreciate its value."

"I do appreciate its value and what it symbolizes. Let me know when you are ready to sell it," said Jack, knowing he had to play his role.

Nazi-looted art didn't just reappear from nowhere. The provenance for the Van Gogh was fabricated. Zurich, 1951?

Conveniently vague. But Jack had the ERR ledgers now—enough to expose Fischer's entire operation.

As the conversation continued, Lily triggered a silent security breach using Yaron's hack from the night before, activating the virus embedded in the gallery's systems. Emergency lights flickered briefly, and the security camera feeds looped, showing an empty hallway while Jack moved toward a restricted office behind the gallery floor. Fischer rushed out of the room, and his voice echoed from the main auction hall, ordering his staff to investigate the disturbance.

Jack and Lily exchanged a brief glance, their silent communication honed through trust and shared experience. "I'll cover you," Lily whispered, positioning herself near the hallway to keep watch.

Inside the office, Jack slipped a data extraction device into the computer, the screen flooding with folders labeled 'Consignments,' 'Private Holdings,' and 'Transfers.' A progress bar inched forward as encrypted files began copying.

Outside, Lily's voice came through the earpiece. "Two guards coming your way. You've got thirty seconds."

Jack's pulse quickened. The download hit 95% just as the doorknob rattled. Lily stepped into the hallway, intercepting the guards with a calm smile. "I seem to be a bit lost. Could you point me to the lounge area?"

One of the guards hesitated, but the other frowned. "Madame, you shouldn't be here."

The final progress bar hit 100%. Jack ejected the drive, slipping it into his jacket's inner pocket and quickly wiping the device history.

Rafi's voice crackled in his ear. "Exit route secure. Service door, north side. Move now."

Jack emerged, nodding once to Lily, who fell in step beside him as the guards' radios buzzed with Fischer's lockdown orders. The lights flickered again—Yaron's subtle interference working to mask their escape.

Once outside, Rafi guided them to a waiting black sedan. "We got what we needed?"

Jack held up the flash drive. "We did. But the art stays behind."

Back at the safe house, the team pored over the data. Yaron and Noa decrypted the files while Jack and Lily stood behind them, impatient to see the spoils.

"It's worse than we thought," Yaron muttered, scrolling through pages of transactions. "The gallery's profits are linked directly to Senator Cain's campaign funds and several extremist organizations. Not just Europe—this extends to the U.S. as well."

Jack leaned over, his fists clenched. " This stolen art is funding a global network of hate."

Lily watched him, then placed a hand on his arm. "We're making a difference, Jack. Look at this—proof, connections, names. We can expose them."

He glanced at her, the tension giving way to something deeper. "It doesn't feel like enough. We left those paintings behind. Pieces of history still in the corrupt hands of people like Fischer."

She nodded, voice softer. "I know. But tonight, we stopped their funding. We hit them where it hurts. And we're not finished."

In the safe house, Jack and Lily sat across from each other, the weight of their recent mission hanging heavily between them.

"You know," Lily began, her voice soft yet resolute, "this painting, *Bildnis Fräulein Lieser*, is a testament to a family's history, a history violently disrupted by the Nazis."

Jack nodded, his expression thoughtful. "The Lieser family," he said slowly. "They were prominent Jewish industrialists in Vienna. This portrait was commissioned by them, a symbol of their cultural and social standing. This type of portrait by a leading artist of the day took serious funds."

"Exactly," Lily replied. "But after the Anschluss in 1938, their world was turned upside down. Their assets were seized, their homes taken. Henriette Lieser, the matriarch, was deported to Riga and murdered in 1943."

Jack's jaw tightened. "And the painting vanished, lost for nearly a century, only to resurface in the hands of those who would exploit its value without acknowledging its dark history."

"Those dirty hands also belong to Fischer, and we know he has the Klimt and a buyer," said Lily. "It's important proof of Fischer's outsized role in Vilar's network."

Jack sighed, running a hand through his hair. "It's overwhelming, thinking about the sheer number of artworks still out there, each with a story like this. But if we can make a difference, even with just one piece, it's worth it."

"It is," Lily agreed. "And it's not just about the art. It's about justice, about righting the wrongs of the past, even if it's decades later."

Jack reached across the table, taking Lily's hand in his. "We'll do it together," he said firmly. "For the Lieser family, and for all the others who had their lives and legacies stolen."

Lily squeezed his hand, a determined smile forming on her lips. "Together," she echoed.

Their shared commitment to the mission deepened their bond. Their partnership was a united front against the injustices of history.

Jack exhaled slowly, the weight in his chest easing. "You're right. We're not finished."

The quiet resolve between them was palpable, their shared mission no longer just professional. It was personal—an unspoken vow to see this through.

Getting back to analyzing the night's work, in a separate room, Yaron and Noa decrypted the files while Jack and Lily recounted the night's events. The team traced connections leading from Fischer's holdings directly to Senator Cain's re-election fund, exposing a significant funding channel fueling hate campaigns across Europe and the U.S.

"They're not just fringe voices anymore. This is becoming the new face of power across Europe. It starts with stoking fear—fear of outsiders, fear of losing tradition, fear of falling behind. Then it grows—manipulating public discourse, restricting press freedom, rewriting history. The extreme right gains public traction, cannibalizes the center, and starts to look mainstream. And don't think it stops there. The U.S. is next. Look at Cain's rhetoric—it's the same playbook. Corrupt financial networks fund extremism while laundering their influence through events like this D.C. fundraiser. If we don't shut this down, we'll be watching history repeat itself—not in distant capitals, but on our doorstep," said Jack.

The laundering operation was more complex than they had imagined. The documents detailed how Fischer had used Galerie Moreau as a front for laundering stolen art sales. High-profile auctions would mask the transactions, while proceeds were funneled through a web of holding companies, converted into cryptocurrencies, and finally distributed to extremist groups under the guise of 'art preservation' grants. Rare pieces, including those stolen during World War II, were traded for inflated sums among conspirators, further obfuscating the source of funds.

Jack stared at the screen, stress simmering beneath the surface. "We have proof, but it's not enough. We need more than financial records—we need physical evidence tying Fischer directly to these crimes."

Lily nodded, determined. "I know just where we must go next. We will hit him where it hurts. We will take the stolen art back and expose everything publicly. This isn't over yet."

Rafi interrupted. "I know where you're planning to go. My father worked there for many years before moving back to Israel."

"Did he work for The Office?" said Lily.

"Yes. My dad became an expert on dealing with criminal networks, such as the one on the island. He taught me a lot. I can be very useful—let me go with you."

CHAPTER 16

Sicily

The tarmac at Le Bourget Airport, once Paris's principal airport, the landing side of Charles Lindbergh's transatlantic flight in the *Spirit of Saint Louis*, was unusually hectic for this time of night. Gulfstreams, Falcons, and other private jets were still coming and going. Fuel trucks moved among the many planes on the ground.

The security official looked at the documents from the driver of a black sedan and let it pass through the gate without an inspection. Jack exhaled, signaling to Lily and Rafi a small sign of relief.

"The Office has made all the necessary arrangements. We're unofficially hitching a ride on an empty plane being returned to Catania," said Lily.

The jet left under the cover of night, with the three stowaways secure in their seats. After the close call at Galerie Moreau, there was no time for celebration. Jack sat by the window, watching the lights of the city disappear below. Lily, seated opposite him, remained quiet, lost in thought as she reviewed encrypted documents on her tablet. Rafi, in the seat next to Lily, looked over her shoulder.

Mossad had arranged a private flight to Catania, bypassing commercial scrutiny. The plan was simple: vanish from Paris and regroup in the isolation of Sicily. The pilot, a trusted contact from her

Mossad days, said nothing beyond confirming their destination.

Jack used his trusty Canadian passport, traveling as James Oberling from Vancouver.

Catania's airport, Fontanarossa, located near the Ionian coastline, pulsed with a blend of modern efficiency and old-world charm, a key gateway to Sicily's rugged beauty. Its history was as layered as the volcanic soil it rested upon—originally a small airfield, it had expanded significantly over the decades, now serving as a primary link between mainland Italy and the island. The sight of snow-covered Mount Etna looming in the distance, smoke curling faintly from its peak, was both a reminder of nature's power and the island's deep historical roots.

Upon landing, as prearranged, a driver greeted them, holding a placard with "Oberling" above his head. Bracing against a chill winter breeze sweeping in from the sea, he led them to a waiting SUV with tinted windows and a second driver at the wheel.

"Why two drivers?" asked Lily, suspicious of anything that veered from the plan.

"To idle here, instead of parking farther away," answered the first driver, loading the bags into the back of the SUV.

"It looks good, now," said Jack. "The big risk at the airport was being identified while walking to the car. The three of us will squeeze in back."

Their destination was Rifugio Citelli, a converted mountain lodge that offered both seclusion and security, featuring stone walls, reinforced windows, and a sophisticated surveillance system.

The Rifugio Citelli itself was a remote retreat steeped in history. Built in the early 1930s as a shelter for mountaineers exploring the volatile slopes of Etna, its stone walls had seen decades of both nature's fury and human resilience. Over the years, it had been repurposed, serving as both a base for scientific expeditions studying the volcano and, more discreetly, a haven for covert training exercises. Its isolation and harsh conditions made it ideal for sharpening survival instincts.

For Lily, Rifugio Citelli was home to some of her most formative training experiences. During her early Mossad years, she spent weeks navigating the hostile terrain surrounding the refuge, learning endurance, countersurveillance techniques, and physical resilience under the mentorship of retired operatives. It was here she built the quiet confidence that defined her fieldwork, shaping her into the strategist she had become.

The drive to Rifugio Citelli was marked by fog and the looming presence of Mount Etna.

"You missed the turn," said Lily to the driver.

"Don't worry about it," said the driver.

The man in the passenger's seat turned around and pointed a handgun at the three of them in the back seat. "There's a change to your itinerary. Put these on," he said, throwing three black hoods at them.

Relying on years of training, Jack, Lily, and Rafi understood there wasn't much they could do at this moment. The best course of action would be to obey and buy some time.

The man said something to the driver that Jack couldn't understand.

"Cosa Nostra," whispered Lily.

If Vilar is behind this, his network includes the Cosa Nostra, the Sicilian wing of the Mafia. Had Mossad been compromised—was there a mole working at the safe house who alerted Vilar that they were coming here? Maybe Vilar knew all along, thought Jack.

The SUV turned sharply onto an unpaved road and bounced from pothole to pothole before coming to a jarring stop.

Lily groaned as they were yanked out of the SUV, their arms pulled behind them, their wrists secured with zip ties. They were led into a building that whistled in the wind.

Inside, their steps echoed as if in a large warehouse, and a sharp, acidic smell of industrial chemicals filled the air. More guards approached them and separated them, two of them taking Rafi out through a rusting metal door. Other guards forced Jack and Lily to sit on a weathered wooden bench in the middle of the room.

A tall, familiar figure came into the room as the guards pulled off their hoods. The silver-streaked hair, the suit, the shoes, the way he carried himself.

"We warned you, several times, but you kept popping up—Rose Lake, Titus Lake—and we suspect that it was you at Galerie Moreau. You knew the risks."

"We meet for the last time, Mr. Berman. You will dissolve without a trace," he added, motioning with a finger across his throat as he walked out of the room.

Jack couldn't remember the last time he felt this powerless. Could they rush the armed men with their wrists tied behind their backs? Could they talk their way out of this—maybe bribe them?

He was out of ideas.

"We were a good team," Jack said to Lily.

"We may not be around to see it, but my people will avenge…" said Lily.

Before she could finish, the doors exploded open from every direction, followed by muffled popping noises, flashes of light, and short, crisp commands in Hebrew.

It was over in seconds. Their captors were spread on the ground all around them—some twitching, most not moving.

The commander of the Mossad team untied Jack and Lily. "Are you alright?"

He added, "We track all our vehicles. We scrambled to investigate as soon as your car went off course. We found the driver sent to pick you up—in a ditch near the airport—killed. *Alav Ha-Shalom*."

"Yes, may peace be upon him," said Lily.

"This man is one of our agents with a high security clearance," said the commander, looking down at one of the dead men. "He must be the mole that we suspected in our midst for a long time. I never thought he could betray us. Someone must have been very persuasive with him."

"Did you rescue the man who was with us. They took him through that door," said Jack, pointing with urgency in his voice.

The commander and several of his men rushed through the metal door, guns raised at shoulder level. He came back with the bad news. "I'm sorry, we were too late to save your friend."

Jack and Lily looked at each other for a long time in disbelief. Finally, with bravado betrayed by her quivering voice, she said, "We all know the risks."

Driven by two Mossad agents, they rode in silence to Rifugio Citelli. It had begun to fully sink in that they would never see Rafi again, and just how close they had come to being killed and disposed of with industrial acid.

"I've known Rafi for over seven years, from the time he was a wet-nosed gofer to when he became one of Mossad's best field operatives," Lily said, tears streaming down her cheeks.

"It was an honor to have known him," said Jack, putting his arm around her shoulders.

"He always put everyone ahead of himself—always ready to risk his life to save others. He was my friend," said Lily, wiping her face with her arm.

"It never gets any easier," said Jack, thinking back to his days at the CIA.

Returning to Rifugio Citelli now, after what they endured, felt both nostalgic and heavy with purpose. The walls that had once echoed with the barked orders of trainers now bore silent witness to a new mission—they had to shake off their ordeal and get back to work. Jack and Lily's return wasn't just about hiding—it was about regrouping where Lily had once learned the cost of standing still in the face of threats.

Inside the Refugio, the atmosphere was both tense and focused. The rustic interior, complete with wooden beams and a central hearth, contrasted sharply with the tech-heavy command center Lily had set up in the secured room. Screens illuminated maps, financial logs, and intelligence reports.

Going forward, the security at the safe house became more

compartmentalized. All discussions were on a need-to-know basis. Information about Jack and Lily's movements was only revealed to a select few.

Lily reminded Jack that the stakes had risen for him once again. "There's no reason to believe that someone won't make other attempts on your life. And if you don't lose your life, you may lose your liberty—we don't know how close police agencies of Europe and Interpol are to apprehending you."

Jack nodded and took the lead. "Fischer's network is layered but not unbreakable. We target Marigold Holdings and Victor Adler's offshore accounts. Our goal: expose his financial vulnerabilities while maintaining leverage."

Jack's expertise in private equity gave them a unique advantage. Years of structuring investment vehicles and handling high-value portfolios meant he understood how to mask assets behind complex financial instruments. He explained how hedge funds, shell companies, and layered trusts could be systematically peeled back. Their strategy would focus on uncovering the weaker, less protected accounts—those linked through recently restructured holding companies.

"We need to identify the patterns in Fischer's account activity," Jack continued. "Start with transfers through low-regulation jurisdictions—Luxembourg, the Caymans, and now Zurich. Lily, I'll need you to run penetration tests against these offshore entities. Simulate typical auditing scenarios. Look for batch transactions that don't match declared asset values. Also, look for authorized signers who are present in multiple entities. This could signify a possible string for us to pull at."

Lily nodded, already well along in configuring Argus. "We can also look at real estate acquisitions and art transfers. He may be using high-value collectibles as collateral in private equity loans. If we can flag those as fraudulent or inflated, we can trigger regulatory scrutiny."

Jack adjusted a couple more Argus parameters. "Julian hinted at Adler's accounts but deflected when pressed. We need to ask him directly. Here's what we need clarified: Why the recent shift to Zurich? What changes occurred in account accessibility? Is there a secondary entity we haven't seen yet? And who authorized the last compliance review?"

The team reviewed cases like the Bouvier Affair, where art dealer Yves Bouvier manipulated the pricing of artworks, creating artificial value to siphon funds through inflated collateral. Fischer's network exhibited similar patterns, using rare art acquisitions to mask financial transfers. This precedent made it clear how high-value art could serve as both a laundering mechanism and a tool for wealth concealment.

The real challenge was ensuring Julian's cooperation without tipping Fischer off. Jack and Lily agreed to press him subtly in their next call, focusing on the accounts while cross-referencing his data for inconsistencies.

A video call with Julian Stokes followed. His face appeared on the screen, backlit by the Lisbon skyline. Calm, professional—but something felt off.

"We need clarity on Marigold Holdings," Jack began. "And Victor Adler's assets. How vulnerable are they?"

Julian hesitated. "They're... layered, but manageable. The Adler account was recently shifted, less exposed than Lily's assessment suggested."

Lily frowned. "That's not consistent with what we have, Julian. The data shows active vulnerabilities."

Julian shifted in his chair, the slight pause betraying discomfort. "Data fluctuates, Lily. This is the most recent intel."

Jack leaned forward. "Julian, you mentioned a compliance review that limited access. Who authorized that shift?"

Julian blinked but recovered quickly. "It was internal, under Fischer's oversight. The specifics were kept confidential."

Lily crossed her arms. "Confidential? If Fischer had oversight, it means he knew how to protect his most vulnerable assets. Julian, we need some insight here."

Julian exhaled. "I understand. I'll review the files again. But be careful—if we push too hard, we might trigger alarms we can't control."

"I'll see what I can do, but I have expenses," added Julian.

"Just do it," said Jack, "I'll cover your expenses."

The video call ended. Jack and Lily exchanged a glance, both aware they were skating on thin ice with Julian's answers but determined to push forward.

The team gathered around the central screen, reviewing everything they knew so far. Maps of financial transfers, shell companies, and account trails covered the table. Jack stood at the head, arms crossed as he began.

"We need to finalize our next steps," Jack said, his voice calm but intense. "Julian's evasiveness raises concerns, but we have enough to move forward. The question is, do we target the Adler offshore accounts first, or do we pressure Julian for clearer data?"

Lily frowned. "If we push Julian too hard, he might alert Fischer. On the other hand, going after the Zurich accounts without confirmation could backfire. We need solid evidence before we trigger any regulatory inquiries."

Jack nodded. "I'll have Marcus double-check Julian's background. Something isn't adding up."

"It's something that's been bothering me for some time," said Lily. "Julian is doing less and less, asking for more and more."

"Titus Lake, Paris, and now here. Vilar always seems to be a step ahead of us. I think someone is tipping him off."

After a few seconds, Jack and Lily uttered in unison, "Julian."

"I think he's working both sides—snitching on everyone, squeezing everyone," said Noa.

"He's outlived his usefulness," said Jack, "Insufficient ROI—the returns no longer justify the investment."

Lily reminded the team of the upcoming political fundraiser in Washington, D.C. "This event isn't just another target; it's a critical opportunity," she said. "Right now, we have Vilar, Fischer, and Harrington tied to the conspiracy. But a network this large doesn't stop there. The fundraiser is where we'll find the hidden supporters— politicians, corporate magnates, and financiers who've been operating in the shadows. If we can gather intel there, we'll expose the full scope of this operation."

Lily leaned back, considering further. "We should also call Elena for insight on the art itself. She might offer better strategies for using the art pieces to pressure the network further."

Elena Kovacs joined the next secure call. Her face, stern yet composed, filled the screen. Behind her, the dimly lit walls of her Geneva office were lined with folders and artifacts from past restitution cases.

"I've prepared the files on the stolen pieces that you found at the gallery," she began, referencing the meticulously compiled documents detailing the looted art. "These records trace the acquisitions back decades, some as far as Nazi-era transfers. I can release the data to international media channels once you give the signal. But understand the legal implications—this will open formal investigations across multiple jurisdictions."

Jack nodded. "That's the goal. We need the fallout to be loud and irreversible. Vilar needs to lose control of his narrative completely."

Elena closed the call with a final warning. "Make sure your case is airtight. Public exposure without proper evidence could backfire disastrously. And remember—timing is everything."

As the plan solidified, tension grew between Jack and Lily. Late that night, they sat by the stone hearth, the flames crackling softly.

Lily broke the silence, voice calm but edged with steel. "Jack, this isn't enough. We're leaking data, yes, but it's too passive. People like Fischer don't crumble with a scandal. We need to take direct action."

Jack's brow furrowed. "Direct action? What are you suggesting?"

Lily met his gaze. "I trained for this. In The Office, we didn't just expose. We neutralized threats permanently. Fischer has already crossed lines. If we don't shut him down fully, he'll just rebuild."

Jack exhaled, shaking his head. "Lily, I know they tried to kill us. But this isn't black ops. We're trying to stop them legally. If we go beyond that—"

"Legally?" Lily interrupted, voice rising. "This isn't personal. He's funding extremist movements. Laundering stolen history. There's no courtroom justice for men like him."

Jack stared at her for a long moment. "You're asking us to become what we're fighting against."

Lily's expression hardened. "No. I'm asking us to make sure they can never do this again."

Silence fell. The fire crackled, shadows dancing across their faces as both weighed the cost of their mission.

The plans were set, but the execution awaited the perfect moment. The team knew the risks—one misstep could unravel everything.

Jack stared out the window at the darkened slopes of Mount Etna, the distant glow of lava barely visible against the night sky. "We wait for the right moment. Then we finish this."

CHAPTER 17

D.C.

"Jack, I have a surprise for you," said Lily.

"Haven't we had enough surprises?" said Jack. He was in a hurry to leave Sicily. "I have to worry about getting back to the U.S. safely. It will be harder than ever to avoid detection, both leaving Italy and entering the U.S. I can feel the noose tightening around my neck, a little more every day."

"You'll like this one," said Lily, with a sly smile.

"OK."

"The DCM, the deputy chief of mission, at Israel's embassy in Washington, D.C., has been vacationing here in Sicily. He remembered me from a family dinner years ago. His dad is friends with my dad. He's the second-highest-ranking official of Israel's diplomatic corps in the U.S. He has generously offered to let us fly to D.C. with him. Full diplomatic immunity—no facial identification, no passport control, no questions asked. What do you think?"

Jack felt a huge weight lift from his shoulders. "That's fantastic. When do we leave? From where?"

The next day, in the early morning hours, Jack and Lily boarded a Gulfstream G280 at Falcone-Borsellino Airport in Palermo.

The DCM, sitting next to a stack of documents, looked up and greeted them. "*Shalom.*"

"*Shalom,*" said Lily, and Jack nodded.

"It's nice to see you again after all this time," said the DCM to Lily, adding, "It will be my pleasure to have you as my guests for this trip."

Besides the pilot and co-pilot, the DCM's executive assistant and a flight attendant accompanied them on the flight. The cabin was spacious and comfortable, but not private.

"There's nothing we can do but relax for the next ten hours," said Lily, sinking into her plush leather seat.

"Yes," said Jack, noting that the DCM and his assistant were easily within earshot.

On arrival at Dulles International Airport, the passengers were met by a US State Department official and escorted through a line for diplomatic arrivals. A limo picked them up and, in less than an hour, they arrived at the Embassy of Israel to the United States.

Once inside, the DCM turned to face Jack and Lily. "I wish we had more time, but I know you must be on your way. I wish you safety and success in your mission. *Behatzlacha.*"

"Thank you," said Jack and Lily, shaking hands with the DCM.

They walked out the side door of the embassy into the chilly early evening air. They were back on their own, back on high alert.

"Secure arrangements are in place for our visit. A car should pick us up shortly," said Lily. "My people are being extra careful. They're still a little embarrassed about the incident in Sicily."

A few minutes later, a car approached and flashed its lights in a predetermined signal.

"That's it, that's our ride," said Lily.

By this time in the evening, there was little traffic left on the streets of Washington as they passed long lines of amber streetlights toward Georgetown, only fifteen minutes away.

"Georgetown brings back a lot of memories," said Jack, as the car rumbled along the waterfront on the uneven cobblestone streets of the historic district. "We ran many operations through here, as did the other side."

Georgetown was a natural backdrop for intrigue, with both domestic and foreign intelligence agencies setting up operations in the classic, red-brick townhomes and vintage carriage houses. It was easy for agents to blend in with a steady stream of new faces—government officials, diplomats, and academics, who were always arriving and leaving.

They pulled into an alley and through thick wrought-iron gates into the courtyard of a carriage house covered with climbing ivy and surrounded by tall, manicured hedges that shielded it from the street.

Jack gazed at the vaulted ceilings with exposed beams and reclaimed oak floors. "This will have to do," he said with a wry smile.

"It's been swept thoroughly," said Lily, "and there's a full complement of intrusion detection systems, including motion detectors and hidden cameras everywhere. In the unlikely event we are compromised, there is an escape tunnel in the basement."

"Nice work," said Jack. "Get some sleep. We have a long day tomorrow."

The fundraiser for Senator Gerald Cain in Washington, D.C., was meant to add the final, grand touch to his presidential campaign. He was gaining in popularity, attracting increasingly large, enthusiastic gatherings, and this event was intended for his most exclusive, wealthiest supporters. This would be an opportunity for Jack and Lily to observe Vilar's endgame unfolding and maybe identify a way to disrupt it.

Jack and Lily made their final preparations to attend the event, leaving nothing to chance.

"Here are our new documents, clean burner phones, and earpieces through which Noa will be our second set of eyes," said Lily. "Cain's fundraiser is in the Dolly Madison House. Our ride will be here in twenty minutes."

Short of prosthetics, Jack altered his appearance the best he could. He dyed his hair, darkened his skin with a little makeup, and put on a pair of fake glasses. To look the part of a wealthy donor, he wore a finely fitted Brioni suit. Lily wore a sleek Vera Wang dress, a wig, and colored contacts, ensuring she looked nothing like her usual self.

They remained hypervigilant as they drove through the city. Were street cameras tracking their movements? Were they being trailed by unmarked vehicles? They couldn't be sure. The car dropped them off at the north entrance of Lafayette Square, not far from the Madison House. Once on foot, they crossed the park toward their destination, scanning their surroundings for signs of surveillance—for mechanical and human eyes tracking them.

Arriving early, they scoped out the location of the event in advance, noting both primary and secondary exits. Jack identified the side entrance as a potential escape route, while Lily confirmed a service corridor that offered additional cover if they needed to retreat quickly.

Midway through the event, Senator Cain took the stage, and the crowd erupted. As he spoke, they hung on every word. "This nation was built on principles we must reclaim. Our legacy, our culture, our strength—these are not up for negotiation. Together, we can take back what is rightfully ours and restore the values that made this country great." His speech echoed themes of white nationalism, carefully cloaked in patriotic language, but the subtext was impossible to ignore for those paying attention.

Gerald Cain was born on a farm in rural Oklahoma. Growing up, he witnessed globalization firsthand. Money was always tight. The small family farm struggled to compete with a flood of cheap farm products from Canada, Mexico, and China. Starting from a young age, he worked odd jobs to help ends meet.

He graduated with a law degree from the University of Oklahoma College of Law. He joined the Navy Judge Advocate (JAG) corps, but only practiced law for a short time before entering politics, running for a state congressional seat on a populist platform. He naturally gravitated toward a career rooted in an America First philosophy that promised protection for the farmers in Oklahoma and beyond. After serving only one year in the state house, he successfully won a US Senate seat as the law-and-order, strong borders candidate. Senator Cain quickly distinguished himself, bringing a disciplined military courtroom presence to the Senate floor.

Cain's rise to national prominence had been remarkably rapid. As a low-profile congressman from a district known more for its farmland than political influence, he had spent a year as a background figure—

hard-working and competent—but a name rarely mentioned beyond local circles. It was the financial crisis that changed everything. In its aftermath, as the nation faltered, Cain seized the moment, casting himself as a voice for the forgotten, railing against government overreach and coastal elites. His speeches, once polite policy talks, turned fiery, tapping into simmering frustrations across rural America. Media attention followed, amplifying his message until donors with deeper, more dangerous agendas took notice. They polished his image, sharpened his message, and gave him a national platform. Now, as he stood before the crowd, his words were no longer just rhetoric—they were a rallying cry:

"For too long, we've stood idly by while the foundations of our way of life were quietly chipped away. The institutions that once gave us strength—family, faith, service to our country—have been eroded in the name of democracy. But our democracy has become decadent and soft.

"Tonight, I speak out of duty to reverse the decline of our country. We live in a country that does not suffer from a lack of innovation or wealth—it suffers from a lack of leadership. It suffers from a loss of shared values and a loss of belief in who we are and what we stand for.

"It is time to reverse this decline—not with divisiveness, but with resolve. We must rekindle the moral clarity that once defined us. That is why I propose a national effort to restore the soul of this nation— an effort to take, what I call, 'civilizational responsibility.'

"This is not about exclusion—it's about preservation and continuity. We are the stewards of a great inheritance."

In his speech, Cain presented themes from his bestselling book, *Restoring America*, which introduced the Cain Doctrine, a blueprint for a 'national renewal' based on cultural restoration and American exceptionalism.

Jack and Lily exchanged several glances, the tension escalating as Cain's words hung in the air like a challenge. The historic Madison House, their target, was a study in power and influence. Once the residence of a 19th-century railroad magnate, its grand façade featured neoclassical marble columns and intricate stonework that whispered old money and political legacy. The mansion had been the site of numerous controversial gatherings, from whispered wartime negotiations to the private deals that shaped the modern power structure. Marble columns and velvet-draped windows framed the grand ballroom where the city's elite gathered. Chandeliers sparkled overhead, classical music filled the air, and the aroma of champagne mingled with the scent of polished wood.

"Did you check out the art here?" Lily said, scanning the room. "Carefully curated displays of culture meant to impress this elite crowd. Interesting to note that displaying it makes dangerous or fringe political ideologies look legitimate, tasteful, even morally grounded."

Jack nodded. "Case in point. Here comes Dr. Annalise Riedl from ICS. She and her institute wield a big influence over Cain—their imprint is found in every chapter of his book."

Jack thought back to Lisbon, to the dossier on Eduardo Vilar and *Directive 88*. It appeared that Dr. Riedl and ICS were making progress, relentlessly supporting nationalists' movements and extremist politicians like Senator Cain.

Senator Cain was a towering testament to the effectiveness of their efforts. Their contributions—whether publicly declared or, more often, funneled through dark channels—contributed to his huge war chest and made him the clear favorite to become the next president of the United States.

Dr. Riedl served the attendees the usual nationalistic fare and concluded her speech with: "For decades, mainstream politicians have promised economic progress, personal freedoms, and unity. They have failed on all counts, including preserving our culture and values. Senator Gerald Cain does not make promises that he cannot keep. He will succeed where others have failed."

Jack moved through the crowd, playing his part as an investor curious about strategic partnerships. He made eye contact with diplomats and CEOs of the most recognizable companies in America, letting his Wall Street bona fides drive the conversations.

Engaging an older gentleman in a navy suit, Jack raised his glass slightly. "Quite the collection here tonight," he remarked, gesturing toward a nearby painting.

The man nodded, adjusting his cufflinks. "Indeed. Some of these pieces have fascinating histories. You a collector?"

Jack shook his head. "More of a financial strategist. Always curious about high-value assets and their stories."

Meanwhile, Lily navigated the event from a different angle, moving gracefully among the waitstaff as if checking for quality control. Her eyes scanned the exits, noting a service corridor near the rear where security presence was light.

Over her coms, Noa confirmed the all-clear. The rest of the team had made their way back to Sun Valley from Sicily to regroup, with Noa providing remote surveillance for Jack and Lily.

Jack overheard a hushed conversation between a defense contractor and a sitting senator near the wine table.

"You'll find the shipments are completely concealed. No traceable links," one of them whispered, voice tinged with the confidence of someone who had done this before.

Jack tilted his head slightly, feigning interest in the wine selection but focusing intently on their bits of the conversation. "Lisbon's channel remains the most secure... critical hub... finance Cain's political ambitions. Vilar's influence ensures no interference, reinforcing Cain's power base through hidden sources and international leverage," the senator added, swirling his glass of red wine as if discussing a simple business deal.

The defense contractor nodded, lowering his voice further. "It's not the funds. It's the network—cultural assets, private auctions—it's about control. Making sure the right people owe Cain favors. Entire sectors are in play here."

Directive 88, thought Jack.

"Look a little to your left," whispered Noa to Lily. "The man in the dark-blue suit is one of Cain's campaign managers. He's been celebrating as if Cain's already the next American president."

Lily turned to her left just in time to see Senator Cain walk up to and shake hands with a balding, middle-aged man holding a stack of campaign flyers. She noticed what an untrained eye would miss. Right after the handshake, the campaign manager discreetly slipped something into his jacket side pocket, something small enough to be completely concealed by their hands.

"I saw a transfer," whispered Lily back to Noa. "Cain passed something to the campaign manager. I'm going after it."

Lily made her way through the crowd of supporters to the campaign manager, bumped into him, and brushed down with her hand, sending the flyers flying to the floor in front of them.

"I'm so sorry, let me help you," said Lily.

The campaign manager, clearly surprised and unsteady, clumsily started collecting the flyers as well as he could. Lily helped him and expertly lifted the contents from his jacket pocket—it was a flash drive.

Lily quickly found Jack. " I have a flash drive that I took from Cain's campaign manager. We should get out of here."

Suddenly, a man at the bar locked eyes with Jack—former CIA, now a private security consultant. Their cover was fraying. Jack could feel his shoulders tighten, the telltale sign of a trained operative recognizing another. The contractor didn't break eye contact; his posture shifted, signaling awareness without a word exchanged.

At the same time, "Over there. That's her!" shouted the campaign manager from the other side of the room, pointing at Lily.

"Yes, time to move," Jack whispered, setting his glass down, voice calm despite his adrenaline spiking. They made it halfway to the door when Jack felt a firm grip on his shoulder. The contractor. Jack twisted sharply, knocking the hand away with a precise movement. The man staggered and moved away, but his eyes remained fixed on Jack's face, calculating.

Jack feigned calm, forcing his breathing steady as he grabbed another champagne flute from a passing server. Engaging a guest in light conversation, he used the reflective surface of a nearby silver platter to monitor the contractor's movements. The man was speaking into a cufflink—communicating with another security person who likely was wearing some kind of concealed earpiece.

Meanwhile, Lily disappeared into the service corridor. She barely made it ten steps before a uniformed security guard emerged from a side door, blocking her path. "Ma'am, I need to check your bag," he said, stepping closer.

Lily shook her head, gripping the strap tightly. "This is personal property. Let me pass."

The guard reached for her arm. Lily drove her knee into his ribs, forcing him back. He grunted but didn't go down. His radio crackled to life—backup was on the way. Lily spun, using her elbow to strike his jaw, but he managed to catch her wrist, twisting it painfully.

The struggle intensified. She dug the heel of her stiletto into his shin, but the guard wrestled her into the wall, pinning her. Lily was restrained, her breath ragged from the fight.

Jack caught sight of Lily's capture and knew he had to move fast. With a running start, he slammed into the first guard, knocking him into the second—both of them sprawled on the ground. The second guard, momentarily distracted, gave Lily the opening to break free.

A subtle alarm chirped from a nearby security console. Jack's heartbeat surged. The entire room seemed to shift as the first layers of security tightened—an usher now stationed near the main entrance, the side doors quietly closing. Jack knew they were moments from full containment, and only seconds remained for their exit. Noa guided them to the closest exit through their earpieces. Jack and Lily ran into the street, barely evading the security guards as they attempted to close in on them.

The first SUV tailed them as they left the estate, headlights cutting through the misty night. Jack and Lily split at the next intersection, with Jack darting down Constitution Avenue toward the Federal Triangle DC Metro stop. His steps echoed against the pavement as he slipped through a side entrance, weaving into the rush-hour crowd. The packed station slowed their pursuers temporarily, but Jack knew it wouldn't last long.

"Two tails, black and silver sedans. They're circling near the National Mall," Noa's voice crackled in their ear.

Jack emerged from the Metro near Smithsonian Station, the broad expanse of the National Mall stretching before him, a canvas of pale stone and historic grandeur under the dim glow of streetlights. The Smithsonian Castle, with its red sandstone towers, loomed like a silent sentinel in the distance. The Washington Monument stood stark against the low clouds, a pale spear of marble catching ambient light. Clusters of late-night tourists lingered near the museum entrances, their laughter soft but distinct against the quiet hum of the city.

He scanned the streets, heart pounding. Lily was across Independence Avenue, moving past the modern lines of the Hirshhorn Museum, her dark silhouette barely visible. She kept to the edges of the sidewalks, angling towards a narrow side street where the concrete barricades of federal security framed the path.

The silver sedan came into view, its headlights dimmed but unmistakable, shadowing her every step. The driver moved with patience, matching Lily's pace without drawing attention. Jack felt the urgency coil in his chest. Lily was playing it cool, but they both knew time was running out.

Suddenly, Lily made her move. Without breaking stride, she adjusted her steps, angling closer to a waist-high metal traffic barrier near the corner. Just as the sedan crept closer, she pivoted sharply, catching the barrier's edge with the heel of her shoe. The barrier shifted, its base scraping loudly against the pavement as it tipped into the vehicle's front wheel well.

The driver reacted too late. The sedan swerved, its front bumper smashing into a concrete planter, jolting the passengers inside. Tires squealed as the driver overcorrected, turning too much in the other direction and clipping the side of a stone security barricade.

Lily didn't wait to see the damage. She slipped between two parked cars and vanished into the shadows along a pedestrian pathway leading toward the National Museum of American History. The collision drew a lot of attention and gave Jack enough cover to evade the car following him. He caught up with Lily, his pulse steady but his mind racing. They'd bought themselves enough time to slip away, but safety wouldn't come until they reached Georgetown.

Hours later, safe in the carriage house, Jack stared at emptiness, thinking about the fundraiser and their narrow escape. They had witnessed so much—Senator Cain openly aligning with controversial figures, whispered negotiations involving high-profile defense contractors, and a series of coded exchanges hinting at illicit art sales funding political ambitions. The room had been filled with power brokers, all carefully hiding behind their expensive suits and polite smiles.

But they had nothing concrete to prove any wrongdoing. Lily remained near the window, scanning the streetlights, her jaw tight with frustration. "We saw Cain meet with that lobbyist from the Lisbon auctions. And the defense official... he practically admitted laundering money through those art deals," she said, voice low but edged with tension.

Jack exhaled sharply, pacing the length of the room. "And yet all we have are vague memories of conversations. Nothing that would stand up in court or the press."

"We have this," said Lily. She fidgeted with the flash drive and inserted it into the USB port of a computer sitting on the desk by the window. "Can't read what's on it—the drive looks to be encrypted."

"We'll have to wait until we get home," said Jack.

Lily nodded, but her expression remained guarded. "We're getting closer to Vilar. But someone's feeding him our moves. Think about it—how else would they have known to intercept us tonight? They knew where we'd be and exactly what we were after."

"It's apparent that we are not safe—Vilar is casting too wide a net," said Jack. "And there's not much they can do if the police apprehend me. With Vilar's influence, I'm not guaranteed a fair trial—who knows where I would vanish—even here, in the U.S.?"

She paced the room, glancing out the window again. The street was quiet, but the sense of being watched lingered.

CHAPTER 18

Wood River Drive

Jack stared out the frost-coated window of the Cirrus SR22T, the engine's steady hum a quiet backdrop to his racing thoughts. Mossad had arranged for one of their pilots in D.C. to fly him to Idaho in a private plane, possibly the only way he could get back home a free man.

"How long will it take?" Jack asked the pilot.

"About ten hours. We'll need to make two fuel stops. You know there are better ways to fly cross-country than in this small plane."

Jack knew that his travel options were very limited. Not so for Lily, who took a commercial flight to Idaho and probably was in Sun Valley by now.

The trip felt longer than it was, but the stops to refuel gave Jack a chance to stretch his legs. Over the Rockies, the weather started to deteriorate as storm clouds darkened. Approaching Hailey, a report came through from Friedman Memorial Airport:

"Attention all aircraft. Due to low visibility, all runways are closed until further notice."

The airport was socked in, so the pilot rerouted to Boise, a two-and-a-half-hour drive to Sun Valley. Jack would have to rent a car; his local debit card was blocked thanks to Vilar, and his European credit card could be problematic.

"I'll rent a car for you," said the Mossad pilot, "The Office will pick it up from your home tomorrow."

Starting with a forty-minute stretch to Mountain Home, Jack knew the route like the back of his hand. The longest leg, between Mountain Home and Bellevue, gave him plenty of time to think.

D.C. had generated little new intel. Paris had promised answers but delivered only more questions. The Titus lead had revealed stolen art, yet every critical piece of proof had slipped through their fingers. Trails ran cold just as they grew promising. It was a game of inches, like Marcus said, but the inches weren't adding all the way up yet. But Jack's business instincts, learned the hard way on Wall Street, and his intelligence work refused to accept failure. If the art was moving, so was the money—and he was determined to follow every financial thread until he found the source.

It was early evening by the time Jack neared Bellevue, only two miles from the airport at Hailey, where Jack should have landed hours ago. The Idaho sun was just starting its descent, splashing red on the peaks of the Smoky Mountains.

As Jack made his way into his home, snow draped over the slopes of Sun Valley like a heavy curtain, masking the world in stillness. His home, which sat in the frost-covered woods only 200 yards from the base of Bald Mountain, was normally a perfect location for getting in a few runs to start the day. But life was not normal—his mind was worlds away from gliding down the mountain.

This house was never meant for this. Jack had built his Sun Valley retreat as a sanctuary where he could finally leave the remnants of his former life behind. The crisp mountain air, the snow-draped woods—it was supposed to be his post-career refuge, a quiet space for reflection. Yet now, instead of peace, the house felt more like a bunker. He was huddled with Mossad agents, chasing stolen Nazi art funneled through offshore trusts, the profits fueling a dark web of influence threatening to destabilize America. The danger was closing in, and the illusion of peace he'd constructed here was a distant memory.

Jack struggled to suppress his growing suspicions: Was it too easy to leave Georgetown to return here? Could he trust Noa or Lily? Was Vilar setting a trap for him in Sun Valley?

Jack stripped off his coat, but the suspicions clung to him.

To make things worse, his situation was more critical than ever. His cover was broken in Washington, and, if caught now, he wouldn't be able to fight extradition. His prospects in the Austrian justice system looked bleak; it was unclear whether he would even have his day in court.

Jack pondered his dwindling options if he failed in his mission. Disappearing into the wilderness of northern Idaho, or the forests of neighboring states, seemed the most promising—nothing else was viable. His skills as an outdoorsman might see him through. Eventually, by cashing in some IOUs, he would create a new identity in the States or somewhere overseas.

Their return to Sun Valley wasn't supposed to feel like this. They had returned mostly empty-handed from Paris and D.C., but Jack had pieced together fragments from their previous leads—transaction patterns and crypto activity tied to the stolen art trade—transaction records linking stolen art sales to extremist funding and a Cayman Islands trust obscuring millions in dark money. Argus pulled its weight, again, finding obscure connections from disparate sources. Proof, if handled correctly, that could dismantle the network they had spent months chasing.

The team was unable to break into the flash drive that Lily had taken from Cain's campaign manager in D.C. "It's very strongly encrypted, AES-256. It could take months to break into it, even with the world's fastest supercomputer," said Noa.

"They've taken special precautions with this drive," said Lily, trying not to think about how valuable the contents of the drive could be.

Settling in front of his laptop, Jack stared at blockchain records from the recent operations in Paris and D.C. Glimpses of massive data sets had appeared—an intricate web of high-value art sales, the proceeds seemingly funneled into anonymous digital wallets before vanishing into offshore accounts. Yet every trace had been just out of reach, the pieces visible but never fully obtainable, leaving him chasing shadows instead of proof.

Jack understood the complexity of the system he was up against. Crypto wallets weren't like traditional bank accounts. They were digital vaults, each protected by a unique cryptographic key—a code so complex that it would take a supercomputer hundreds of years to crack. Transactions moved through a decentralized web, each payment divided and masked across thousands of blockchain nodes. Once funds were sent, they became nearly untraceable, stored behind a string of encrypted addresses that concealed both the sender and recipient. Some wallets were cold—disconnected from the internet entirely for maximum security—while others, like the one tied to Vilar's Cayman trust, were hot, constantly participating in crypto transactions in the cloud. To penetrate the wallet, one needed to exploit a flaw in the encryption itself. And Jack knew the cracks in the system, however small, were where people like Fischer thrived.

The Cayman Islands trust stood at the center, a financial fortress shielding payments to extremist groups and shadowy political donors. But it wasn't impenetrable. Jack had already isolated several crypto wallet addresses tied directly to the trust. If they could break into that core system, the entire financial network would unravel.

"This is it," Jack muttered, highlighting a cluster of suspicious transactions. "These wallets lead back to the Cayman trust. Known for its lax financial regulations and secrecy laws, the Cayman Islands permit the creation of trusts that conceal true ownership, making them ideal for laundering funds through anonymous transactions. If we penetrate it, we can collapse the entire operation."

"Noa, are you making progress breaking into the Cayman Island server?"

"Not yet. I'm trying. It's the most secure server I've ever encountered," said Noa, clearly frustrated.

"By the way, where's Yaron?" said Jack.

"I haven't seen him," said Noa. "I thought he came here with you."

"No, he didn't. I'll call him on his burner phone," said Jack.

After no response from Yaron, Jack said, "It's not like Yaron. Usually, he lets us know what he's doing."

As Jack ran through a mental checklist of Yaron's possible whereabouts, his burner phone buzzed, the shrill sound breaking the silence. "Who would know this number?"

"Only someone on our team. It must be Yaron—he's the only one not here," said Lily.

Jack answered.

A distorted voice hissed through the line. "We have your hacker. Give back the flash drive—or he disappears."

Jack's stomach twisted. "You have one of my people?"

"We will give you the time and place for the exchange."

Silence. Then the call went dead.

"They, Vilar's men, have someone from our team. It must be Yaron, and they will kill him if they don't get back the drive we took in D.C.," said Jack.

"What? How did they get him?" said Lily.

After a moment, Jack answered. His voice was measured, but the tension bled through. "I don't know how they got Yaron, but we must get him back at all costs."

Lily appeared behind him, eyes hard with determination. "We need to find out where they're holding him. We need to extract him. Now."

Jack shook his head, jaw tight. "We need to buy time. We're on the verge of crippling their financial core. If we stop now, we lose everything."

The sky was darkening, and the clouds were gathering. Soon, a white fury would engulf Sun Valley. Roads would vanish beneath a rising tide of snow. Trees and shrubs would groan under the weight of the thick blanket.

As the storm outside was brewing, wind rattling against the frosted windows, the pressure in Jack's chest tightened. Choices were dwindling. Time was slipping away. And with it, the margin for error.

Jack's burner phone buzzed again, the distorted voice returning, calm but sharp as static crackled along the line.

"You want him back alive? Here's how it works."

Jack's jaw tightened. "Go on."

"Tonight. 8 p.m. Base of Bald Mountain. River Run Lodge. Bring the drive. No games, no backup, or your man doesn't get out alive."

"And if we refuse?"

A low chuckle echoed through the line. "Refusal means we send Yaron back to you—piece by piece. If you're lucky, we might start with his hands."

Jack's grip on the phone tightened. "Proof of life. Now."

A pause. Then came the faint sound of rustling fabric. "It's me." Yaron's voice was hoarse, pained but clear. "I'm still here, keeping my head in the clouds."

The line cut out abruptly, the voice returning. "He's breathing. For now. Do as you're told, and he stays that way."

Jack's mind raced. "If we give you the drive, what's stopping you from killing him anyway?"

"We're not monsters, Berman. We want the drive, not a body count. You have your instructions. If you're not there tonight with the drive, then—"

A click. The line went dead.

Jack's hands shook slightly as he lowered the phone. "They want us to bring the drive to River Run Lodge tonight."

Lily's voice was sharp. "It's a trap, but we must step into it."

CHAPTER 19

River Run

Jack sat at the head of the long farmhouse table in his home near Bald Mountain with its slopes blanketed in white. The fire crackled quietly in the background, but the tension in the room remained ice-cold. The snowstorm had built steadily, wind battering the windows as if the storm itself were closing in.

Marcus had arrived from Lisbon earlier in the day. He would be a welcome addition to the team that could use all available manpower.

The exchange of the flash drive for Yaron would take place in a few hours. Until then, they continued their attempt to break into the Cayman trust. They worked in silence.

Jack's laptop illuminated his face, the screen a maze of blockchain transactions, red-flagged crypto wallets, and half-traced financial trails. Each dead end was a reminder of their failures in Paris, D.C., and Titus, the disappointment of missed opportunities pressing down like the storm outside. He needed to find a clue, anything, maybe a misplaced password, to help them break into the Cayman trust server.

He inhaled slowly, forcing calm. "We must keep trying," Jack said, breaking the silence. His voice was measured but tight with frustration. "The Cayman Trust is the key. If we crack it, we can trace the stolen art sales directly back to Vilar's network, tie every sale back to the offshore accounts funding his operation.”

“And if we can take his crypto wallets, we can throw a wrench into his financial machinery,” said Lily.

The others remained silent, the implications sinking in. This was it.

Lily leaned against the far wall, arms crossed, her jaw tight. The glow of the firelight danced across her face, deepening the tension in her expression. The storm outside howled louder, wind rattling the windows like an audible countdown pressing against their fragile sense of control. She stared into the flames before speaking, her voice tinged with frustration. “Progress report, please.”

“Slow progress. I’m checking for mistakes in setting administrative privileges,’ said Noa and continued to work in silence.

“Nothing, yet,” answered Jack.

“And if we can’t crack it? What if this fails, too, Jack? We’ve been circling dead ends for weeks. What if Vilar’s already ahead of us? And he has Yaron.”

Jack sat motionless in front of the computer, the screen a reflection of his own gnawing uncertainty. He wanted to reassure her, but the evidence was thin. The web of transactions they’d uncovered was complex, distributed. His instincts told him they were zeroing in—but how close was close enough?

The fire cracked loudly, and for several minutes, neither of them spoke. The silence wasn’t comforting—it was the kind that only intensified the pressure.

Julian wasn’t in the room with them. He sat alone upstairs in the study, the door half-closed, as if he didn't quite belong in the heart of the conversation unfolding below. The fire didn't reach that far; the space was colder, quieter, the storm outside pressing against the windows, a pale, oppressive gray light filtering through the frost-lined glass.

He had arrived early that morning. A few days earlier, he had told Jack in a phone call that he had some new information best delivered in person. Intrigued, Jack agreed and suggested that Julian should stay at his home. Lily would help make the travel arrangements.

He sat in a worn leather armchair, a half-empty glass of scotch resting untouched on the side table beside him, forgotten. His hands trembled slightly as he stared down at his phone—scrolling through the last message he'd received. The words replayed over and over in his mind:

"You were warned. Betrayal carries a heavy price."

No signature. No demand. Just a chilling reminder that Fischer's reach extended further than Julian had ever imagined.

His journey here had been shadowed with fear. Julian's role had shifted from informant to a pawn dangling dangerously close to exposure. A coded message on his personal encrypted server was the first sign. Then there was the figure in the black coat tailing him through Heathrow the night he'd boarded the flight for Salt Lake City. He hadn't told Lily about that part—he wasn't sure if it was paranoia or real.

The flight itself had been long and tense. Julian felt the eyes on him. He'd barely slept, checking the cabin for passengers watching him, his mind racing through worst-case scenarios. Flying on a smaller jet from Salt Lake City to Hailey was easier, and he arrived just before the snowstorm, but it was still stressful.

Now, here he was. Holed up on the second floor of a snowbound house in Idaho, feeling every bit the compromised asset they all thought he was. And the worst part? He *was* compromised.

From downstairs, he could hear muffled voices—the low hum of Jack and Lily discussing the plan. The plan that hinged on him. His pulse hammered harder.

He didn't belong in this world.

Not like them. Not like Jack, who spoke in strategic layers and saw threats before they happened. Not like Lily, who could lie, manipulate, and bend the truth without missing a heartbeat. Julian wasn't built for this. He was an information broker, a financial manipulator, yes—but *this*?

And yet, here he was.

When he couldn't take the tension anymore, he called down from the top of the stairs. His voice was thin, barely steady.

"They sent someone to warn me, Lily. A message—coded, but clear. I'm compromised. If I show my face, I'm dead. You're playing with my life here."

The words echoed back at him, the silence in return more unsettling than the storm outside.

The wind outside had settled into a low, steady torrent, pressing against the cabin walls like a warning. Jack stared at the dying fire, the last embers fading. In his mind, Jack walked through each step of the proposed exchange. He thought of all the things that could go wrong—it was likely that they would not get Yaron back, *assuming that*

Yaron was still alive.

Marcus spoke from the corner, voice grim. "And we all know this won't be a clean handoff."

Jack exhaled slowly, his eyes narrowing. "No. But we play their game—for now. Because we're getting Yaron back."

No one spoke for a long moment. They didn't need to. Each of them felt it—the significance of what lay ahead, the razor-thin line they were about to walk.

"Team, it's time to go," said Jack.

They piled into Jack's SUV as the storm thickened, visibility shrinking as wind gusts swept across the road.

"There's no way they're going to play this straight up," said Jack. "I'm getting out here, so I can move into position behind the handoff location."

About a hundred yards from the lodge, the SUV slowed down just enough to allow Jack to slip out into the dark. They parked the SUV, and Marcus and Lily walked to the front of the lodge and stood by the black, life-size bronze statue of the grizzly bear. The cold wind cut through the valley, snow swirling under the floodlights of the lodge entrance. Julian and Noa stayed behind.

Within minutes, they were approached by three men wearing heavy winter jackets.

"Do you have the flash drive?" asked the man who appeared to be in charge.

"Yes. Where's Yaron?" said Lily, sensing a trap.

"He's been delayed," said the man.

"That's unfortunate," said Jack, as he stepped forward from

behind, pointing his Glock at the back of the man's head.

The men turned around. "There are three of us and only one of you."

"Yes, but which one of you wants his head blown off?" said Jack. "Now, one at a time, slowly reach into your coats, remove your weapons, and place them on the ground."

Not prepared to answer Jack's question, they did as they were instructed. Marcus and Lily quickly and discreetly picked up the handguns.

"Here are the zip ties," said Jack, pulling out a bag from behind his belt. "I thought we might need some."

"Arms behind your back," said Marcus to each man as he yanked their arms behind them and secured their wrists.

"Let's take a walk. This way," said Jack to the men, nodding in the direction of a gentle, lightly-snow-covered slope.

Near the bottom, about fifty yards away, in a small thicket of trees, Jack said, "This will do. Marcus, secure their feet."

Marcus herded the men into the thicket, pushed them to the ground, zip-tied their feet, and stuffed their mouths with cleaning rags that Jack had brought for this purpose.

Finally, with more zip ties, he attached each man to a tree.

"You'll want to free yourself in the next few hours," said Jack. "Otherwise, you're in for a long, cold night."

The team safe, back at his home, Jack was philosophical.

"What happened tonight was to be expected—there was no reason to think that Vilar would keep his word," said Jack.

"We need to find out where they're holding Yaron," said Lily, then abruptly turned to Jack. "What did Yaron say on the phone?"

"Something about his head in the clouds," said Jack. Lily's eyes lit up, her mouth pensive. "I think I know where they're holding him," she said. "Yaron gave us a clue. We had lunch at the Roundhouse the day before he was kidnapped. He said he felt like his head was in the clouds when we were looking out the restaurant windows. And the failed exchange was near the Roundhouse. That's got to be it."

Noa, silent until now, interrupted, stepping forward as the firelight flickered across her face. She set her laptop on the table, turning the screen toward Jack and Lily. A map was open, centered on a snow-covered mountain restaurant perched high above the valley—the Roundhouse.

Her voice was calm but tight with urgency. "There's an auction at the Roundhouse tomorrow. This isn't just any private event—it's bigger than we thought."

Jack's eyes narrowed as he leaned closer. "What tipped you off?"

Noa tapped a few keys, pulling up a series of encrypted financial transactions, each linked to offshore accounts they'd been chasing for weeks. "Remember the wallets we traced from the Cayman breach? I cross-referenced the activity with recent high-value insurance contracts. Several were filed under corporate shells we now know are controlled by Vilar's network—listed for pieces marked for private sale. And then, this."

She enlarged an invitation on the screen: a gilded, minimalist design with a single phrase— "An Evening of Rarity and Prestige." The location was confirmed as the Roundhouse on Mt. Baldy.

"A remote restaurant halfway up a mountain you can only access on a gondola, an exclusive invite, and all tied back to Vilar's network. What are they selling?" asked Jack.

Noa hesitated, glancing at Lily before answering. "I can't verify everything yet. The details are heavily redacted. But from what I've pieced together... it's significant. High-profile. Historic pieces. The kind that could disappear for decades if they fall into the wrong hands."

Jack folded his arms, voice sharpening. "You're saying this isn't just another illegal auction—this is a statement."

Lily nodded slowly, her voice quieter now, calculating. "It's more than that. Vilar's moving stolen pieces and showing his clients he's untouchable. If this auction goes through, it'll be a power play to prove his network can operate above the law, without fear."

Jack stood, the flame's shifting shadows against the walls. "This is it. This is where we disrupt Vilar's network for a long time. We must prepare a plan."

"Where's Julian?" asked Lily. "We'll need his help."

Jack approached the stairs leading to the second floor and paused at the bottom. "Please come down, Julian," said Jack. "We need to talk."

Julian came downstairs and shook his head, voice trembling. "You don't understand. I can't help you anymore. They're watching every move I make. If I slip, even for a second—"

"Who's watching you and why?" said Lily.

Julian took a deep breath to compose himself. "I have a confession to make. I don't have new information for you."

"Then, why are you here?" said Lily.

Julian took another deep breath. "I'm sorry, Jack… I told—I sold—to Fischer the discovery you made about Harrington. Fischer sent his men to intercept the shipment you showed me. There was no shipment. Fischer thinks I played him."

Jack gave Lily a look as if to say, "I'll explain everything." Lily understood and didn't ask about Paris or the shipment.

Jack leaned forward, voice quiet but intense. "What's done is done. We won't let anything happen to you. You were always part of this plan. We're close, Julian. Closer than we've ever been. We need your help."

"Fischer is holding an auction at the Roundhouse tomorrow for Vilar's operation. It has to be big money—it may be his biggest fundraiser of the year, right here in Sun Valley," said Lily.

"We need you to help us disrupt the event," said Jack.

Julian looked up from where he sat, his voice quieter but no less strained, the emotion pressing hard against the quiet hum of the storm outside. His pale face was drawn, his hands flexing and clenching against the arms of the chair as if trying to ground himself in the moment. "And you expect me to just walk into the auction? Walk among them like nothing's happened? They'll be watching me the second I step into that room. If Fischer sees me, I'm finished."

Lily stepped forward, her expression softening but still strained. Her voice lowered, steady but compassionate. "That's exactly why it has to be you, Julian. You've been playing the part, and Fischer still needs you. If you walk into that auction, play it right, he'll see a man desperate to buy back trust."

Julian blinked, his jaw tightening. "And if I slip?"

Jack leaned forward, his voice incisive. "You won't. Because we won't give them the chance." He gestured to the screen where the Roundhouse floor plan glowed, the layout divided between the gallery, auction hall, and secure manager's office. "We split up. You're the lookout. You keep watch over the auction hall—act the part, make bids if you have to. Keep them focused on the spectacle."

His gaze shifted to Lily. "You and I will handle the extraction. Yaron most likely is being held somewhere in the basement, at the level below the restaurant's main hall. It's the most likely place he could be. His life is in serious danger, and we must get him out right away. We'll go back to the auction after Yaron is safe."

Noa, seated near the window, added with a nod, "The basement is by the lower patio where they keep supplies and firewood. The security we've mapped confirms the office is downstairs from the main hall. Physical access only. I'll provide Jack the credentials and access code."

"Good. You and I will get into the office," said Jack.

"How do we get into the auction, past the security?" said Marcus.

"I've got that covered," said Noa. "I discovered they sent QR codes to buyers invited to the event. They've been told to put them on their left forearms, like a fake tattoo."

"How about these QR codes for us?"

"I created QR codes for the team and a way to apply them," said Noa.

Jack nodded. "OK. The plan is set. We hit them from all sides. Extraction. Distraction. Disruption. They'll be too disoriented to react in time."

Julian exhaled, his face pale as he shook his head. "And if it goes wrong?"

Jack's eyes narrowed, his voice turning colder now. "Then we adapt. Because this time, Julian, we control the narrative. They've spent months controlling the flow of information—shaping the perception of power. Now we turn their arrogance against them. You're the key to this."

Silence stretched, the wind rattling the windowpanes harder, pressing in.

Julian nodded slowly, his voice quieter but more grounded. "OK. But I'm trusting you to pull me out if it falls apart."

Jack's gaze didn't waver. "We won't let it fall apart."

The wind outside pressed harder against the windows, rattling them with sharp gusts. Snow swirled in dense sheets beyond the frost-lined glass, the wind's howl rising in frequency, a steady drumbeat echoing the tightening coil of tension in Jack's chest.

Julian shifted, his face illuminated by the flicker of firelight. His eyes searched each face at the table, lingering on Lily, then Jack. The crackling of the fire was the only warmth in the room. His voice was cold, barely a whisper when it broke the silence.

His concerns persisted. "You're asking me to walk into a den of killers. If Fischer's men realize I'm compromised—if Fischer wants me dead—I won't leave that room alive." He swallowed hard, his hands curling into fists on the armrests, knuckles whitening as he struggled to suppress the tremor in his voice. "You don't understand the way they look at you, Jack. I've seen it firsthand. They can smell weakness. They know when someone's scared."

Jack held his gaze, steady but unyielding. His own pulse pounded harder, not from fear, but from an acute awareness of what they were walking into. He could feel it pressing in on him—the risk, the cost—but there was no room for hesitation now. His voice, when it came, was calm and controlled, but edged with steel.

"They won't, Julian." His words cut through the room. "We have the element of surprise. Vilar thinks he's untouchable, thinks his network is invisible. But that arrogance—it's his blind spot. And we're about to tear it open. The art, the money, the entire campaign to control the U.S. government with Cain. We're stopping this sale and dismantling everything he's built."

Lily nodded, stepping closer, her expression softer but no less resolute. "Julian, you're not alone in that room. We'll have eyes on you the whole time. The second something feels off, we'll be ready. But we need you to trust us."

A violent gust of wind slammed against the cabin walls as if daring them to break. The shadows seemed to stretch longer across the room, flickering across Julian's face as he exhaled shakily, nodding once. "I'll do it." His voice was hoarse, but steadier now. "But you need to promise me... if it goes wrong, you get me out. No questions. No second-guessing."

"None. If anything goes wrong, we'll get you out," said Jack, as he watched Julian wander back upstairs.

"Let me bring you up to date," said Jack to Lily, checking that he was out of Julian's earshot.

"I gave Julian some intel in Paris," said Jack. "A controlled leak of fake information about Harrington to see if Julian would betray a trust—which he did; he said he sold it to Fischer."

"I can see how Fischer was not happy when he found out the intel was fake," said Lily. "Julian is in real danger."

"Yes, he is, but I have an idea," said Jack.

Jack had spent decades thinking in systems: complex interrelationships, network effects, and feedback loops. He had quickly analyzed the situation, weighing the pros and cons of the available options.

"I thought of a way to put Julian back in Fischer's good graces, at least temporarily, and to weaken Fischer's security at the auction," said Jack, and filled her in on the details of his plan.

As Julian came back down the stairs, Jack met their eyes one by one. "Stay sharp. Trust the plan. We only get one shot."

CHAPTER 20

Roundhouse

The next day was tense. Everyone was focused—each member of the team rehearsed their roles—no one wanted to drop the ball.

Just after dark, the team stepped into the gondola, which was adjacent to the River Run Lodge at the base of Bald Mountain. The heavy glass doors slid shut behind them with a mechanical hiss. The cabin swayed slightly as it began its ascent toward the Roundhouse. The storm had started up again, and snow was blowing around the lift system, clinging to the glass, obscuring their view.

The irony was not lost on Jack. The grueling odyssey that began when he boarded another gondola in Kitzbühel—that seemed like many lifetimes ago—was coming to an end with a gondola ride.

"Everyone clear on the plan?" asked Jack, followed by nods all around.

River Run Lodge was no longer visible behind them. They all stepped out of the gondola and headed towards the Roundhouse. The strain deepened as they ascended the old concrete staircase toward the Roundhouse, the snow lashing the windows. Built in 1939, the structure was originally designed as part of the region's first major ski lodge expansion, and its age showed in the weathered stone walls and the creaking steps. The Roundhouse had hosted countless elite events over the decades, but tonight, its legacy felt tainted as it bore witness to something far darker.

"It's time to split up. Lily and I will find Yaron," said Jack.

"Julian, Noa, and I will join the auction," said Marcus, as they continued up the stairs.

"I think the most likely place they're holding Yaron is in the basement," said Jack. "I've been to the Roundhouse many times. There's a second patio here, but how do you get to the basement?"

The patio on this level of the Roundhouse had been closed for years. Weathered, warping chairs were stacked up and secured against the walls. Deep snowdrifts impeded their search.

"I don't see any doors leading from the patio," said Lily.

"Keep looking. There must be a way into the basement."

"Look at this," said Lily, pointing to something she caught out of the corner of her eye.

"I see the corner of what appears to be a delivery hatch," said Jack, looking behind a stack of firewood.

Lily and Jack cleared the logs to reveal a sloped entrance, barely three feet across, with a wooden cover splintered along the edges, its hinges rusting. It wasn't the main entrance to the basement, but it would have to do.

Behind the hatch was a dark, dusty passageway with damp, musty-smelling walls and not much headroom.

"This service tunnel probably hasn't been used in years," said Jack.

"Watch your head," said Lily, stepping inside, pulling out her LED flashlight. The red beam was easier on the eyes and less likely to be noticed by anyone at the other end.

Crouching, they slowly made their way through the passageway that first turned left, then right, and ended at another old, small wooden door.

Through cracks in the door, Jack and Lily peered into a dark room with concrete walls and exposed pipes, illuminated by a single dim light bulb. Dust-covered chairs with torn cushions, old tables, crushed cardboard boxes, rusting equipment, and other junk littered the room. A mildewy, oily smell seeped into the passageway.

Yaron sat bound to a chair at the center of the dimly lit room. His face was pale, his clothes disheveled, but his eyes were clear and alert.

"Is there anyone guarding him?" said Lily, straining to see more of the room.

"I don't see anyone," said Jack.

Just then, a man passed in front of them, barely two feet from the door.

"Is there only one guard?" she whispered.

"I can't tell," said Jack.

They waited.

Finally, Jack said. "There's just the one. We can't wait any longer. The next time he's close to the door, I'm going for him."

"What? Through the door?"

"Yes, through this rotting door," said Jack, as he stepped back to give himself a small running start. "Tell me when he's in front of the door again."

A few minutes later, Lily whispered, "Now."

Jack covered his face with an arm and lunged. The door gave way easily, and Jack slammed into the guard, both men hitting the floor hard. They rolled and both jumped to their feet.

The man was massive, broad-shouldered, his face cold and professional. He responded without hesitation, driving into Jack with a bone-jarring shoulder check that sent him crashing into the wall.

Lily had followed Jack inside. She reacted on instinct, snatching a steel candlestick from a nearby table and swinging it hard at the guard's head. He caught her wrist mid-swing, twisting brutally. Pain flared through her arm, but she pivoted, driving her knee into his ribs. He grunted but barely staggered back, his size absorbing the impact.

Jack recovered, lunging back into the fight, but the guard was relentless. A vicious blow to the jaw sent Jack staggering again, crashing into a glass display case that shattered under his weight.

Lily adjusted, rolling to the side as the guard advanced on her. She spotted a piece of a broken wine bottle, grabbed it, and slashed low. The glass caught his leg, blood seeping through his dark pants.

He roared and backhanded her, knocking her to the floor.

Breathing hard, Jack found his footing. He surged forward, slamming the man into the wall. The guard groaned, but his size was overpowering, twisting Jack into a chokehold.

Lily grabbed the shard of glass again. This time, she drove it deep into the man's forearm. His grip on Jack faltered, long enough for Jack to spin around and deliver a forceful blow to the guard's temple.

The man crumpled to the ground, collapsing into a motionless heap.

Silence.

Lily wiped her hand across her bloodied face and moved toward

Yaron. "Can you stand?" she said, slicing through the zip ties binding his wrists and feet with the shard of glass.

"No."

Lily couldn't see how Yaron was injured, but she knew better. Yaron had been beaten professionally, in a way to minimize the bruising, the external evidence. Maybe they used a rubber hose or a phone book, hitting Yaron's major muscle groups and organs.

"Help me carry Yaron. He can't walk," said Lily.

Jack and Lily, Yaron's arms slung over their shoulders, helped him limp out of the basement and into the gondola.

"He's had a little too much to drink," Lily quipped to an elderly couple exiting the gondola.

Back in Jack's home, they laid Yaron down on the couch.

"How do you feel?" asked Lily.

"It hurts all over, but I'll be alright," said Yaron, adding, "You better get to the auction."

"You may have a lot of internal injuries. It's going to take some time to heal," said Lily.

There was nothing more they could do to make Yaron more comfortable except bring him some food and drink.

"Let's get cleaned up and make ourselves presentable," said Jack.

Jack and Lily washed off the evidence of their brawl with the guard. Soon, the transformations were complete—they were in their formal attire, ready to attend an upscale event.

"Let's go," said Lily.

Jack started toward the door, then stopped, mid-step, as if he just had an epiphany.

"There is a loose end to take care of. Let me make a call," said Jack.

"Who are you calling?" said Lily.

"I'm just making sure we will have a clean-up crew."

CHAPTER 21

Bald Mountain

As they turned a corner in the stairwell leading up to the main hall of the Roundhouse, Jack and Lily were greeted by a young woman in a full-length, black evening gown.

"Good evening. May I see your invitations, please?"

A few steps behind her stood two athletic men, holding their hands at the ready in front of them, in the style used by US Secret Service agents.

Each in turn, Jack and Lily pulled up their left sleeve to uncover a QR code that would either allow them into the auction or be assaulted, or worse.

With a plastic smile, the hostess scanned each code with her phone, saying, "Welcome to the auction. This way, please," pointing to the rest of the stairs.

The further Jack and Lily climbed, the more disturbing the sight on the walls became. The lighting had been deliberately curated to draw attention to the centerpiece: Raphael's *Portrait of a Young Man*, a painting both iconic and haunting.

Jack flashed back to Titus Lake, where he first encountered the painting—pulling it out of a dust-covered crate, in the corner of a cluttered room in a snow-covered lodge.

Yes, as he'd thought, the art at Titus Lake—it's here. The lodge was used as a waystation for Vilar's stolen art.

Surrounding it were other masterpieces—each more unsettling in context than the last. The lighting cast a golden hue over the stolen works, as though daring the audience to marvel at their beauty while ignoring their tragic history. These were the pieces they had seen stored at Titus, each a fragment of a legacy stolen and twisted into symbols of power.

Art long thought lost, taken during the Nazi occupation, now flaunted in warm spotlights for sale as if its past never occurred. The textured stone walls, part of the lodge's original design, only heightened the historical weight pressing down on the space. Framed beneath the glass, some pieces looked hauntingly familiar. Art long thought lost was now shamelessly displayed as symbols of wealth and power. Masterpieces stolen by the Nazis hung on display as if trophies of conquest: Michelangelo Buonarroti's *Madonna of Bruges*, Vermeer's *The Astronomer*, Degas's *Place de la Concorde*, and *The Beautiful Gardener* by Max Ernst.

They were in but had to be careful. Vilar's men were positioned at key points in the room, their eyes carefully tracking their every movement.

The auction hall itself was a cathedral of wealth and influence. The Roundhouse exuded historical charm, its octagonal form perched high on Bald Mountain. Large picture windows framed the snowstorm outside, barely visible through the frost clinging to the glass. A four-sided stone fireplace dominated the center of the hall, flickering light across the room. The wooden beams overhead were original, their dark patina adding to the lodge's sense of aged grandeur. The floors were polished oak, worn from decades of elite gatherings, their quiet creaks barely audible beneath the hushed conversations. Towering windows, partially fogged from the storm, lined the far side of the room, revealing hints of the swirling snow outside.

The artwork on display seemed almost out of place—too pristine, too haunting for a venue with such a storied past, while conversations punctuated the soft strains of classical music.

The guests included elite art collectors, global financiers, and power brokers, some present out of genuine interest in the art, others with far more sinister motivations—key players in extremist funding streams—mingled with dignitaries and discreet operatives.

Among them stood Senator Cain and his campaign team, their presence more than just symbolic. A protective detail of two Secret Service agents always accompanied him, with another six agents positioned around the room and near the entrances. In dark suits and discreet earpieces, their eyes swept over the crowd, noting its every movement.

Cain worked the room like a professional, smiling as he shook hands with potential donors, blissfully unaware—or perhaps willfully ignorant—of how deeply tied the event was to blood money from stolen art. If tonight's evidence were to surface, his career and the institutions backing him could collapse overnight.

Jack and Lily moved among the attendees, fitting in seamlessly. They passed Marcus and Noa and exchanged partners. Jack and Noa moved in the direction of the office while Marcus and Lily continued to mingle.

"Do you see Julian, over to your left?" said Marcus.

"Yes, he certainly looks the part of a serious buyer in his tailored suit," said Lily.

Julian adjusted his cufflink, the concealed camera inside his lapel capturing every detail and sending a live stream to Noa's encrypted feed. The stakes were clear. Their operation was focused on disrupting the auction and recovering stolen art. Every face caught on that feed was evidence.

Faces of power, influence, and legacy blurred with the disturbing reality of extremist funding streams—some of whom Jack had identified from their financial web weeks earlier. The stakes heightened as Fischer arrived, taking personal control of the event, an unspoken sign that the auction's importance had escalated.

Jack and Noa peeled away from the main floor, slipping through a side staircase that led to the lower levels of the lodge. The air grew cooler as they descended, the ambience shifting from opulence to stark, reinforced security. What was once a bar was now unadorned concrete walls, the lighting dimmer, emphasizing the fortress-like design beneath the glamour above. The office, guarded by its recently installed biometric security system, stood at the end of the hall, its large door imposing and flanked by cameras that tracked every movement.

Two of Vilar's operatives stood like statues near the office, their expressions impassive but their alertness undeniable. Jack exchanged a glance with Noa, adjusted his jacket, and stepped forward with calm authority, his forged Secret Service badge flashing as he approached. "Security inspection. Level clearance required."

The bluff worked—for the time being. The guards stepped aside and allowed Jack to reach the terminal by the office door. He keyed in the decryption code extracted from Yaron's earlier work, watching the screen pulse as the system processed the input. Then, a soft beep. The screen blinked green.

"Access Approved."

The heavy wooden door of the office opened partially, as if it were spring-loaded.

"Thank you, you may go." Jack said to the guards and walked into the office with Noa.

Several paintings, each with its own attached tag, were propped up against the walls. At the far end of the office, there were three crates, like the ones Jack had seen at Titus Lake. To the side, there was a narrow, steel table with a stack of folders.

Jack opened one of the folders. "Escrow contracts, appraisals, provenance documents, and more."

"Check out the markings on these crates," said Noa.

"Yes, I know," said Jack. "They're similar to the ones we've found before."

"And look, here's a cash box filled to the top with large-denomination bills," said Noa.

"Probably escrow money, in cash, so it's untraceable," said Jack, adding with a wry smile, "Just leave it. The clean-up crew will take care of it."

Upstairs, the auction was starting. The lights in the room were dimmed, and the first painting was wheeled out and unveiled on the stage, triggering a murmur from the crowd. A single bright spotlight illuminated the painting, magnifying the drama.

In the background, Jack could hear the auctioneer say, "Ladies and gentlemen, please look at your brochures. This is a magnificent example of a Post-Impressionist painting by Paul Cézanne titled *La Montagne Sainte-Victoire.*

"Cézanne has captured the distinctive mood and atmosphere of the mountains that surround his hometown of Aix-en-Provence in southern France. His use of contrasting colors suggests a feeling of expanse and breadth. The areas painted in green and yellow accent the towering Sainte-Victoire.

"The bidding will begin at three million dollars. Do I have three million?"

"The auction is in progress," said Noa, just as the first "Sold!" could be heard behind her.

"Go back upstairs. It's time to make the call," said Jack, pulling out his cell phone.

"Sold for $5.5 million," said Lily. "That's just the first painting."

The second painting brought to the stage was *Five Dancers on Stage* by Edgar Degas.

"This painting is the finest example of the artist's fascination with the world of the dancer, capturing a moment of movement and elegance. It portrays an evocative blend of texture, light, and visual unity."

The starting bid price was considerably higher as was the interest in it, judging by the "oohs" and "aahs" from the crowd.

"Lily, look by the stairs. Julian is talking to Fischer," said Marcus.

"That's part of the plan," said Lily.

"What plan?" said Marcus.

"Julian is telling Fischer there's a cargo plane departing Coeur d'Alene airport late tonight with a load of art that's being diverted," said Lily.

"Diverted by whom?" said Marcus.

"By Harrington," said Lily. "It's a long story."

"Look. Some of Fischer's men are leaving," said Marcus.

"That's another part of the plan," said Lily. "No doubt they're on their way to intercept the cargo plane—fewer guards here will make it that much easier for us."

Just as Jack finished the call, Fischer entered the office.

His face was red, sweat beading along his temple despite the chill in the air; his suit was slightly rumpled as if he had been pulled from the auction floor. His blue eyes were sharp and predatory, narrowing as they locked onto Jack across the small space. His gaze shifted to the progress bar on the terminal, creeping closer to its final stages.

"Berman," he hissed, stepping forward. His voice was a low, dangerous whisper, heavy with restrained rage. "You have no idea what you've gotten yourself into."

His right hand twitched near the opening of his jacket. Jack recognized the movement instantly—a reach for the shoulder holster. A weapon waiting. But Jack didn't flinch.

"I know that the Titus Collection will be returned to its rightful owners, and there will be no windfall for you, Vilar, and Cane in Sun Valley," said Jack.

Suddenly, the steady rhythm of the auctioneer's voice was interrupted by shouts of, "This is the FBI", "Everyone stay where you are."

Fischer's face twisted with barely controlled fury. His lips curled back as he took a step closer, his hand fully disappearing beneath his coat.

Jack reacted first. In a split second, his Glock was out and aimed.

Fischer's breath quickened, his fingers tightening—but he clearly thought better of it. The pistol never cleared the holster.

With a snarl of pure frustration, he pivoted and bolted for the door, his footsteps echoing in retreat.

Jack didn't move. Despite Fischer being out of earshot, he said, "Run all you want. There's no escape."

Marcus tapped Lily on her shoulder. "Look, it's Fischer running up the stairs."

Not seeing an agent nearby, Lily said, "Let's go. We can't let him escape."

Lily and Marcus followed Fischer onto the rooftop, their breath fogging the freezing air as the storm howled louder, ice swirling around the exposed platform. Snow clung to their clothes, turning every step treacherous as they fought against the bitter wind. The platform was slick with a thin layer of ice, and each footfall had to be carefully placed to avoid slipping.

A sudden crack—sharp, distinct—cut through the roar of the wind. Gunfire.

"Get down!" Marcus shouted, his voice barely carrying over the storm. He crouched behind a concrete barrier as another shot rang out. The bullet ricocheted off the metal railing, the spark nearly lost in the blinding snow.

Lily dropped to one knee, heart hammering, her pulse roaring in her ears. She scanned the ridgeline, the storm masking nearly everything. Then, for a fraction of a second, the wind shifted—and there he was—the sniper.

Half-hidden in the skeletal structure of the chairlift across from the Roundhouse, nestled between the support beams and tangled cables. The Christmas Chair, which normally took Jack to the top of the mountain, was now a sniper's perch. The faint glint of a rifle barrel caught the low light as the sniper shifted, steadying for his next shot.

"Top of the chairlift—eleven o'clock!" Lily called, raising her weapon. Two sharp bursts echoed as her rounds sparked harmlessly against the steel supports. The sniper ducked, shifting position.

The wind kicked up again, obscuring everything in a flurry of ice. "We're sitting ducks out here while Fischer is getting away!" Marcus growled. "We have to move!"

Suddenly, Jack burst onto the rooftop from the service door, his weapon already raised, face taut and pale from the cold. "Cover me!"

He advanced, firing measured, controlled bursts toward the chairlift as Fischer ducked in a thicket of pine trees.

Another shot cracked. The bullet missed by inches, sparking off the metal frame near Lily's boot. She returned fire again, this time targeting the steel structure itself, forcing the sniper to reposition once more.

Pinned down by the sniper's barrage, there was little they could do but watch Fischer climb onto a snowmobile hidden among the pine trees, one he must have positioned for just this eventuality.

Lily kept firing bursts toward the sniper's position, but the figure had disappeared—swallowed by the storm.

Jack directed two shots toward the snowmobile, just out of frustration, knowing it was out of range. He glanced back toward the chairlift, just in time to see the faintest movement—the sniper retreating, slipping back into the storm, his task to provide cover for Fischer, complete.

"Let's get back inside," said Jack.

A tall, dark-haired man wearing a blue jacket marked "FBI" in big yellow letters approached Jack.

"Jack Berman? I'm Agent Henderson, Special Agent in Charge of the FBI Salt Lake City Field Office."

"Yes, I'm Jack. We spoke on the phone. I hope this was worth battling the snowstorm," said Jack with a knowing smile.

"We have the organizers in custody," said Henderson.

Except for the big fish that got away, thought Jack, flashing back to Fischer and the snowmobile.

"And the paintings?"

"We're carefully cataloging and removing them."

"Some of the art came from GalerieSV in Sun Valley," said Jack. "I can get you a lot of incriminating information."

"Thank you. Here is how you can reach me," said Agent Henderson, handing Jack a card.

Jack paused, while looking at the card. "What happens to the buyers?"

"We have their information. They'll be investigated to determine if they're in possession of stolen property."

"Thank you, Agent Henderson," said Jack. "Oh, just one more thing."

"Yes?"

"There's a perp you overlooked," said Jack, motioning to Julian standing next to him. "Julian Stokes. I can provide the evidence that he's involved."

"You are under arrest, Mr. Stokes," said Agent Henderson. "Come with me."

"Jack, what's going on? I'm on your side. I've been helping you," said Julian.

"You've been mainly helping yourself—working both sides," said Jack as he walked away.

Jack stared out into the void below, his face hard, unreadable. The mission was over. They had won the battle, but the war wasn't over.

The team, back in Jack's home, celebrated their victory but knew they would soon need to resume the fight.

"We accomplished a lot," said Jack. "The tide is turning in our favor."

"Thanks, you guys," said Yaron. "I was sure I was on my way to the big hackathon in the sky."

"No need for thanks," said Lily, as they all clapped.

Still, the looming goal was to get into the Cayman Island trust. The team had been trying to break into the system for days, with little to show for their efforts.

"Any luck breaking into the Cayman server?" Jack asked Noa. He was almost afraid to ask, knowing that Noa had been working on it diligently, without success, for many days.

"Almost there… just one more minute… I'm in!" exclaimed Noa, raising her arms.

"Copy everything. Delete everything," said Lily.

Noa's face went pale. "There's nothing here. The server has been wiped clean," said Noa.

"I could have told you that," said Yaron.

"What?" said Jack.

"I overheard Fischer talking to Vilar on his satellite phone. Vilar has moved the crypto wallets and a trove of documents from the Cayman Islands server," said Yaron.

"Everything? Where?" asked Lily.

"It appears that Vilar combined the hot wallets into one cold wallet and saved it, along with all the documents," said Yaron. "They're probably saved to an external drive."

"Vilar has physical control of the digital wallet. His Cayman Island crypto fortune is out of our reach," said Jack, not sounding very happy.

"Unfortunately, as long as he still has the means to finance his operations, we haven't heard the last from Vilar," said Lily.

"True. But let's not forget that we disrupted a major auction and recovered a large collection of stolen art," said Marcus. "We have to take our wins as they come."

"The biggest win is that we stopped Senator Cain," said Lily, "The Manchurian candidate is neutralized."

"At least for now," said Marcus. "It will take Cain a long time to restore his reputation."

Jack could not force himself to take a victory lap. *The big fish got away*, he thought.

In his mind, he replayed the long journey that started with an innocent ski trip to the Alps and ended in a major disruption of a worldwide conspiracy to destroy his heritage.

A message appeared on his phone: *First round goes to you. The next round will go to me.*

Epilogue

The world reacted to the disrupted auction in Sun Valley.

The New York Times led with a piercing headline: *"Global Conspiracy Unraveled: Stolen Art, Secret Deals, and Political Fallout Exposed."* Every major network followed. BBC. CNN. The story ignited across continents, capturing global attention with every unfolding detail.

Images of priceless stolen artworks filled the screens—pieces that had vanished decades ago, now traced to secret dealings among elite financiers and political figures. Survivors of stolen works appeared on broadcasts, their voices trembling with long-suppressed pain as they described not only the thefts but the erasure of their cultural identity. Art historians weighed in, emphasizing the importance of restitution and justice. Public pressure mounted, with viewers demanding accountability not only for the theft but also for the institutions that had enabled the secrecy for so long.

Jack sat in his home at the base of River Run, the snow gently falling outside. The fireplace snapped and popped, its warmth a sharp contrast to the cold truths being aired across the globe. The television played the unfolding coverage on mute, the ticker at the bottom scrolling relentless updates. Yet, his name never surfaced. He had made sure of that. His role in exposing the conspiracy was hidden beneath layers of anonymity, designed to protect himself and those closest to him. The official statement detailed the recovered art, the falsified documentation, and the financial webs that had kept the stolen works hidden for years, carefully worded to reveal the crime but shield the hunters.

Lily worked beside him, focused and precise. She was orchestrating the strategic release of evidence—one piece at a time. Financial ledgers cross-referenced with auction records. Unsealed shipping manifests documenting the illegal movement of artifacts. Transcripts of Edward Fischer's communications with high-profile collectors and politicians.

The evidence painted a damning picture: a global conspiracy in which wealth and influence had conspired to tip the presidential election—and with it, the future leader of the free world.

The fallout was swift. German and Israeli diplomats pressed Washington for cooperation in the investigation. Wealthy patrons who had unknowingly—or knowingly—acquired stolen pieces began returning them under the pressure of public scrutiny. Edward Fischer's financial network crumbled as frozen accounts in Switzerland, the Cayman Islands, and Luxembourg revealed the depths of the scheme. Funds recovered from Fischer's holdings were seized and anonymously redirected toward the restitution of stolen art and compensation for families affected by the thefts.

Edward Fischer disappeared completely. Arrest warrants in his native Germany and an Interpol Red Notice yielded nothing. Numerous sightings, in Europe and the U.S., all turned into dead ends. Reports that placed him in Russia, where he formerly had ties to the Russian Mafia, also could not be substantiated.

The Institute for Cultural Sovereignty was discredited and shut down. But Dr. Annalise Riedl landed on her feet. Her track record of publishing influential papers made her a strong candidate to work for think tanks or academia. It is rumored that she will accept a position with the Konrad Adenauer Foundation, associated with Germany's center-right Christian Democratic Union (CDU).

And then came the political earthquake. Senator Gerald Cain, once a rising star and a key figure implicated in the conspiracy, faced immediate and relentless scrutiny. Major networks broadcast excerpts of private emails leaked from the investigation, revealing Cain's direct knowledge of the stolen art dealings as a source of campaign funds. Investigative journalists uncovered a series of offshore donations linked to his campaign, adding fuel to the public's outrage. The bipartisan criticism was swift. Political commentators from both sides of the aisle condemned Cain's involvement, with some calling it a "betrayal of public trust."

As pressure mounted, Cain attempted a last-ditch effort to salvage his career. He held a tense press conference, visibly shaken, where he declared, *"This is a coordinated attack on my integrity. I will fight these baseless accusations."* Yet the media was relentless, dissecting his statements and comparing them against newly released financial records. Former allies, including senior members of his own party, publicly called for his resignation. Ethics proceedings in the Senate accelerated, and within weeks, Cain was forced to withdraw from the presidential race entirely. His career was finished, though the ripples of his downfall lingered.

Galerie Moreau, once a celebrated institution, became a symbol of scandal and betrayal. Within days of the revelations, three major French agencies descended upon the gallery: the Central Office for the Fight Against the Trafficking of Cultural Property (OCBC), the Ministry of Culture, and the Parquet National Financier. Each agency scrutinized every corner of its operations, from acquisition records to financial statements, leaving no document unchecked. The OCBC led the investigation into the provenance of the artworks, while the Ministry of Culture focused on ethical violations and the restitution process. Meanwhile, the PNF examined potential financial crimes, tracing money trails linked to the illegal art trade. Several key pieces from its collection were confiscated, while thousands more remained unaccounted for, fueling rumors of private caches and black-market dealings.

Luc Moreau, the gallery's director, was arrested during the sweeping investigation. Official charges included complicity in the trafficking of stolen cultural property and financial fraud. As the inquiry deepened, evidence surfaced linking Moreau to secret deals with high-profile clients, falsifying provenance records, and concealing stolen works in offshore storage facilities. Though his defense claimed ignorance, the mounting evidence painted a picture of complicity and greed.

A series of lawsuits followed, filed by families whose stolen artworks had passed through the gallery's hands. Former directors and curators, once respected figures, faced mounting pressure to explain how stolen masterpieces had ended up in their exhibitions without proper documentation. While some claimed ignorance, evidence suggested complicity, with whispers of high-level deals brokered behind closed doors.

Yet not all traces of the gallery had vanished. Investigators uncovered evidence of a secret storage facility, a freeport located near the Geneva airport, holding dozens of unregistered art pieces tied to the conspiracy. The discovery raised more questions than answers. Who still had access? And how many pieces remained hidden? Rumors circulated that Vilar, despite his public denials, still held influence over what was left of the collection, using it as leverage in ongoing negotiations.

The conspiracy involved other galleries in the U.S. and Europe, including GalerieSV in Sun Valley. Many of the pieces recovered at the Roundhouse restaurant had passed through this small, unassuming gallery. Jack provided the FBI with more than enough evidence, which forced its closure.

Jack knew the gallery's downfall was only part of the picture. There were still shadows where truth remained buried—and he couldn't shake the feeling that someone was working to keep it that way.

Julian, who had been entangled in Vilar's financial web, emerged as a surprising ally in the aftermath. Faced with mounting evidence and pressure, he chose to cooperate with authorities, providing crucial intel on Vilar's remaining assets and laundering tactics. While his involvement was significant, Julian was far from guiltless. Seeking redemption, he worked alongside international investigators, helping trace stolen art still unaccounted for. Yet, the shadows of his past lingered, and Jack knew there were parts of the truth Julian hadn't shared—whether out of self-preservation or deeper loyalties remained uncertain. His carefully crafted public statement cast him as a victim of Fischer's betrayal. He emphasized his cooperation with authorities while quietly moving assets to secure locations. His network, though damaged, was far from dismantled.

William Harrington retreated beyond reach. An army of lawyers shielded him from the speculations of his complicity. Disappearing from public view, he returned to running his empire, for now. Jack knew that Harrington was still out there, watching, waiting, and perhaps already plotting his next move.

The Mossad, having played its role in exposing the conspiracy, quietly withdrew. Their primary mission complete, most operatives returned to Israel. However, a select few remained in Europe and the U.S., their presence obscured but unmistakable. Jack noticed a familiar face in the crowd during a brief press appearance—a Mossad agent he'd worked with before, lingering just long enough to be seen. Conversations with Lily confirmed his suspicions: the Mossad believed other pieces were still in play. There were rumors of hidden accounts left untouched, and encrypted communications between Vilar's network and other unnamed figures continued to surface. The silence was tactical. Someone was still moving in the shadows, and the Mossad had no intention of leaving them unchecked.

Jack presented the encrypted thumb drive to Special Agent Henderson in Salt Lake City, who, in turn, passed it on to the FBI's Operational Technology Division (OTD) in Quantico, Virginia. It is expected that OTD will collaborate with the National Security Agency (NSA) in Fort Meade, Maryland, to access its powerful cryptoanalysis capability.

Marcus was gone. No trace, no loose ends. An exit only someone like Marcus could manage—calculated, precise, absolute.

A week after the disruption of the Roundhouse auction, a sealed envelope arrived at Jack's Sun Valley cabin, slipped under the door in the dead of night. No postmark. No courier. Inside, a single line scrawled on unmarked paper:

"The forest is quiet. Let it stay that way."

No signature. The handwriting deliberate, stripped of sentiment. Jack read it twice, the edges of the paper rough, as though torn by hand. It wasn't a farewell. It was a statement of intent.

Lily suspected South America. Somewhere remote, off the grid. Jack wasn't convinced. Marcus never ran. He just knew how to disappear.

The message lingered in Jack's mind long after the snow melted. Not an ending. Just Marcus, retreating to a place where ghosts couldn't follow.

Lily nodded, both knowing this fight was far from over. The threads they had pulled had unraveled part of the tapestry, but so much remained hidden. They had recovered only a few dozen stolen artworks, while thousands more, worth untold millions, remained unaccounted for—each piece holding the potential to unleash the same kind of havoc. Outside, the snow kept falling, masking the truths yet uncovered, while the art world's darkest secrets lingered just out of reach.

Despite the mounting arrests, Eduardo Vilar, like William Harrington, remained untouched, shielded by layers of deniability and proxies who took the fall in his place. He had retreated to his lavish compound in Monaco, a sprawling estate perched above the Mediterranean, where the sun-drenched luxury masked the fortress-like security protecting him from judicial authorities. Monaco, with its complex financial privacy laws and lack of extradition agreements with the United States, offered him a haven just beyond the reach of investigators. From behind the estate's tall gates, Vilar continued to orchestrate subtle moves, ensuring key figures remained silent and portions of his network stayed intact, leaving just enough distance between himself and the crimes to avoid direct prosecution. His influence lingered behind carefully crafted legal barriers and offshore financial networks, with enough plausible deniability to avoid direct connection to the crimes. Investigators struggled to tie him to the stolen art, as evidence revealed his involvement only through intermediaries and indirect communications. Whispers persisted that he had personally orchestrated key elements of the operation, yet every traceable link seemed to dissolve before reaching him.

But Vilar did not escape unscathed. Although he had managed to rescue his crypto wallets in the Cayman Islands, he was not as successful elsewhere. It's estimated that well over half of his total cryptocurrency holdings were recovered. With the assistance of the Monuments Men and Women Foundation, as with other recovered illicit wealth, Vilar's crypto was liquidated and restituted to the families of the owners, who perished in the Holocaust, of the stolen art.

From the terrace of his estate, Vilar watched the media storm unfold with quiet satisfaction. The arrests, the investigations, the public outrage—it had all played out exactly as he had anticipated, sparing him from consequence. The news anchors' voices echoed faintly from a screen inside, recounting the latest legal actions against those beneath him in the chain of power—figures he had ensured would be visible enough to absorb the fallout, yet distant enough not to implicate him directly.

Vilar leaned against the ornate iron railing, the sea breeze carrying the scent of salt and jasmine, masking the staleness of old secrets. The headlines scrolling across the muted television declared justice served—*Gallery Director Arrested, Financial Web Collapses, Stolen Art Recovered.* But Vilar knew better. Only some had been exposed. The true depths of his empire, the vaults of stolen masterpieces hidden behind layers of false identities and confidential trusts, remained beyond the reach of the authorities. The setback of losing a fortune in crypto was irritating, but, in time, it would be restored.

He smiled faintly. The world's outrage was temporary. Scandals faded. Investigators moved on when the evidence grew thin, and public attention turned to fresher crises. Already, his lawyers were working on subtle countermeasures—statements of plausible deniability, carefully leaked documents shifting the blame further down the chain.

And yet, a whisper of unease crept into his thoughts. Moreau was already behind bars. Julian had betrayed the network in a bid for redemption. Fischer had vanished, but Vilar knew better than to believe in total disappearances. Shadows always shifted when observed for too long.

Still, he remained untouchable. For now.

The world could scream for justice, but from the sanctuary of his sunlit terrace, justice felt like nothing more than an inconvenience kept comfortably at bay.

Afterword

Thank you for reading my first thriller! I greatly appreciate you taking the time to join me on this journey. I hope you had half as much fun reading this novel as I did creating it.

The Titus Conspiracy is a work of fiction inspired by actual and current events. I have taken liberties to alter some settings and give them fictional characteristics to enhance the narrative.

The Nazi's vile campaign of Aryanization made theft of Jewish art a central part of their failed ideology over 80 years ago. Yet, deep antisemitism in Europe and the United States remains today, while right-wing ideologies are making their way back into mainstream political systems. This novel imagines what would happen if the two were connected and left unchecked.

Sun Valley is my happy place, where I aspire to be at all times and during every season. As the author, I couldn't imagine having my protagonist retire anywhere but in Sun Valley. While the skiing is indeed epic, the Pio has the best prime rib in the world, and the freshies in the backcountry cannot be matched, there is no hidden cache of art in the Sawtooths. Titus Lake is a favorite hiking and backcountry spot, and Galena is a wonderful experience after a day on the mountain. But there are no secret cabins full of priceless art to be found anywhere in this spectacular slice of the country.

If you do visit Roundhouse, don't pass up the best espresso martini known to humanity. And, if you go outside on the patio to enjoy the drink and the view, tread carefully, as there is a secret entry to a hidden basement below. Although if you look closely, you are more likely to find timber for the fireplace than a hidden Mossad agent.

Those reading this book may be tempted to enjoy an incredible meal at Huberbräu-Stüberl. While you will find delicious Austrian foods and even photos of Sun Valley, none of them have Nazi insignias, and you will not have to worry about a killer bartender.

In Paris, the Hôtel Du Continent offers a lovely repose from the busy shopping streets. However, you won't find the Gallery Moreau. If there were one, it would be located at the spot of The Paul Rosenberg Gallery on Rue La Boétie before it was confiscated by the Nazis in 1941.

Lisbon was indeed neutral during the war and home to some very special wines. However, Adega Viúva Gomes, a winery in the small town of Almoçageme, is just that—A lovely multi-generational winery and not the headquarters of a global terror mastermind's annual symposium.

On the Italian island of Sicily, skiers can find snow and a lovely *rifugio* on Mt. Etna, perfect for recharging over pastries and coffee. And, while there are Israeli cherry tomato farms nearby, no Mossad agents are making it their base of operation.

All of the art that Jack and Lily found in Titus was confiscated illegally by the Nazis and remains missing to this day. The most famous missing piece is Raphael's "Portrait of a Young Man" (1513-1514), which depicts the renowned artist of The School of Athens in the Vatican as a young man. Its theft and disappearance is a loss for all.

I owe a huge debt of gratitude to my friends and family for indulging me as I took this journey and for their support along the way. Also, many thanks to Ann, Erin, Patrick, and Stuart for their support in the editing and presentation of the book. Of course, I tip my hat in grand appreciation to the great thrillers in whose shadows I've found inspiration. Reading and re-reading these works as I waded through my manuscript was one of the best parts of the journey. I also thank my friends and editors for reading and giving me feedback. Your input was invaluable.

About the Author

David Asher is the pen name of a Seattle-based writer. He focuses on thrillers that explore hidden histories, financial intrigue, and global power dynamics. His work is informed by research, travel, and the intersection of finance, politics, and art.